The Conscripted Extremist

A Novel

By

A. Marc Ross

CHAPTER ONE

Gabe forced his way through the battling crowd. He struggled forward, shoving and elbowing, making slow progress toward the front. The front—where the speakers had been working up the crowd before the fighting broke out. Extremists on the far left fighting those on the far right, trapping protestors in their midst. Around him men and women screamed in rage while others cried out from pain and fear. Police flood lamps lit the long city street, revealing peoples' cuts and bruises and blood glinting in their bright lights. Fallen bodies from both sides dotted the street, some trying to crawl to safety. Others lying still.

A woman, her logoed tee shirt ripped partway off, clenched her bleeding head and lurched into him. Gabe saw bearing down on her a bearded man brandishing a short wooden bat, his open leather vest exposing his bare beer barrel belly. Gabe lunged and grabbed the man's bat-wielding arm with both hands, staving off the blow. The man hit Gabe in his side, but Gabe shrugged it off. They wrestled then fell to the street, rolling over each other. Pieces of broken glass stabbed them. Several people, forced by the mob's pressure, stepped on them. Others fell over them. A kick caught Gabe's neck and he lost his grip on his foe. They both rose to their knees, glass shards embedded in Gabe's bare knees. Gabe's chest rose and fell slightly while the man was panting, and his stomach jiggled with each gasp. He swung the bat. The swing was feeble enabling Gabe to catch the bat with one hand, wrench it away, and shove the man down. The man stared up at Gabe, his face twisted in fear and his arms raised for protection, but Gabe resisted the urge to strike him.

Bat in hand, Gabe headed forward again, stepping around and over bodies strewn in the street. He didn't strike anyone with the bat. Instead, he held it up, waving it to deter potential attackers. His mouth was pursed in a tight line and his unblinking light brown eyes kept looking around as he concentrated on continuing, his determination pushing aside any fear. Near Gabe a young woman fired a paint gun at an alt-righter, catching her target along the outer edge of one eye. Her victim grabbed his face and crumpled, screaming. A wrench struck the woman's forearm, sending her paint gun flying. Despite the surrounding noise Gabe heard bones crack. His stomach heaved, but he kept everything down. A woman wielding a hockey stick and wearing a goalie's mask stepped in front of the injured woman, protecting her. Gabe didn't stop to help. Instead, he pushed on to reach his friends up front. Gabe could see somewhat above the crowd and he spotted one of his friends' head over the sea of flailing arms, raised weapons and bouncing heads. He angled toward the towering head.

Suddenly, Gabe was yanked backwards as someone grabbed his wrist from behind, wrenching and twisting it. He yelled as pain shot from his wrist up to his shoulder and the move forced him to drop the bat. He managed to twist his head enough to see who was gripping him. His eyebrows rose and his eyes widened in surprise; it was a man wearing the black bloc outfit of the extreme left and a dark helmet with a visor covering his face. The helmeted figure's left hand had a powerful hold on Gabe's bent wrist. With his right he threw several quick jabs to

Gabe's side and along his ribs, making Gabe yell and bend away. Gabe tried to turn and face the man to strike back, but his assailant danced around him, maintaining his hold and continuing his assault. He twisted Gabe's wrist further, forcing Gabe to one knee. His mouth opened and he let out a sharp cry. The man didn't let up. He began pummeling Gabe between his shoulder blades. It hurt. It hurt bad, and Gabe was helpless. The man twisted Gabe's wrist even further. Screaming from the added pain, Gabe was sure his wrist would snap. The man drove Gabe's face onto the asphalt street. The grit rubbed against his cheek, drawing long scrapes. A hard rod pressed against the back of Gabe's neck, immobilizing him. His wrist was released, but before he could react a restraint was strapped around both wrists, and they were pulled tight behind his back.

Now that Gabe was bound, the pressure came off his neck. He was yanked to his feet while thinking *Why is a black bloc attacking me? I'm wearing shorts and a tee shirt. He can see we're on the same side.* Before he could think further, out of the corner of one eye Gabe saw by his side a second helmeted man in black bloc. The new man punched Gabe in the stomach, making him gasp and knocking the wind out of him despite his solid abs. Gabe started to double over and collapse but the first man kept him standing.

One of the men pushed and the other man pulled the breathless, dazed and helpless Gabe through the melee, the men shoving aside anyone in their way. Without a free hand to protect himself, Gabe took several shots from the crowd, bloodying his face, until the three of them finally emerged from the scrum. The men continued pushing and pulling him along for a block; Gabe stumbling while struggling to keep his feet. The men finally stopped and held Gabe up against a van's rear door. Gabe stared vacantly, then one of them hit him in the chin and they shoved him into the van.

As he passed out, Gabe thought *But it had been such a good day.*

////

Early that morning Gabe had thought *It felt good. It just felt so so good. It had been a long time. Everything they'd all gone through, and now they were back.* For this day he'd dropped eight pounds, worked his abs to the core and had his suit jackets let out to fit his bulked-up shoulders and chest.

A few minutes earlier, a fine silk weave had caressed his legs as he'd pulled up his black trousers with their pinpoint white stripes. The designer socks had been a treat for his feet. He'd used his shoehorn with its long rigid leather handle to help slide on his custom-made low-rise cordovan dress boots. As he had cinched the boots' straps tight, their embrace had given him a sense of solidity and strength. The brand-new custom made high thread count blinding white shirt had been next. The collar fit his neck just right—secure but not too tight. Then there'd been the leather belt, broken in perfectly—not yet showing wear, but supple and enhancing the solid feel of the boots. Next had been the French silk patterned tie of red and gold to add a splash of color, tied properly and centered directly below his Adam's Apple. Finally, in his mind like a matador putting on his *chaquetilla*, he'd donned his suit jacket. He'd pulled the jacket's sleeves so they fell to the exact right length on his shirt cuffs. He was ready for battle as it had been fought in his world before the pandemic and would now be waged again.

Later that morning, suitably clad, Gabriel (Gabe) Bentley paused outside a conference room, ready to make his entrance. Gabe was a lawyer at a large New York City law firm. He was a mid-level associate, meaning he was a few years out of law school. Normally someone his level would not be allowed to do what he was about to do—lead a high stakes meeting such as this one. "Run the deal" as they called it. However, both the senior partner and the client had confidence in him.

This would be his first in-person mask-less face-to-face negotiation since the pandemic. Masks had ended a good while ago and then offices had reopened, but few workers had showed up. When people finally had returned to their offices, for a good while they'd still avoided in-person meetings. From the start of the pandemic Gabe had participated in countless Zoom meetings, but to him they weren't as effective as being face-to-face. You couldn't read body language well when you could only see someone from the shoulders or neck up, or properly judge the resolve in their eyes through the screen. You couldn't give your team a side look which could convey so much or pull them aside when needed. He'd thought of it as dancing at a distance, but you can't really dance some dances that way. Whether it's swing, the jitterbug, ballroom dancing or a waltz, you need that proximity, that contact, to really perform and to really enjoy it. Today, for Gabe, the music was starting again.

Gabe entered the conference room. Scanning the room, he saw that his clients hadn't arrived yet, but three others were there. Across the long glass table sat the principals on the other side of the deal, a married couple in their sixties, and their lawyer. Gabe's client was negotiating to buy their company and, in the process, make the husband and wife obscenely rich. Introductions were made, hands were shaken, and cards were passed out, just like the old days. Gabe took a chair across from them and spread out his papers as they engaged in small talk. Gabe's client, a large technology company, had two employees acting for it, the CFO and his assistant. They arrived shortly, and once again the rituals were observed. All the men wore suits and ties – the return to formal dress and casting off business casual in their field had been one response, albeit an unexpected one, to the pandemic's end.

Once everyone was settled the CFO gave his opening speech, as he always did, telling the couple how excited his company's management felt about buying their business and stressing how the deal would be a home run for everyone. The husband and wife exchanged quick glances then lowered their eyes, nervous yet excited by the fortune awaiting them.

After a bit more, the CFO looked toward Gabe. "Take it away, counselor."

Gabe nodded at the CFO then turned to the lawyer across the table. "I suggest that we begin by you raising any questions or comments you might have on the deal documents we've sent you."

The seller's lawyer, an overweight man in his forties with an early morning five o-clock shadow, began. It was usual for his side to raise issues and try to negotiate matters, but right away this lawyer went too far, making Gabe lean back in his chair and set his jaw. As the man went on, Gabe thought the objections ranged from unreasonable to over-reaching to just plain absurd. Moreover, Gabe found him offensive as he insulted Gabe's client and Gabe personally and began yelling at Gabe.

"Whoa," Gabe said, trying to calm the man down. The lawyer ignored Gabe. Gabe thought *perhaps this guy's putting on a show for his clients or maybe he really means what he's saying and this is his style.* Either way Gabe wasn't about to let this approach benefit this loudmouth or his clients.

After several minutes of this barrage, Gabe interrupted the lawyer and said, "We need to talk in the hall."

"I'm just fine right here."

"We need to talk in the hall," Gabe repeated as he walked towards the door, leaving the other man no choice but to follow. The man slowly strutted out behind Gabe, smirking to his clients.

Once in the hall and the door had closed behind them, Gabe stared into the man's eyes and lashed out. "You clearly don't have a damn clue what you're doing or how to do it."

Before the lawyer could respond, Gabe launched into his own tirade, his voice firm but quiet. "Let me make this very clear to you. You want to be an asshole, fine. I can be an asshole. You want to take extreme positions, I can do so too. We served up a reasonable agreement. If you won't or can't do your job properly, I'm going back in there and telling your clients the positions you're taking and your manner on their behalf are unacceptable to us. I'll tell them this gives us grave concerns about their judgment in using you and, as a result, in their judgment in general, and if they don't fire you on the spot we'll end the meeting. Furthermore, in that case I'll rewrite the documents, making them drastically worse for your client and tell them to either take it exactly as rewritten or pass and leave those hundreds of millions of dollars behind."

The man bent toward Gabe, bringing his face within inches of Gabe's. His voice was raised but he was no longer yelling. "You punk. I'm doing my job."

Gabe ignored the insult and maintained the close eye contact. "No, you're not. Your job is to see if a deal can be made. You're killing the deal. We don't greatly care. My client has a lengthy list of other businesses it can buy. Despite our CFO's b.s. speech, this deal matters fairly little to it. I think it matters the world to your clients though. Now, we're going back in there and I'm going to reject your first point very politely. If you politely accept my position or politely offer a reasonable compromise we'll continue. If not, I will tell your client what I just said I would say. The meeting will be over and you can go home. The same applies to every other point."

Sweat had broken out on the other's face, making his forehead glisten, and lines run across his jowls. His pale skin had turned red.

"I can't believe your client would let you do that."

"They absolutely will. Want to try me and find out?"

Without another word Gabe returned to the conference room, not saying anything to anyone, only staring across the table with a rock hard expression. The sellers were whispering to each other and casting nervous looks at Gabe while Gabe's clients were busy texting on their phones, seemingly uninterested in what was happening. After several minutes the other lawyer rejoined them, his face still bearing traces of red color and sweat.

"Returning to your first point," Gabe said in a civil tone, staring directly into the other lawyer's eyes, "Unfortunately, that won't work for us. Are you sure you can't accept our position? We think it's fair."

Beads of sweat forming again on his brow, the lawyer leaned over and whispered to his clients. The whispering went back and forth for a minute or so. Gabe could see the women's hands shaking slightly while her husband used his handkerchief to wipe off saliva at the corners of his mouth.

Done with the whispering and avoiding any eye contact, with a strained expression the lawyer replied quietly, "In the spirit of getting the deal done and knowing how much the parties want to work together, we accept your position."

The rest of the meeting proceeded almost verbatim in the same smooth fashion, the outcome pleasing Gabe's clients. Later they asked him what he'd said to the other lawyer, but Gabe refused to say, not wanting to embarrass the man any further.

That evening Gabe took a car service to his apartment, mentally reviewing the meeting and thinking how much he'd enjoyed his return to the deal-making wars.

CHAPTER TWO

That night, after getting home from his victorious 'corporate battle', Gabe changed into shorts, a bright yellow tee shirt and worn-out basketball sneakers. He messaged a few people and after receiving responses headed out to meet up.

Walking along he received a text from his friend Matt. "Jasminn at City Hall protest. I'm worried. Come."

Jasminn and Matt were Gabe's closest friends, the three of them going back to college. Jasminn's being at a protest was no surprise since she was quite involved in the New York left wing activist scene. By comparison, Gabe joined occasionally, and Matt rarely. Gabe stared at the text then messaged back, grabbed a cab and headed downtown, but thinking it incongruous to cab it to a protest.

The driver, clearly a newbie, took a poor route, got cut off left and right and seemed to hit most every red light. Gabe struggled to keep his cool, Jasminn on his mind. He often worried about her. She was an organizer for a non-violent left-wing protest group. However, these days many protests ended up with violent people on the left and the right fighting, the police storming in, and the original peaceful protestors being trapped in the middle. So, despite Jasminn Cummings being strong and tough, Gabe still worried.

They'd met their freshman year of college. She was on a basketball scholarship, although her father was a successful dentist who could have paid for her schooling. The women's team often practiced against male students, generally guys not good enough to play Division

One college ball, but who'd played high school ball, and most of whom could have played in Division Two or Three. Gabe was a low Division Three caliber player, but he'd showed up for the women's practices like clockwork so he'd gotten a lot of playing time. He and Jasminn had first met on the court, where they'd often guarded each other. Gabe at six two and one ninety and Jasminn at five nine and one forty-five had made for a pretty fair match-up. His first time guarding her she'd caught the ball down low, shoved back with her butt, catching him in the groin, and wheeled in for a layup. She'd run downcourt giggling and watching him grimace and grab himself. Such was the beginning of their friendship. She'd admitted to her girlfriends that she thought he was cute with his long curly brown hair, pug nose and roundish face. Nevertheless, she'd often teased him by saying the original movie *White Men Can't Jump* was an homage to him. In turn, he'd say that her butt was bigger than Shaq's. That first meeting took place ten years ago. Later, they'd both done graduate work in the Bay Area and ended up in New York City. Although nothing sexual went on between them, they'd grown extremely close.

Jasminn wasn't just a ballplayer—she was smart and driven. In junior high she'd picked basketball and played it year-round, giving up soccer and tennis despite being nationally ranked in both in her age group. Computers had fascinated her from an early age. She'd majored in computer science in college and been aggressively wooed by high-powered tech companies. She'd risen rapidly through her chosen company's ranks but became more and more involved with the left-wing protest scene. Eventually, she'd quit to take a less time consuming, although much lower paying, job, so work would interfere less with her movement activism. Gabe admired her for this, but he'd worried about what might happen during a protest. He'd believed it was just a matter of time.

Finally, Gabe's cab came within walking distance of City Hall and he jumped out. He couldn't miss which way to go; the crowd noises led him to the action. Rounding a corner, he found himself at the rear of a large crowd blocking the street. Hoping to spot Matt or Jasminn, Gabe hooked his arms and legs around a streetlight and shimmied up, scraping his bare legs, and then boosted himself up to sit on a projecting metal arm. He couldn't see everything that was happening, but he could see more of it.

Off to his right, lit by a police floodlight, Gabe saw a cluster of people dressed in black bloc—black from head to toe, including black ski masks or balaclavas with wrap-around sunglasses or ski goggles. He knew who they were—members of the extreme left wing known by various names, but mainly as the Antifa. One of their key principles was "If the right uses violence, we'll defend ourselves and defend those with similar beliefs."

From his lamppost vantage spot, Gabe couldn't see the alt-right but he knew they must be there, and he knew both sides' extremists came prepared for battle. Looking down the long street, he could see the brightly lit steps of City Hall at the far end and just make out figures in dark clothing on its steps. Gabe was too far away to be sure, but he figured they must be a police riot squad, ready for whatever went down. Filling the street for several blocks between Gabe and City Hall stood the non-violent protestors. Jasminn would be somewhere in that crowd, too close to these other people ready to fight. *A battle is coming*, he thought, *but a very different battle than the one I'd fought earlier in the conference room.*

Gabe shifted his head and looked down at the people nearby. Supporters of the demonstrators lined the sidewalks and spilled into the street. Some had booths or tables and many had signs saying "Medical Aide" or "Water." A few advertised legal services, and their workers shoved business cards at passing demonstrators in case, or in hope in the minds of these workers, that the demonstrators were arrested.

Gabe could hear the crowd sounds. Even here, at the fringe, the noise was loud, although not deafening as it must be further in. The sound of people chanting in response to the call leaders with their megaphones hit Gabe with a rhythmic but incomprehensible roar. Like waves crashing against a rocky shore, receding and then being followed by the next wave. Suddenly, from behind him, he heard a different sound—the revving of a car engine.

Gabe looked back and screamed, "Look out!"

A large white sedan roared towards the aide stations. From its roar, Gabe knew the driver must have been pressing the gas pedal, building the RPMs while his other foot had held down the brake until he released it, freeing the mechanized metal weapon to hurtle forward. It came at an angle, plowing through several stations and demolishing them. The volunteers had no chance. The vehicle catapulted some of them into the air and ran down others before crashing into a fire hydrant and coming to a jarring halt. Its front bumper was smashed in and its hood crumpled. The passenger side was covered with deep long marks, dents and blood.

People who had not been in the car's cross-hairs rushed toward it and its victims, trapping Gabe on the streetlight so he could only bear witness. The driver opened his door to escape, but the mob was on him before he was fully out of the car. They grabbed him, pulled him out the rest of the way and began pummeling him. He was on the ground and they kicked him repeatedly, people shoving each other to get close enough to deliver a blow. Gabe lost sight of the driver who was quickly buried under his attackers.

Policemen raced over. Leading with shields and batons, they pushed their way to the fallen driver and drove back his attackers. The police were followed by EMTs, and eventually the police succeeded in forcing the crowd back far enough to make room for several ambulances. The police started arresting most anybody nearby, later claiming in each case that the arrested person had attacked the driver or a police officer. Many others in the crowd fled and the immediate area thinned out. Gabe later learned that three sidewalk stand volunteers died; two from the car's impact and an elderly man who wasn't seriously injured by the car but suffered a massive coronary at the scene. The driver was in a coma and his prognosis was uncertain.

Gabe watched this unfold from his perch, staring and with his mouth gaping, first in horror and anger at the carnage wrought by the car, then feeling conflicted about the driver's beating, and finally anger at the police. He knew there was nothing he could do, so he put this aside. Before clambering down he took one last look at the crowd ahead. It seemed oblivious to what had transpired.

Gabe hoped to spot one particular head above the rest—that of his other close college friend, Matt, who stood six foot eight and had blonde hair. Gabe figured Matt would try to reach Jasminn, and while Gabe knew he couldn't easily locate her in this large churning throng, he hoped to spot Matt towering above them. No luck. He'd have to force his way forward blindly and hope to find them.

At first Gabe made good progress. The people in the back weren't packed too tightly together and didn't hinder Gabe much. He moved some aside, slithered between others and made his way without much trouble. Suddenly, he felt a hand on his shoulder. He spun around, shrugging off the hand and his own arms came up to defend himself. However, it was Matt, not the alt-right. Gabe sighed with relief. Matt bent down some and the two of them yelled back and forth, barely able to hear each other. Then, with Matt leading and Gabe riding in his wake, they forced their way through the thickening crowd, looking for Jasminn. They kept heading toward the front. Gabe knew that the front was where the worst action would be, so if Jasminn got into trouble that would be the most likely place it would happen.

Matt and Gabe were still aways from the front when, from his view above the crowd, Matt picked out Jasminn, pointed and yelled to Gabe, "That way." Matt pushed harder to get to her. Gabe tried to stay with him but couldn't keep up as Matt would part the crowd but it would close behind him, leaving Gabe to do his own pushing.

Up ahead, extremists from both sides stood in the middle of the street, just a few feet apart and yelling and cursing at each other. Suddenly, a shot of bear spray caught an unmasked left winger in the face, and a balloon packed with dirt and paint hit a man belonging to the right, collapsing both victims. Which happened first was unclear, but it didn't matter. Both sides surged forward and the battle was on. The street became an arena of brutal action. Both sides had their preferred weapons and defenses. The black blocs were partial to milkshakes—containers holding quick drying cement—paint guns, garbage can lids for shields and orange traffic cones to cover gas grenades. The right wingers preferred bear spray, bats, other clubs, chains, brass knuckles and good old fists. The police quickly advanced. They had pepper spray, gas grenades, flash/bangs and flexible batons for offense, body armor, helmets and shields for defense, and no name tags or badges for anonymity. The peaceful protestors were caught amidst this and could either try to flee or stand and fight. All was chaos. The crowd felt the danger and its herd instinct kicked in. Some people tried to escape to the rear, creating a log jam. Gabe recognized the signs—the retreat, the chant replaced by a loud roar of people screaming.

Behind Gabe the crowd was rapidly dispersing. He could have retreated safely, but Jasminn and Matt were up ahead so that was his direction. Soon he was swallowed up in the combat. Several minutes later, after forcing his way forward, fighting, being beaten, taken captive, and shoved into a van, he was unconscious.

CHAPTER THREE

Gabe slowly lifted his head as he started coming around. It was several minutes after he'd been knocked out and tossed in the van. From the jostling and sounds he knew he was being driven somewhere, but there were no windows to see out. Gabe gasped for breath and felt an arm pressing against his chest as someone kept him pinned to the floor, making breathing difficult. He didn't fight, but only lay there, confused, gasping and in pain. Every time the van hit a bump it felt like a blow to his ribs. After what seemed a long time to Gabe, he sensed the van driving down a ramp into an unknown space. The man in the rear lifted the arm that had been crushing Gabe and pulled a hood over Gabe's head then dragged him out. Gabe felt someone steering him.

"What's going . . ." Before Gabe could finish one of them yanked on his restraint and the other hit him in the stomach, silencing him other than for a loud grunt.

Despite the hood and his confusion, Gabe could tell they were going up in an elevator. They exited the elevator and walked some, then one of the men yanked Gabe to a halt. He could feel them rummaging in his pockets. They took his phone and wallet from his deep pants' pockets, removed the hood and cut the restraints. Gabe rubbed his sore wrists as his eyes adjusted to the light. He was facing a wall. Turning around he saw he was in a cell and the two men, with their faces still covered, stood outside its bars.

Gabe shouted, "What is this? Who are you? What do you want?"

Their only response was a bottle of water flipped to him before they walked off.

Gabe rushed to the front of the cell, grabbed the bars and stuck his face partway between them, yelling after the men, "Wait. What's going on? Hey! I need a doctor! I think you broke my ribs!"

They ignored him, vanishing from sight around a corner.

Still at the bars, Gabe looked out at a large bare open space. It seemed to him to be under construction—some walls were open and he could see dangling wires and insulation. Other walls had spackled plasterboard. Gabe thought of office space waiting to be finished, but no office Gabe knew of came with a cell. He shook the cell door, not expecting it to open but deeming the attempt mandatory. It had no give. Upset and confused, he retreated and sat at one end of a wooden bench which ran the length of the back wall. He rested his back against the side wall and set one foot on the bench, nursing his aches and sipping the water.

//////

Gabe focused on slowing his breathing, trying to calm himself. He figured that they, whoever they were, probably wanted him to freak out. He was determined not to. His thoughts bounced around, not staying long on any one subject but returning to the same ones over and over. *Who were these guys? Why'd they grab him? Where was he? Why wasn't he locked up with other people arrested at the protest?* Then, *what happened to Jasminn and Matt? Were they OK?*

Gabe tried to figure out why they'd taken him. He'd ended up in the fighting, so the police could've arrested him for that. But that notion didn't fit neatly. His captors wore black bloc, not police uniforms. Plus, his beating seemed extreme, even based on the rumors about what the police sometimes did.

He scratched his head, wincing from the pain.

Moreover, he was taken separately, rather than being tossed into a wagon with others. On top of all that, he couldn't believe this was a real police station. Maybe, he thought, scratching his head more carefully, they were with some other government agency. If so though, why grab him or treat him this way? But if they weren't government, who were they? The only alternative he could think of, and a scarier one, was that they belonged to an extreme right wing group. Some things fit that scenario, although there were holes in this theory too. Why would right wingers bother with him? They couldn't think he was Antifa. He was wearing shorts and a yellow tee shirt. Hardly a combat outfit.

Gabe was at a loss. What was this all about? Did they want something from him? If so, what? He shivered in fear. Fear that they might beat him again. Harder. Or they might do worse. But it made no sense.

To try to distract himself from these questions and fears plus his pain, he examined his prison. He rose and paced it off, calculating it at about eight and a half feet wide and nine and a half feet long. Raising one arm overhead as best as he could with his bruises, he estimated the ceiling was nine feet up, normally a mere hop even for him, despite Jasminn's wisecracks. He studied the walls. At first glance they looked as if they were made of large grayish-tan bricks with grout between each brick. Closer inspection showed otherwise. They were actually gray cement on which slightly lighter grayish-tan vinyl rectangles, representing the bricks, were affixed. *Saving money?* He looked up at the ceiling. It had two narrow grated air vents. No way out there.

Alone in his apartment during the pandemic he'd worked out and gotten a lot stronger. Maybe if he only had to take on one of the men he could handle him and escape. After all, Gabe thought, although one was roughly his size, the other was shorter and thinner than Gabe. He felt a cold dash of reality splashing him, killing that idea. Gabe didn't know how to really fight—until tonight he hadn't been in a fight since he was a kid. Also, these men clearly knew how to handle themselves. He'd bet they were highly trained, so even if he got a chance to try, he'd just get beaten up again. With that thought he grabbed the ribs on his right side, wincing from the pain.

Gabe heard a door open and footsteps coming in his direction. He played it tight, looking tough, and resumed his position sitting with a foot on the bench and his back against the wall, having nothing better to do than wait to see what happened.

CHAPTER FOUR

There were three of them—two men and a woman who carried an old-fashioned doctor's bag. The men weren't wearing helmets but were in black bloc and Gabe assumed they were the same men as before. The three of them entered the cell, the smaller man staying by the door as the other one and the woman approached Gabe.

The approaching man, the one about Gabe's size, said, "I'm sure we didn't cause any serious injuries, but Ms. Doctor here will give you a quick once over. Make any trouble and I'll have no choice but to inflict more pain. Understood?"

Gabe lowered his foot from the bench, sat up and without looking at them muttered, "Yeah."

"Stand and remove your shirt," the woman ordered in a flat seemingly disinterested voice.

She examined him, probing different spots and listening with a stethoscope. She was none too gentle, and every time he coughed on command he couldn't believe how much it hurt. She was oblivious to his discomfort however, showing no emotions when he winced or groaned. To her he might as well have been a slab of meat. While she worked, Gabe looked down at himself and moaned in response to the large ugly red and purple bruises on his ribs, stomach and arms. He thought there was about as much colorful flesh as his normal pale flesh. From the pain, he was sure his back was similarly marked up. He rubbed his swollen aching chin.

Done, she stepped back, hanging the stethoscope around her neck. Ignoring Gabe, Ms. Doctor turned to the man with her and said, "We'd need X-rays to be certain, but I think you did what you intended. I doubt you broke any bones or caused internal injuries. He's going to be in pain for several days, but that should be it. I could give him a pain killer and wrap him. That'd make him feel a little better. Do you want me to?"

The man thought for a second, the two of them looking at each other and ignoring Gabe. "No pain killer. We need him alert. Besides, under the circumstances no point in the wrap."

Gabe didn't know what that meant the man was planning, and while they unnerved him, the situation angered him and he stood up straight and clenched his fists. The woman closed her bag and headed for the door.

"Thanks Ms. Doctor. Great job," Gabe's voice dripping with sarcasm.

She turned her head, looking him up and down without any expression, said nothing and left. The man near Gabe stared at him. Gabe tensed for another hit, but the man just stared.

The other one said, "Let's go, Kid."

Gabe figured he must be "Kid" so went along, wincing as he put on his shirt as he walked with one of them in front of him and the other behind.

"I need a bathroom."

They let him use one, although the shorter man stood watch while Gabe did his business. Once he was done, they continued down an unfinished hall, passing several closed doors, until the lead man opened one, saying, "In here."

They entered a small room—Gabe thought it looked like an interrogation room right out of the movies. A gray metal table was bolted to the floor against the far wall. A mirror took up one wall. He assumed it was a one-way window but couldn't imagine who'd be watching. The lead man pointed for Gabe to sit in a metal chair opposite the mirror. The same man sat across from him while the other took a chair set off at an angle.

They sat in silence. For the first time, Gabe studied their faces. They both appeared to be in their forties. The larger man sitting opposite him had a wide face and a broad forehead with lines beginning to deepen with age. Gabe knew the expression "steely blue eyes" but had never seen a pair. This man had them though, and they were fastened directly on Gabe without blinking. The rest of his face was unremarkable except for his strong chin. The overall impression Gabe had was of a determined, no-nonsense reasonably good-looking fellow. The other one was a dramatic contrast to his companion. He had a long thin face; his nose was misshapen, Gabe assumed from a poorly repaired break, and it had a pointy tip; he had shallow cheek bones; lips so thin as to be almost non-existent; and a weak jaw receding into his neck. His skin was marked with acne scars. Gabe thought he appeared weasel-like, almost outright evil-looking, and Gabe quickly swiveled his eyes back to the man across from him.

Looking at him, Gabe demanded, "Who are you? What do you want?" Before they responded, he yelled, "What the hell am I doing here?"

The no-nonsense man calmly answered. "We're with Homeland Security. I'm Special Agent Smith and," pointing to the weasel man, "this is Special Agent Jones."

Gabe issued an incredulous cough, grabbing his side in response to the resulting pain. "You've got to be kidding me. Smith and Jones?"

Smith shrugged.

"Couldn't you guys come up with better aliases than those?"

Each of them reached into his top, pulled out a folded wallet and tossed it onto the table in front of Gabe, in both cases landing open. On one side were badges. Both badge's lower part was shaped like a shield and on the top stood an American Eagle with wings spread. Right below the eagle, in gold lettering on a dark blue background it read, "Homeland Security Investigations" and on the bottom it read "Special Agent" with a number in small writing below that and fancy metalwork all around. They looked impressive. Gabe picked up one wallet. The shield gave it a hefty feel. He looked at the ID on the wallet's other side. It read 'Department of Homeland Security,' had an intricate colored design in blue and red ink and in black letters said 'Smith,' the first name being covered by tape.

"Nice, but it could be as phony as the ID I used to get into bars when I was nineteen. Besides, I don't have any idea how a real one looks, so I'm not buying."

He tossed the wallet back down, and each man retrieved his.

Smith, at least according to him and his ID, replied, "Gabriel, it doesn't matter whether you buy it or not. We've shown you our IDs and even if we were lying, it wouldn't matter. The bottom line is we're here and you are in an extremely serious situation. The sooner you accept that, the better all around."

"I don't understand this," Gabe muttered while rubbing the back of his head. "You've no right to hold me. I want to call my lawyer."

"No," Smith replied.

"What the hell do you mean 'No'?" Gabe yelled. "I've got the right to a lawyer."

"Gabriel, you have no rights. We're working under a national security directive which basically lets us do whatever we want."

Gabe's eyes widened then blinked and his jaw drooped. "You can't do that. It's not right. And why me?"

"I'll explain 'Why you'," Smith said, leaning slightly toward Gabe. "Just sit quietly and listen."

Gabe straightened up and almost said something snarky, but he let it pass for the moment.

"You remember the protest at Gracie Mansion a while ago?"

Gabe nodded.

"We first spotted you there. Even post-Covid most protestors wear masks to hide their identities. You didn't."

Somewhat defensively, Gabe told him, "Mine'd been ripped off by some right wing guy."

Smith shrugged. "Whatever. Once you shoved your way to the front there you drew our attention."

With a thin smile and a shake of his head, Jones threw in, "Not very polite, shoving like that."

Ignoring Jones, Smith continued. "You spoke to the police, then to several protest managers. After that you made your way to the leftist forces who were primed for combat, in black blocs and everything. What'd you say to them?"

Gabe had a confused expression, not understanding this, but replied, "Right, at Gracie Mansion that day there were many more on the extreme left than on the right. If fighting had broken out, it looked like they'd have done a lot of damage. Although of course, to end it, at some point the police would have waded in and beaten people to take control."

Jones sneered while adding, "Beaten them bad."

Gabe glared at him with his mouth twisted and he shook his head while Smith continued ignoring Jones.

"So my question is, were you responsible for the Antifa holding fast? Do you know their key people and did you persuade them to stand down?"

Gabe's reply had a taunting tone. "Were you two in on the trap, Special Agent Smith?"

Smith leaned back in his chair, extended his legs out straight and clasped his hands behind his head.

"Aah."

"Aah! That's what you have to say? You guys are disgusting," Gabe said.

Jones moved before Gabe or Smith could react. He delivered a chop to Gabe's neck. Gabe collapsed to the floor, grabbing his neck while Jones strolled back to his chair.

From the floor, and rubbing his neck, Gabe yelled at Jones, "And you're a fucking asshole!"

This time Smith was faster than Jones, restraining him until Jones nodded, waved Smith off and sauntered from the room.

Hands on his chair, Gabe pulled himself up partway, then slowly made it the rest of the way. Seated, and still rubbing his neck, Gabe rejected any notion of handling this man in a fight. "Goddammit that hurt."

"I warned you, Gabriel," Smith drew out, sounding like a teacher lecturing an inattentive student.

Jones returned, closing the door behind him. He flipped Gabe an ice pack.

Alternating applying the pack to his neck and his jaw which still hurt from before, Gabe asked, "Standard equipment for when you work someone over?"

"Gabriel, that attitude is not helping. Now, let's return to that 'trap' as you called it. Of course we knew about it, but we had nothing to do with it. Those alt-right gentlemen planned it all on their own. How'd you know about it?"

"About two blocks from Gracie Mansion I passed a warehouse with large double doors, one of which was partway open. I accidentally spotted a group of guys, looking like alt-righters. I snuck closer to get a better look. They were definitely alt-righters—lots of subtle clues such as Nazi helmets, alt-right group patches on army surplus clothes, and several alt-right flags like the Kekistan national flag. Some guy, a lookout I guess, grabbed me. He got my mask but I pulled free and ran."

Smith nodded and picked up from there. "And you figured they were reinforcements who'd come running when the fighting started and so you warned your friends?"

"I warned people I was told were in charge of the left's combat contingent. I don't know any of them though."

"Nevertheless, you convinced them not to charge. You must be quite persuasive. I imagine that goes with being such a good lawyer. What I don't understand though, is why those guys in the warehouse didn't come and start up anyhow."

Despite the situation, Gabe gave a tiny smile. This was the first time he'd gotten the better of Smith. "I showed a police captain a picture. He must not have wanted a bigger ruckus than he already had, so he ordered some of the riot squad to that warehouse. As far as I know the police simply contained them there."

"What picture?"

"Before the lookout jumped me I snapped a shot of a bunch of them in their combat gear carrying weapons."

Jones broke his silence. "So maybe you're not so persuasive. It's just that you had a picture."

Gabe's lips curled up slightly. "Evidence comes in handy."

Smith interrupted the other two. "Is the picture on your phone?"

"Not anymore. After seeing it, the captain had one of his men forward it to his own phone and delete it from mine. They wiped out all traces of it. A good tech person tried to recover it, but it's definitely gone."

Smith leaned back again, legs out and hands behind his neck. Apparently, Gabe thought, this was Smith's thinking position.

Sounding as if this was all run of the mill, Smith said, "After seeing what you did, we figured you might be our guy. When we ID'ed you..."

Jones interrupted, laughed and said, "Because like a fool you weren't wearing a mask."

Smith cut Jones off, "…and checked out your background we became more interested. And now that we've had this little chat, I'm even more convinced you'll be perfect for what we want."

"What do you want?"

"We want your assistance in an important government investigation."

Looking into those steely blue eyes, Gabe chortled. "You beat the crap out of me, drag me off somewhere and hold me against my will and you want my help? You've got a strange way of asking. Fuck you, motherfuckers."

From the corner of one eye Gabe saw Jones tense up, his hands gripping his chair's arms as he shifted his weight and inched forward. Ready to attack.

"Gabriel, I'm glad you've still got some spunk," Smith said, maintaining the same position. "You'll need it for this assignment, but it'll get you nowhere with us. You'll just waste all of our time."

Gabe shrugged in frustration. Wearily, and tired of being hit, he muttered quietly, "Go ahead."

Jones sat back. Smith signaled Jones.

"What we want you to do Kid," Jones explained, "is find out certain information. Per our direction, the NYC cops arrested four men at tonight's demonstration. We know some about these guys, but not much. They're secretive. We think here in New York they may lead left-wing groups or be right below that level. We want you to learn about them, see if we're right, and use them to name others."

Gabe's eyebrows dropped, making a Vee and lines across his forehead. Through tight lips he said, "You want me to spy for you? And be a rat? No way."

Smith sought to placate him. "Don't look at it that way, Gabriel. Look at it as helping your government avert threats to national security."

"Oh come on. You guys are so full of it."

Jumping back in and leaning forward with fists clenched and his teeth bared, Jones' voice rose an octave as he spat out, "No we're not 'full of it' and you will do this. If not it'll be very bad for you and your friends."

"My friends!" Gabe cried, seeing the alligator smile on Jones' face. Gabe knew Jones meant Jasminn and Matt. He could feel his heart rate rising and he felt short of breath.

Smith held up his hand towards Gabe and assured him, "Right now they're both in cells with their fellow protestors. Nothing bad will happen to them there, and they'll be out in the morning."

"However, that won't be the case if you don't cooperate," Jones sneered, the corners of his thin lips turning up, enjoying himself. "The big guy, Matt, would be moved to a cell of alt-righters. I'm sure they're not happy being locked up, but they'd be much happier if he joined them. He reeks of left-wing protestor, and they'd be all over him. Additionally, it just so happens the cops in that cell area would be on a break. He'd end up in the hospital, and who knows how much permanent damage he might suffer."

"You're a fucking asshole," Gabe yelled, lunging at Jones, who sat waiting for him with a big smile, mocking Gabe. Smith moved with a speed which surprised Gabe, and before Gabe reached Jones, Smith had him by an arm and yanked Gabe to him, holding Gabe tightly.

Smith tried to calm him. "You don't want to do that Gabriel. You'll just end up with more injuries, and it won't change Matt's situation."

Jones smirked. "Then there's Jasminn. We don't have a cell with alt-right women, and even if we did, I'm not sure they could handle her. She's tough. We'd have to do something else."

He paused for a moment, observing Gabe's flared nostrils and clenched jaws, enjoying torquing Gabe up.

"What there always are, however, are women picked up for working the streets. We could put Jasminn in with them and while your lady is tough, she's not street tough like they are. Someone always manages to smuggle in a knife or some other sharp instrument. They're called 'Skanks with shanks'." This time Jones' grin was gleeful.

Gabe struggled to get free of Smith and reach Jones, but Smith put him in an arm bar, immobilizing him. Smith pressed him against the table and Gabe felt the pain from his wrist up into his shoulder blade while having trouble breathing.

"You bastard."

Smith maintained the arm bar. "It doesn't have to be this way, Gabriel. Just cooperate."

"And by the way," Jones added offhandedly, flipping one hand, "once those guys are done with Matt you might end up with them too."

"I'm not afraid!"

"Of course you're not, Gabriel. That's one of the things we like about you," Smith said. "I'm going to let go of you and you're going to sit in your chair and you are going to stay there. No more nonsense. Please."

Gabe did as Smith said and sat hunched over, rubbing his arm and shoulder and asked in a cracking voice, "How can you do this? None of this is legal."

"I've already told you, this is a matter of national security so don't talk about what's legal," Smith said, pausing while Gabe stared at him, wide eyed. Smith continued, "Now, are you prepared to listen?" Without waiting for an answer, he explained, "What we want is this. We'll move you over to the precinct and the police will put you in a cell with the men Jones told you about. They should accept you as one of them. Your bruises should be very persuasive—which, by the way, is one reason we worked you over. You spend the rest of the night with them, learn what you can and later tell us. In the meantime, Jasminn and Matt remain where they are—nice and safe."

"If you're after the Antifa-type leftists, why put me with these guys who you said were just part of the protest?"

"We believe we've got a better chance of working our way up in the non-violent sector first. The left's extremist leaders are virtually invisible. It's almost as if they don't exist. But we're sure there's communication between the leftist leaders at both ends of the spectrum. He wound up. "So, if we get to the right non-violent leaders we think we can use that to get to the ones we really want."

Jones chuckled and added, "Beyond that, of course ,we don't care about any non-violent groups."

Gabe sat unmoving, his hands resting on the table and his fingers clasped, thinking furiously. He didn't know what to do. He was sure he shouldn't accept what Smith and Jones said as true. He didn't like the prospect of being hit again by Jones, but he figured he'd survive that if need be. But most importantly, he thought, he couldn't have them do to Jasminn and Matt what they'd threatened. If there really were leaders or other high-level types in the cell or if their identities were really such a big secret, presumably they wouldn't say anything in front of him. In that case he'd just end up spending the rest of the night in the cell with them and no one gets hurt.

"What if I don't learn anything?"

Smith's eyebrows went up and his head tilted slightly.

"I'm told you're a very talented lawyer, Gabriel, and from our chat I have no doubt that's true," Smith cajoled, "so I'd expect you'd learn a lot. We'd be disappointed if you failed, of course. However, you can't guarantee results. If you try, then you get what you get, you and your two friends are released tomorrow safe and sound and that's the end of it."

Gabe sat, thinking further. He didn't trust them, especially Jones, but Smith probably was no better and simply playing less bad cop. He had no choice though. So quietly they could barely hear him, he grumbled, "You win, you bastards."

Jones smiled and nodded slightly as if taking a bow and considering 'bastards' a compliment.

They made him surrender his money, which was all that was left in his pockets, and his belt, promising he'd get them back when the police released him. Jones put the hood back on Gabe and steered him to the van for another ride.

In the van, Jones warned, "Don't mention Homeland Security and if anyone asks who beat you, say it was the police."

After a short ride Jones removed the hood and led Gabe out of the van. Right before entering a brick building Gabe caught sight of a sign which read "New York City Police Department.

A uniformed policeman and a plainclothesman took him from Smith and Jones. Without a word they marched him up several flights and down several halls, stopping in front of a cell with four men in it. The uniform yelled for the cell door to be opened. As it did, the plainclothesman punched Gabe in the stomach and shoved him into the cell. The door rolled shut and locked behind him. The cops walked off, laughing.

CHAPTER FIVE

The shove landed Gabe on the floor, and the punch left him clutching his stomach. Several pairs of hands helped him partway up, then maneuvered him onto his back on a lower bunk. While they moved Gabe, his shirt slid up. Someone exclaimed, "Wow! The cops really worked you over, didn't they?"

Gabe didn't respond at first. After a short time he forced himself to sit up and pulled his shirt down. Staring at the floor, he mumbled, "Yeah."

Another voice sounded impressed. "You must have pissed somebody off good. They're normally under orders not to abuse us that much."

Gabe lifted his eyes from the floor and looked around, getting his first look at his cellmates. They were four men spread out in front of him. Despite the pain, he laughed slightly and said, "Yeah, well I guess they wanted to make sure I got my fair share."

They looked at him blankly. Not *Stones* fans, Gabe thought. Grabbing a pole attached to the cot he tried to stand and with help from two on either side, he made it to his feet. To stay standing, he held himself up against an upper cot.

One man, a white guy across the cell, asked, "What's your name?"

"Gabe."

"I'm Tall Alex." He pointed to an unusually short black man. "That's Short Alex." Pointing at the other two he added, "This is Justin and that's Peter."

Peter spoke up. "It's actually 'Pietrov'. I'm originally from Ukraine, but here I'm Peter."

Gabe briefly studied them. They all looked about his age, give or take a few years, with Justin appearing to be several years older than the rest and Short Alex the youngest. They all were disheveled with some rips in their clothes and a few minor bruises and scrapes, but nothing compared to Gabe's wounds. Tall Alex wasn't any taller than Gabe, probably an inch or two less. He was only tall in comparison to Short Alex. He had dirty blond hair, was wearing khakis and a light blue polo shirt and, but for his bruises and rips and the setting, struck Gabe as a typical preppie.

Shaking his head and acting more dazed than he really was, Gabe checked out the others more closely. The first things Gabe noted about Peter were his stringy black hair, which probably had gone unwashed for too long, and his wispy moustache. He frequently pushed aside strands of his hair hanging over his rimless glasses. Peter wiped his glasses showing Gabe that one stem dangled, perhaps a result of the evening's activities. Short Alex was short, by any standard. He was thin and looked to be in his early twenties. He wore beige drawstring pants and an MLK tee shirt. An odd-looking furrow ran across his lower forehead. It was thin and shallow except for strips above each eye. These ran deeper and darker and curved downward toward the middle of his face. They gave him a slightly puzzled look but, as Gabe soon learned, when he had a determined or stern look, these lines accentuated that. He wore thick-lensed glasses with a tortoise shell frame.. He seemed more roughed up than the other three—Gabe figured it was because he was black. Last was Justin. Medium height, a strong build and brown hair. Of Chinese descent Gabe thought. He was wearing jeans and a plain white tee shirt.

"What'd you do to deserve the honor of getting worked over like that?" Tall Alex asked.

Gabe thought, *Here's an opening to do what Smith and Jones want.*

"They wanted the names of leaders on the left. For some reason they thought I knew some. I kept saying 'I don't know,' and they kept hitting."

Justin's eyes narrowed and he studied Gabe closely while Tall Alex's jaws clenched and his knuckles turned white as he gripped the cell's bars.

"Do you know?" Justin asked, leaning toward him.

"No," he replied with a big sigh. Then he said loudly, "How would I know? I'm just a guy who shows up at some marches and protests like lots of other people. Otherwise, I'm not involved." Gabe looked around, the others concentrating on him, making their interest clear. "Sorry guys, I don't know shit."

"So why'd they pick on you?" Tall Alex queried, stepping forward and getting up in Gabe's face. "They must have a reason for thinking you do know."

"Well they were wrong,"

Gabe's fists clenched and some spit accidently flew from his mouth, catching Tall Alex. He'd had enough of being pushed around.

"Anyway, let's say I did. What's it to you?"

Short Alex slid in between them, one hand surprisingly firmly moving Tall Alex back a step and the other holding Gabe in place. He stared up at Tall Alex, then twisted his head to look up at Gabe. "Cool it you two. Let's not fight among ourselves."

Tall Alex stared at Gabe for a few moments, looked down at Short Alex and with a big exhale said, "You're right." He looked at Gabe. "Sorry man."

Gabe nodded. Short Alex held his position, like a basketball referee between two seven footers. Tall Alex then backed off, ending up again leaning against the bars on the opposite side of the cell.

Tall Alex may have been done, at least for the moment, but Justin wasn't. He tilted his head slightly and scratched the back of his neck, saying, "You know it's strange, and frustrating. I mean we get out there and protest. Sometimes fights break out, and maybe people get hurt or arrested. The cops book us so they know who we are. Everyone knows a few others, such as speakers and some logistics sort of people, but what about the people behind all this? Those who decide, 'OK, let's march from here to there or take over this place or protest that event.' As far as I know, most of them are unknown. Who are they?"

Peter rattled the others by smacking one of the cots and said, "Whoever they are, from my old country I know how dangerous secret leaders can be."

"Maybe these leaders are set up in ranks, or in cells like in spy books, so only their direct reports know them," Tall Alex chimed in. Raising his voice he called across to Gabe, "What do you think?"

Gabe looked back at Tall Alex's face, noting his pursed lips and stare, and felt that the guy had something against him. Small Alex noticed this too, and he rested his hand on Gabe again.

Gabe replied, "I don't know Tall Alex. I never gave it a thought before tonight. You seem like you have though. What's your idea? Or are you secretly one of our fearless leaders?"

Tall Alex looked at Gabe, shook his head, then went and sat on the floor in a corner of the cell. Resting his head on his folded arms, he appeared to ignore what went on.

The rest continued talking about leaders, with Justin and Peter doing most of the talking although, in Gabe's opinion, saying little that was meaningful. They periodically asked Short Alex and Gabe what they thought, but neither contributed much, although Gabe kept repeating that he wanted to know who they were. Eventually the talk petered out and they each took a cot to try to get some sleep while Tall Alex spent the night in the corner he'd staked out.

Gabe had followed what the others were saying, but he mostly thought about his situation. Smith and Jones had told him what they wanted from him, along with telling him not to tell anyone about them "or else." But, he thought, in movies and books, when characters followed these instructions it almost always proved to be a dangerous mistake. He didn't know the right way to handle it but was unwilling to risk Jasminn and Matt getting hurt, so decided that for the moment he'd obey instructions. He wanted to get back at Smith and Jones, but his main feelings were fear for Matt and mainly for Jasminn. He was also scared personally but wouldn't admit it to himself. Instead, he thought, *I'm not too happy about this.*

////

Later, Gabe had no idea how much later, the cell block's speakers let loose with a long loud siren, rousing the inmates and setting off grumbling from those who'd managed to sleep.

"Morning wake up call," Justin announced.

The police wanted to clear the protesters out quickly and they were organized and efficient. Officers went cell by cell, taking the inmates for processing. Gabe's cell was one of the first. Each cell's occupants first received desk appearance tickets, then were escorted to another section to reclaim their possessions. To Gabe's surprise, the police gave him what Smith and Jones had confiscated, including his phone. Once someone had their possessions, they were ushered out a side door, like a guest who'd overstayed their welcome.

Gabe was the third from his cell to hit the street and the last two showed up right behind him. The former cellmates clustered in an uncomfortable silence. Gabe shivered from the cool early morning breeze and enjoyed the sun's brightness and the glistening morning dew. Peter took a crumpled pack of cigarettes from a satchel he was now carrying, took one and offered the pack around. None of the others accepted. Peter shrugged and lit his with a lighter he'd dug out of the satchel.

Short Alex broke the silence. "Hey, Gabe, you got a pen and maybe give me your number?"

"No pen," Gabe replied, "but," reaching into his wallet, "here's my card."

Short Alex studied it.

"This is one of those hot-shot fancy law firms, isn't it? And you're a lawyer there?" Short Alex asked, both surprised and impressed, the dark arcs above his eyes deepening.

"Yeah, I'm an associate there, and being arrested and spending the night in jail is just what the partners want their associates doing."

Perhaps, Gabe, thought, knowing a lawyer was a good thing, since Justin and Peter quickly asked for his card and even Tall Alex did. While Gabe dug out more cards and passed them around, everyone else but Peter tapped phones, exchanging contact information, but still saying little and avoiding eye contact. Peter held up an old clam shell phone and shrugged. Gabe tapped phones with Justin and each Alex.

"I'm going to wait for my friends," Gabe told them. The others nodded to each other and took off, except for Tall Alex, who lingered.

Looking at Gabe but still avoiding eye contact, Tall Alex said softly, "Sorry for how I acted in there. The whole thing hit me hard. You know?'

"I know well."

"Maybe we can catch up on this leadership stuff at some point?"

"Sure Tall Alex," Gabe replied, not expecting the suggestion or any follow up.

"Good, and since we're no longer locked up with Short Alex, I'm back to simply 'Alex'."

With that, Alex left. Gabe looked around for Smith and Jones, but then figured the spot might be too public for them. He didn't doubt though that they'd grab him soon.

Shortly, Matt emerged from the precinct, blinking and rubbing his eyes from the early morning light. He spotted Gabe and rushed over, lifting him up and giving him a bear hug. Gabe let out a sharp cry from the hug's pressure on his ribs.

"You OK?" Matt asked, trying to examine Gabe while still hugging him.

"Yeah, just some bruises. Now, would you put me down?"

They killed time, joking and smiling in relief at being on the outside and in one piece. Knowing what he knew, Gabe was especially relieved Matt was alright and hadn't been tossed in with the alt-right. After they waited awhile, Jasminn finally appeared. Gabe ran to her and without thinking, picked her up and hugged her tight, ignoring his pain and taking comfort in her body pressed against his as he held back tears, surprising himself.

She tilted her head to look him in the face. "Gabe, what're you doing here? Put me down."

He lowered her the few inches to the ground.

"I'm just glad you're OK," he whispered.

"I'm fine, all considered. What're you doing here?"

"I'll tell you, but let's get gone first."

Matt had joined them and he said, "I'm hungry. Let's get some breakfast."

They walked until they found a cab letting out an investment banker-type. Gabe gave the driver his address and they drove off.

CHAPTER SIX

After delivering Gabe to the police, Smith and Jones had gone home. Jones was back at the station early, watching Gabe from a distance once he was released. When Gabe and his friends left, Jones followed them then reported to Smith.

When Jones called, Smith had already completed his workout, showered and was out on his small patio, sipping the day's first cup of coffee, black. His feet were up and he was gazing across the Hudson to his panoramic view of the City. Smith lived in a small apartment on the flats in Weehawken, New Jersey. Often, he was up early enough to catch the sun peeking through the city's cross streets, its rays pointing toward him, and he'd follow the light as it climbed above the city's rooftops.

After Jones' call Smith hiked up to Port Imperial, grabbed his second coffee from a fast food stand and hopped aboard a ferry.

Smith stood on deck as the ferry crossed the Hudson, shifting his weight from one leg to the other to balance against the river's chop. He reflected on this assignment, rubbing his free hand across his jaw and his neck. He believed in the DHS and this assignment's objectives, but aspects gave him pause. He had qualms about how they'd coerced Gabe. Convincing someone to volunteer, or threatening jail for someone's misdeeds, were both fine by him. But Gabe hadn't volunteered, and they had no legal claim against him. Moreover, kidnapping and beating him violated many laws, despite the national security b.s. he'd given Gabe. To Smith, the worst part was the threats they'd made. Smith didn't intend to follow through on them, but he wasn't so sure about Jones.On top of that, Smith didn't know whether Harry Einner, Smith's immediate superior, would order them to carry these out.

The ferry eased into its slip and its passengers made their way off. Stepping onto the cement pier, Smith reminded himself '*It was all for the greater good*,' and resolved that he'd do whatever was needed.

////

Several months earlier, in Washington, D.C., a man in a dark suit and a black Borsalino hat reached the bottom of a staircase leading from a dark alley and ending at the sturdy-looking metal door facing him. He'd arrived by a circuitous route. His driver had dropped him off at the luxury apartment building of his current mistress who, if need be, would swear he was with her all night. From there he'd strode several blocks to a bar where he didn't think he'd be recognized. He had had the bartender call him a cab which had dropped him a block from the alley. Now, rapping on the door using the code given to him, the whole scenario struck him as being out of a film noir.

A young woman let him in. He amused himself by saying, "Swordfish," although he highly doubted she was a Marx Brothers *aficionado* so wouldn't know what he referred to, but sweeping by her he knew she knew who he was.

At the end of a short hall he entered a room which killed the film noir notion. It resembled a suburban rec room, with its large TV, deep chairs and sofas, a small bar and ashen wood paneling. About twenty people were scattered about. They were split evenly between men and women by happenstance, were almost all white, and at least in their late thirties. When he entered, those who'd been sitting quickly rose and everyone went to him, shook his hand while introducing themselves and saying 'What an honor it was' or words to similar effect. He scanned the room then took the most prominently positioned chair. He put his hat on a table, crossed his legs and sat at ease while Harry Einner, their host, brought him a straight up rye made in the man's home state. He sniffed it, enjoying the aroma, sipped it and swirled it around in his mouth, enjoying the taste and texture, and finally let it slide down his throat. He quietly sighed with pleasure.

Before they started, Harry squatted by him and they whispered back and forth. Harry had spent his career in government. He'd moved to the Department of Homeland Security shortly after it was organized and was now one of its highest ranking non-political appointees. He knew all the others personally, vouched for them and had brought them together that evening.

Harry returned to the bar and leaned against it while the rest sat, several on the edge of their seats, and all leaning toward the man. Harry officially greeted him, "Welcome, Senator. I can't properly express how excited we all are at having you here with us."

The group broke into hearty applause. As senators go, the Senator was quite young, and was only in the third year of his first term, but he was a burgeoning star. He'd started with a typical background—wealthy family, and Ivy League undergraduate and law degrees. These were followed by a clerkship with a conservative appellate judge in Chicago who often served as a direct conduit to a Supreme Court clerkship with one of the right justices. After the Chicago clerkship though, he had made a radical shift from the well-trodden path and went to work back in his home state. He'd joined a not-for-profit, but high paying, law firm financed by serious right wing money. The firm primarily defended right wingers facing criminal charges stemming from their political activities. He'd become well-known among many of the ordinary people who shared his views. They came to consider him one of their own and backed him when, in his first foray into elected politics, he ran for an open Senate seat and resoundingly won.

The Senator hit them with his beaming smile, acknowledging his host and the rest with a small proffer of his glass.

He responded, "Thank you, Harry."

Looking about, he continued in his deep baritone, "Thank you all. I understand from my good friend Harry you are patriotic Americans prepared to do whatever is necessary to restore our country to its former greatness."

His audience enthusiastically nodded and kept their eyes on the Senator, waiting for the gems to fall. He disappointed them, however.

"I'm not going to give you a lengthy speech about the sorry state of our country, our government's complicity in its woeful condition or our need to act. That'd be preaching to the choir." They laughed and he gave them a big grin, showing his pearl white even teeth. "If you want to hear that though, be in the Senate balcony when I'm orating and I promise you, you will get your fill."

Uncrossing his legs he shifted slightly toward Harry. "What we're here to talk about this evening is action. Isn't that right, Harry?"

"That's right, Senator," Harry replied, beaming over this recognition.

"I've briefly met several of you before, and Harry's given me dossiers on each of you. I know you're all senior figures in one enforcement arm or another. I'm sure you do your best to carry forward our ideals, even under this administration. I'm also sure that unfortunately you receive criticism from some of the ignorant on our side who don't understand that to succeed we need covert people like you on the inside. On behalf of myself and my Congressional colleagues in arms, thank you for your hard work and perseverance."

He tipped the rye glass toward them again and they responded in kind with their glasses and large smiles. The Senator had another sip.

"So I'm not here to talk big picture. We don't need to do that. I'm not here to talk specifics. I leave it to you great warriors to handle this— developing action plans and seeing them through. Instead, I'm here for other reasons. First, I want to remove any doubts any of you might have about your support in high places. By coming here and meeting you face-to-face I am making my support clear, despite the risks involved. If any of you doubt that or have questions, speak up. Please."

He scanned the room. They were all older than him and had risen to positions of power within the jungle of the government's institutions by being smart and tough survivors, besides, in most cases, ruthless. Nevertheless, as the Senator had assumed, his statements went unchallenged.

"Certain of my fellow Senators and a good number of Representatives over in the House not only agree with us, but are actively working with me. I'm not naming names, but I don't doubt you know who many of them are." He chuckled and his audience chuckled along. "I know from Harry that to some extent you're investigating the left. You need to step this up. In particular, you need to uncover and deal with the leaders on the left, both of the violent groups and the non-violent ones. This will not only undermine them but will alleviate pressure on the right and placate those of our constituents who feel our government ignores the radical left.

"Now I know that according to the left-wing think tank stooges and the manufactured news from the lying left-wing media, on the streets the left doesn't have many real leaders and instead they act mainly as a movement, whatever that means. Right! Sure!" His audience laughed. "They just all happen to show up at the same places at the same times for the same causes! And black bloc groups just happen to be there to fight for protestors and to wage their own attacks and rampage and engage in looting on our streets! My god, these people must think we're fools to believe this. No! We must find these leaders and chop off the dragon's heads!"

He let them reflect for a moment while taking only a small sip, trying to avoid indulging his worsening habit of overindulging and, as a result, requiring extra workouts to work off those extra drinks.

"The more successful you are, the more successful my colleagues and I can be in making the political appointees ease up on the right and apply more pressure against the left. This can affect policies and critically affect the outcome of the next election and the cycle after that. I'm not interested in, and don't want to know, how you conduct matters, although," his smile was disingenuous, a crocodile's grin, "you must of course obey the law. One other point. There are some serious crazies out there."

At this, several people laughed. However, seeing the Senator's tight mouth and glaring eyes they ceased and adopted their own frowns.

"Sad to say, but I mean on our side. People believing in cannibalism by senior officials, believing in fake Supreme Court Justices and lots more." Shaking his head he added, "Can you imagine? We'll use these naïve fools for the present, but at the right time we'll strip them of any power. The power is for us here and our fellow patriots. I trust this is clear." The audience nodded.

Finished, the Senator stepped to the bar, chatting with people for several minutes. He made a point of lavishing extra attention on counterparts of Harry's at the Bureau and the Justice Department, knowing how useful they could be. Soon, leaving Harry to make his apologies, he slipped out, followed a different circuitous route back to his mistress' apartment, and spent the rest of the night in her arms, seeking relief from his weighty duties.

CHAPTER SEVEN

Once at Gabe's apartment, Jasminn and Matt immediately raided his fridge. Gabe took several aspirins and a shower. The jetting hot water aggravated the bruises, and even soaping himself hurt. Afterwards, wearing only shorts with a towel hanging around his neck, Gabe joined the other two who sat eating at his kitchen counter.

Matt saw Gabe first, taking in the bruises on his body. Matt slammed his fist on the counter then turned away from the other two.

Startled by Matt's pounding, Jasminn glanced up, looking at Matt, then at Gabe and stopped chewing mid-bite.

"Oh my god, Gabe! Those look bad."

Gabe tried to make light of the marks. "I'll survive, but you should see those other guys' fists."

She ignored his mangling of the old line, her mouth twisted in concern.

"Really, how'd you get those?"

He couldn't mention Smith and Jones, so had to lie. "A bunch of alt-righters got in some blows. I'm not hurt, but I guess if the cops hadn't pulled them off me it might've gotten a little serious."

They wouldn't let him slough it off.

"Come on Gabe, that looks really bad," Matt said, surprising Gabe by how concerned he was.

Jasminn came around the counter, gently touched a few of the reddest bruises with her fingertips then ran a hand across the left side of his rib cage. "You need X-rays. You might've broken something."

Her hand rested on his side a few moments longer than necessary for her examination.

Matt nodded.

Jasminn snickered, "And Gabe, on the court this could really mess up your A game."

He tilted his head slightly and tightened his lips, but was glad she teased him, rather than just being upset.

"Seriously, you've got to be examined," Matt pushed. "We'll be heading back to our places and will drop you at an emergency room or a walk-in clinic, your choice. If you don't agree, I'll carry you in."

Gabe gave a weak smile and nodded again. He knew this wasn't going to be avoided, plus they were probably right—he should get checked out. He grabbed two power bars and some soda, a morning favorite, and joined them. While they ate, he embellished his story about being beaten by the alt-right and saved by the cops. In turn, he asked how they'd escaped unscathed.

Jasminn answered, continually shifting her eyes back to his bruises and shaking her head. "When Matt reached me we found a spot partway to one side. Suddenly, several cops made a beeline for us and grabbed us. They didn't hit us, only cuffed us and deposited us in a van. It was weird. As if they'd targeted us."

"It was probably my fault," Matt said, "Maybe they saw my size, figured 'He could be trouble' and wanted to take me out right away."

Jasminn raised one eyebrow, finding the explanation weak, but having no better answer she let it go except to say, "Modest, aren't we?"

Jasminn and Matt maintained a nonchalant air, but Gabe picked up signs—Matt's fork kept clanking against his plate as if he didn't have a solid grip on it and his left knee kept jerking slightly, while Jasminn kept wiping her eyes, complaining about allergies. Gabe could tell that the night's events had gotten to them, regardless of what they said.

Done eating, Gabe threw on some clothes, wincing as he moved. He picked a button-down shirt because a pullover would've hurt too much. Finding he couldn't button it himself, Jasminn ended up doing it. While she did so, he blushed slightly and she carefully avoiding making eye contact, but neither said anything.

Shortly, they headed uptown in a car Gabe called. It was still fairly early, but rush hour traffic was already heavy. Go-getters crowded the sidewalks. Normally they would have been part of this.

Looking out the window, Jasminn mused, "It's amazing. We were at a protest and in a riot then spent a night in jail." the driver gave her a nervous look, seeking to determine whether his passengers were trouble. "Now it looks as if nothing happened. Just another day in the big city." The others said nothing in response.

The first stop was a walk-in clinic. Matt had the driver wait until he saw Gabe enter and talk to the woman at the check-in desk.

After checking in, filling out many forms and showing them his health insurance card, his prescription insurance card and his driver's license plus his pharmacy information, Gabe took a seat in the waiting room.

Unexpectedly soon, a nurse's aide called him. Gabe followed her to an examination room, where a young doctor was waiting for him.

Gabe grimaced as he slowly managed to ease his shirt off. The doctor carefully, and much more gently than Ms. Doctor from last night, probed various spots. The diagnosis matched Ms. Doctor's, but the doctor ordered X-rays to be sure.

The doctor said, "I'll send in a prescription for a pain killer in case you need it. Be careful though, you don't want to get addicted." The doctor reeled off some of its possible side effects.

Gabe nodded.

Job done, the doctor departed, and the same nurse's aide helped Gabe on with a paper robe and brought him to the X-ray room. Gabe looked at the technician. The man was well into his sixties, much older than his fancy X-ray equipment.

Gabe's robe accidently parted, making the technician whistle at the sight of the bruises. "You steal some guy's girl you got all those?" he asked with a big grin.

Gabe immediately liked him the man. He managed a weak smile and went along. "How'd you guess?"

The technician maintained his grin then got busy having Gabe assume a different position on the slab for each slide, causing Gabe to wince from the hard surface pressing against his bruises. finished, the technician said, "Wait here Romeo while I make sure these came out properly and we don't have to redo any."

He returned in a few minutes. "Alright, you're done."

"Any breaks?" Gabe asked.

"Only the radiologist is allowed to discuss that."

"Come on, you've probably seen thousands more X-rays than any radiologist here. Give me a clue at least."

The technician studied Gabe's face, judging how trustworthy he was. "Don't tell anyone I said anything, but you'll be fine. In the future though, find single ladies."

"Good advice and thanks."

"Yeah, and you be careful now."

////

Back in the examination room, Gabe painfully changed back into his shirt, then started to leave. Passing an open door, he heard, "Get in here Kid."

Shit. Gabe knew that was Jones. Smith gently tugged Gabe in by a sleeve and closed the door behind them.

Gabe sighed, "Should I bother asking how you followed me or got in here?"

"No, don't bother, Gabriel," Smith said, adding, "I'm glad you're smart and got yourself checked out. Despite what the doctor said, if you pee blood, only worry if it lasts more than two or three days."

"What, now you're a doctor?" Gabe came across as both sarcastic and angry.

"Just the voice of experience."

Jones pointed to the examining table, ordering "Sit." Gabe sat at its edge.

"What'd you learn?" Jones asked.

"Not much."

"Come on Gabriel, please cooperate."

A thought occurred to Gabe. He asked, "Didn't you record us?"

Jones shook his head in disgust while Smith smiled.

"Think back to your Constitutional Law class, Gabriel. You did get an A in it."

Gabe's fists clenched and his muscles tightened, as once again Gabe was angered by them knowing so much about him. He did recall a lesson from the class though. "You did. The Supreme Court has ruled prisoners don't have a reasonable expectation of privacy. You could've recorded us."

"It's slightly more complicated for people who've only been arrested but not Mirandized or convicted, but yes we would've taped you anyhow," Smith admitted, adding to Jones, "I told you he was smart."

"What they didn't teach you in law school though are the practicalities. It's impossible to record every cell and track what's said. The equipment and manpower costs would be huge."

Gabe shot back, "I get it about the equipment cost, but I'd bet you have NSA key word recognition software to know which taped conversations are of interest."

Smith shook his head in admiration, saying to Jones, "See. We have got to get Gabriel to join the Department after this is over."

Jones banged his fist on a countertop and complained, "Unfortunately, the fuckin' cops screwed up. Only some cells have cameras and they were supposed to put all of you in one of those. Instead, they put you guys in the cell next to the monitored one. We got nothing."

"Life's a bitch," Gabe retorted with a big grin.

Jones looked at Smith, who shook his head, forcing Jones to keep back from Gabe.

"Alright, what'd you learn, Gabriel?" Smith asked.

Gabe had been mulling how to answer this question since his release. He stared down at the tile floor then eased off the table, now standing on equal footing with them.

"You picked those guys. You really think they're important?"

Jones growled, "We're talking about what you think, not what we think."

"Okay, Okay."

Gabe raised his hands in mock surrender. He collected his thoughts then began. "My first feeling is they're an insignificant unimpressive group, and it's hard to believe any of them are leaders of anything. The one possible exception is Tall Alex."

Smith interrupted, "Tall Alex?"

"You know you put in two guys named Alex. Before I was thrown in they'd already been tagged 'Tall Alex' and 'Short Alex'."

"Not 'Black Alex' and 'White Alex'?" Jones asked.

"I guess that's one difference between them and you," Gabe replied, his brow furrowing slightly and his eyes rolling up.

"Or maybe they're heightists, not racists," Smith said with a small grin. "Anyway, go ahead."

"Short Alex looked young and seemed rather naïve but a nice guy. I can't see him as a leader, although I give him credit for guts for stepping between Tall Alex and me. Justin and Peter talked as if they hadn't thought much about the question before but got very interested the more we talked. They kept on about it after the rest of us had had enough and tried to get some sleep."

"And Tall Alex?" asked Jones, emphasizing the word 'tall'.

Gabe knew he'd have to give them somebody and had decided it'd be Tall Alex. "I wouldn't rule him out. He's smart, very presentable and has a good presence. When he thought maybe I knew some leaders he seemed concerned. I'm not saying he's one of these leaders you're looking for or is connected, but of all of them he seemed the most likely."

They made him go through as much of what had been said as he could remember, paying particular attention to what Tall Alex said and both of them watching him closely. He told them what he remembered, afraid to lie to them since he thought they might be lying to him about the absence of a recording.

"What's your read of their impression of you?" Smith asked.

"I'm not sure. I'd say it varied. Tall Alex was definitely suspicious of me, at least at first." He paused. "Justin and Peter. . . hmm, I'd guess they thought I might be in the chain of leadership, but not too high."

Gabe gave them a sliver of a smile. "I'm sure they didn't think I was an informant. Short Alex said very little, but I'd say he thought I was just someone who got caught up in the scene."

Smith was silent for several moments and looked away from Gabe He turned back. "This is how you'll proceed…."

Before Smith got any further, Gabe cried, "No way. You promised I'd only have to do that one thing. We're done."

"Don't be naïve Kid. Of course we're not done with you," Jones said, chuckling at Gabe believing them. "This is just the beginning."

Gabe clenched his fists again. He spotted a scalpel resting on the counter. He flashed on grabbing it, stabbing Jones and running.

Reading Gabe's mind, Jones taunted, "Go ahead Kid. That'd give me an excuse to really work you over."

"Don't do anything stupid, Gabriel. Let's talk," Smith almost pleaded.

Gabe hesitated, staring first at the scalpel and then the distance between him and Jones. He'd bet Jones couldn't stop him from getting ahold of it. But then what? He certainly wasn't going to seriously hurt him. And he was sure Smith would intervene.

Deciding, Gabe shook his head, saying, "You're not worth it, Jones."

Jones laughed. "Chicken shit!"

"Enough," Smith ordered in a harsh voice.

"Gabriel, if you'd delivered what we needed, that might have ended this. But you didn't, so it doesn't."

"And what if I refuse? Will your Doberman here attack me again? If so, at least I'm in the right place for when he's done."

Smith sighed, "Gabriel we don't want to work you over again, and I hope we won't have to. However, if we do, we do." He paused and sighed again. "More than that, the real leverage is your friends."

Jones spoke up, "You'll learn, Kid. Having friends can be dangerous."

Smith's look at Jones was one of exasperation. Refocusing on Gabe he continued, "Ignore that. However, they do provide leverage. Your friends could easily end up back in a cell and put through what we described last night. Or they could vanish into the system."

Gabe's rage kept growing, but he could only clench his hands helplessly.

Smith shook his head. "Gabriel, I don't know why you don't admit it to yourself, but you and Jasminn care deeply for each other. Maybe you're each waiting for the other to make the first move. Whether you two do or don't isn't my concern. My point is, you couldn't bear anything happening to her, especially if you were responsible. And believe me, anytime we want, something can happen to her. Funny enough, that's not too different from how you and Matt feel about each other."

Jones interrupted in a snide tone. "You got the hots for Matt, Kid?'

Gabe struggled inside but managed to ignore Jones. After shaking his head and a long pause he asked, "What do you want me to do now?"

"That's much better, Gabriel. See Jones, Gabriel is very rational, and we don't need all that violence."

The corners of Jones' lips turned down and his eyes looked away from both men. His disappointment was clear.

"We had our eyes on you outside the jail. We saw you guys exchanging contact info. That's a good sign and useful. Don't do anything for the next few days, just go to work and carry on normally.

Let's wait and see if any of them contact you. If none of them do, then we'll decide on next steps."

"How do I reach you if I've got something to report?"

Smith produced a card and handed it to Gabe. On it were only two phone numbers, one with an S next to it and the other with a J.

"We don't need your card. We've got your number," Smith pointed out.

"In more ways than one," Jones added.

Smith waited for Gabe's reply, but Gabe had nothing left to say.

"Two more things, Gabriel," Smith cautioned, "Don't mention any of this to anyone. That includes Jasminn and Matt. If you do, things might become unpleasant for them. Plus, you're not our only concern, so you won't necessarily see us or hear from us every day. However, don't think for a second that doesn't mean that we won't know where you are and what you're doing at all times, so don't play games."

After Smith and Jones left, Gabe sat on a rolling stool, sliding back and forth and thinking, but getting no further with any ideas than he got by rolling in the small space. Someone knocked on the door.

"Are you alright, in there?"

"Fine. I'll be out shortly."

Within minutes Gabe was gone from the clinic, on his way back to his apartment and hopefully, he thought, to get some work done. Late that afternoon he received two emails from the clinic. One was the radiologist's report confirming no breaks or fractures. The other was a bill for his co-pay.

CHAPTER EIGHT

Back at his apartment Gabe emailed the firm, saying he was sick but would do what he could from home. He spent an hour mainly staring at his laptop without getting anything done, so decided to get a change of scenery. His customary refuge was a nearby non-chain coffee house. As was normal at this hour it wasn't crowded, so Gabe was able to secure his favorite seat, a large old heavily cushioned wingback chair.

After he drew the waitress' attention, she brought his usual without his having to ask, and sat. They chatted while he avoided staring at her. She had a bull nose ring, a stud below her pierced lower lip and multiple tattoos. She often flirted with him, and he liked her, but didn't get her look. He supported people's rights to generally do what they wanted—if his waitress wanted to wear her bull ring, more power to her. Gabe would defend her right to do so, the look just didn't work for him.

He tried again to work, but still couldn't focus. He couldn't stop rehashing the prior night and pondering what to do. Looking around the restaurant with a vacant stare he wondered again why Homeland Security was going after the left. From everything he'd read, including a bulletin the Department itself had issued, the right posed a much greater threat of domestic terrorism. He grabbed an arm of the chair and squeezed it hard. This wasn't politics, this was just a fact.

He nibbled on his muffin while assessing his own situation, crumbs falling on his lap. He considered going to the police or the FBI. He didn't know if Smith and Jones' scheme was legal, although he thought it probably would be with the proper authorizations, *"Whatever those might be,*" he said to himself. Assaulting him though had to be a crime, although he figured they'd just claim he resisted arrest and any charges would probably go nowhere. Coercing him by threatening to harm Jasminn and Matt must be a crime. Unfortunately, he couldn't prove this, plus he assumed they'd plead 'national security.' He highly doubted that the police or FBI route would work and was afraid that'd only make the situation worse. After staring off a while longer and letting his drink get cold, he decided that the best course would be for Smith and Jones to decide he was useless and drop him. They'd made it clear though if he failed to do as instructed Jasminn and Matt would suffer, and he couldn't risk that. While gulping his cappuccino, he decided that, for now at least, he'd have to go along. Decision made, once again he tried to work, but he still couldn't focus on it and accomplished little.

////

The next day was Saturday. The aches from his beatings had lessened but Gabe planned to take it easy. While Gabe was resting, Matt showed up in the early afternoon.

"You get the X-ray results?" he demanded to know as soon as he was in the door.

"Yes, and nothing's broken except my wallet from the co-pay," Gabe replied, tossing Matt an energy drink.

Matt sprawled on the sofa. "Don't bitch man. Be glad you're OK. You're lucky. Anyway, you're a hot shot lawyer. You can afford it."

"Yeah, me and my student loans. Remember, I wasn't on scholarship like you."

Matt could only shrug. He'd had a free ride in college to play basketball. Coming out of high school, scouts had considered him a serious pro prospect down the road. He was six eight, two-forty, built like an Adonis with great natural athletic ability. He topped most NBA players with a forty-two inch vertical jump, and could run stride for stride with sprinters. What he lacked though was the 'drive', frustrating many people over the years, especially his coaches. He'd never 'put in the work'. He'd never done those ten thousand repetitions supposedly needed to reach the highest level. Even with this attitude though, he'd made Second Team All-Conference his junior and senior years and All Defensive Team three years running.

Jasminn had been particularly frustrated by Matt. She'd put in that work and was naturally talented, but had nothing like Matt's gifts. Her hard work and talent got her her own athletic scholarship and a chance to play Division One college ball, but she didn't have the ability to go further, no matter how hard she worked. Matt frustrated Gabe as well, but more for Matt's own sake. Gabe had the willingness to work but knew from early on he had nowhere near the requisite talent. He was content playing high school ball and then helping their university's nationally ranked women's team by practicing against them.

"Sorry, Matt, I didn't mean it that way."

"Don't worry. I know."

Gabe pushed Matt's legs off the sofa and joined him there.

Matt told him, "I'm going to a court in Brooklyn. It's got a good game. It'll be a good place to work off some stress. Wanna come watch?"

"No, I'll take it easy here." Gabe smiled at Matt and slapped him on the back. "You go dazzle them. I'll check the Twitter raves."

Matt hung out a bit longer before taking off. Watching him go, Gabe thought how the crowd was in for quite a show. He knew what a kick Matt got out of showing up at new courts and wowing everyone. Sometimes Gabe thought of Matt as an overgrown kid. This was absurd though. Matt worked in finance at an investment bank where he was a rising star, putting in the effort there he'd never devoted to his game.

Later, Jasminn unexpectedly showed up. Gabe got a big grin when he saw her. On the sofa they talked about what had happened.

"Nothing's broken?" she asked.

"No. Just a lot of ugly bruises."

"Let me check it out," she said with a sly smile while grabbing his shirt and trying to pull it off.

"And I'll make sure you're OK," he said, reaching for her shirt.

She hit him with a pillow and neither got to check the other.

He couldn't tell her about Smith and Jones or what they were making him do, but since she was so involved with the protest movement he thought maybe he could get some useful information from her.

"Hey Jaz, you ever think about how all these demonstrations and marches come together and how everyone, including both sides' fringes, know where to show up?"

"Not really, but it's no big deal. Sometimes we get a city permit so the police aren't supposed to be able to call it an unlawful demonstration." She added, "One of their favorite gambits. Anyone who cares can find out through the permit process. To get people to show we spread the word—mainly through social media sites everyone checks. Other than you, of course." She smirked at him. "And we want media coverage, so we usually tell them in advance. With all that it's easy for anyone to know."

"What about the decision to hold the rally or march in the first place ? How does that come about?"

She stared at the ceiling and thought.

"Sometimes it's kinda organic. Something happens, perhaps a bad shooting by the police of a person of color, or a b.s. court ruling, and we respond. A few people say go here or there and we coalesce around that. Other times we hear others are planning something so we join. Or some of our people take the lead."

He pressed her. "Don't you think certain people play the key roles in planning all this—basically leaders?"

"Yeah, sure, some people are more proactive than others."

"But are they effectively leading the left, whether or not they're labeled 'leaders'?"

She studied his face, trying to see where this was coming from. "Very few officially, to my knowledge. But some in effect, I guess."

"Do you know any of them?"

She gazed around the apartment, thinking for another moment. "I don't think so."

"Doesn't that bother you?

"What bother me?"

"Come on Jaz, you're no puppet and you're no fool. You're as independent-minded and smart as anyone I know. Maybe smarter. It doesn't bother you that you don't know who's directing things?"

She tilted her head and frowned, giving him a confused look. "It's really not like that," she replied. "It's more a consensus approach."

"You're telling me you don't think there are leaders who play key roles? And maybe the way they work they intentionally stay out of the limelight?"

She shook her head. "Maybe. Sure. Like I said, some people are more involved than others and they're in a better position to plan."

Jasminn's view was muddled, but Gabe took it to mean there were at least quasi-leaders—people who often called the shots. These would be the ones Smith and Jones wanted.

He leaned toward her. "Let's say you wanted to meet them. Could you?"

Jasminn pushed him back, jumped up from the sofa and planted her hands on her hips, glowered down at him. "What's this all about?"

Seeing he'd pushed too hard, Gabe backpedaled, leaning back and saying, "While I was in the cell the others talked about this whole leaders issue, so it made me wonder. Nothing more than that. Sorry, didn't mean to upset you."

She let it pass, gave him a wicked grin and plopped back down. "You're too full of yourself if you think you can upset me. You're out of your league boy."

They didn't speak for a bit, neither sure what to say, until Gabe suggested ordering Thai food and playing video games. Jasminn went along, leaving Gabe relieved that she'd dropped the matter, and leaving her wondering whether what he'd said about his cellmates was really what that had been about.

She left soon after they'd eaten and split several games. Once she was gone Gabe paced around his living room and thought about their conversation. He decided there must be a small group who played a key role in the movement. These were the people Smith and Jones wanted him to reach to get to the extremist leaders. Gabe had no idea how he was going to get to any protest leaders or, assuming they really existed, and assuming there was a connection, from there to the leaders at the far ends. Nevertheless, he was determined that if he could help it he wasn't going to get Jasminn any more involved. It wasn't long though before he couldn't help it.

CHAPTER NINE

The next morning Gabe dragged himself out of bed. Still sore; he'd slept poorly. His body was healing, but not quickly enough to satisfy him. He'd resisted taking painkillers during the night, so however he laid had hurt some part of his body. He'd dozed off several times. Once he'd dreamed he was naked, bound to a metal rack with Smith and Jones looming over him. Jones had a devil's face with horns, and the Jones devil branded Gabe's thigh with the likeness of a spy from *Mad* magazine's old *Spy vs. Spy*. Smith's face was his own but sat atop a cherub's body. The Smith cherub made soothing sounds and had a sympathetic look while dripping burning hot liquid on Gabe's bare torso.

Drinking coffee and aimlessly looking out the kitchen window, Gabe relived the dream. He rarely remembered his dreams. This one he remembered clearly though – *how could he not*. Its meaning seemed straightforward—he didn't need an analyst to interpret it--Smith and Jones had different approaches but were both evil and dangerous. To him the *Spy vs. Spy* branding meant he was a spy, but an inept one. Another thought made him chuckle—did the old Dutch painter Bosch have dreams like this, and if so, did they plague him or inspire him?

Gabe sprawled on his sofa, grabbed his laptop, and spent the morning and early afternoon researching extremists on both sides. From his first search query it was obvious that there was much more online information about the far right than far left. The extreme right, or alternate-right, called alt-right for short, was basically extreme right-wing groups which mostly held certain common beliefs, including white-nationalism, white supremacy, racism and antisemitism. All this Gabe already knew. He was struck though by how many different groups there'd been over time and how many there were now. There were older ones such as the Ku Klux Klan, the American Nazi Party and the Aryan Brotherhood, and many more recent ones. These included the Proud Boys, the Boogaloo Boys and the Three Percenters plus others new to Gabe. It didn't appear to him that these groups were affiliated, but he got no sense whether they coordinated their actions. From his reading he believed that many would resort to violence when they thought it necessary, plus in some cases under even less dire circumstances.

As Gabe continued with the alt-right, many groups' high degree of organization and public leadership leaped out at him. Websites often named their founders and leaders, and these people were featured in articles. Leaders appeared in pictures and were often shown participating in marches. What struck Gabe most and made him sit back and stare at his screen was that in so many images these men—and yes it was overwhelmingly men—were heavily armed. Gabe knew little about guns, but they clearly carried pistols and long guns, seemingly to him a mix of automatic machine guns, military rifles, plain old rifles and shotguns. He could only shake his head as none of this resonated with a Northerner who'd grown up in a progressive household in a big city and had attended a liberal college. Sitting back from his screen, he thought *Their beliefs are horrible, but I give them credit these days for being willing to back them openly, rather than hiding under cowl and robes.*

After what he'd seen, topped off by all the weaponry, Gabe took a break and to relax played an online two-person shooter game. He normally played well, but was too distracted by what he'd learned, and his avatar's head was soon blown off. *A warning?* he wondered.

Returning to his research, he switched to the extreme left or the antifascists as many called them: Antifa for short. He found little information and even less specifics about them. So much of what he did find consisted of theory and generalities. He didn't find the names of any activist leaders nor, with one exception, any openly avowed militant antifascist organizations. This one group had roughly a dozen chapters, mainly in the Mid-West and West. Even for them though, there were no names on the websites, or in any of the few articles about them.

This one organization's umbrella website provided some insights and established several tenets. Although its authors might deny this, Gabe interpreted it to mean that they would not only defend themselves, but would use force to defend other, less extreme leftist groups. Plus, they were willing to seek out and confront the alt-right and, under certain circumstances, law enforcement.

Gabe found no clues about how these groups communicated with each other or even internally. Even the best source he found, an article from several years ago in a prominent weekly magazine, had no definitive answers. By the end, Gabe wasn't convinced that the Antifa constituted an organized group.

Gabe's few hours of research weren't exhaustive, but he believed that further research here wouldn't unearth much more, and it certainly wouldn't unearth the information Smith and Jones were looking for. Of course, he thought, *if that could be found online, Homeland Security would have found it and wouldn't need me*. So, while Gabe had no sympathy for Smith and Jones or their mission, he understood why Homeland Security might conclude infiltration was necessary. Gabe jabbed a pen he'd been holding into a sofa cushion, realizing that this meant it'd be all the harder for him to get out of his situation.

None too happy, Gabe hunted in the fridge and flipped open cabinets, rummaging for some lunch, but only coming up with a can of soup. Partway through his soup, Gabe flung his spoon across the small kitchen, hitting a knife rack and sending three knives plummeting to the countertop. The plastic bowl was next. It bounced off the refrigerator, spraying soup all over. Gabe's tantrum didn't make him feel any better, but cleaning up the mess provided a brief distraction.

Still frustrated, Gabe decided to go for a run despite his bruises. Running was a common outlet for him. He hoped running couldn't further injure him. He was sure it would hurt but he'd deal with it. He threw on a pair of shorts and a shirt with cut off sleeves, then two pairs of thick socks, hoping the extra layer would cushion the impact. Sneakers laced and keys and a ten spot zipped into the shorts' pocket, he headed out.

On the street he stretched against a wall, loosening up briefly. Then he started, moving slowly, his muscles too tight for long strides. Gradually, they stretched out, his stride lengthened, and his pace increased. Meanwhile he cursed to himself as he was passed by a hefty middle-aged woman and a boy who looked as if he belonged in junior high.

Gabe headed east, crossed under the FDR and onto a pedestrian strip along part of Manhattan's eastern shore. The East River flowed past, moving in the opposite direction as he headed north. It was a pleasant day, sunny with a light breeze. It felt good to be out and running. *But damn each stride hurt!* Making it even worse, his sore ribs prevented him from taking deep breaths. Worst of all, he couldn't outrun what he'd read. Much was unclear to him. However, one point that he'd believed before then, and was made clearer from his research, was the greater danger posed by the alt-right. *So why was Homeland Security focused on the left and forcing him to infiltrate the Antifa?* His thoughts synched with his footfalls. *Why? Why? Why? Crap! Crap! Crap!*

Gabe was not a natural runner, however from junior high school on he'd run for conditioning, and he still kept it up, although now covering less distance and moving slower than back when. He'd run with broken toes, sprained ankles and once, despite warnings, with a mild concussion, but it had never hurt this much. He cut through Stuyvesant Town, forcing himself to ignore the pain and try to keep moving. In the middle of Peter Cooper Village his pace slowed further then dropped to a walk, although he'd run much less than usual. Catching his breath, his elbows sticking out like bird wings as he clutched his ribs, he scowled and cursed some more, mad at himself for giving in to the pain.

He drifted back down to Stuytown, eventually sitting in a plaza with a large circular pool with a fountain in its middle. Gabe's gaze wandered over Stuytown's nearby red brick high-rise buildings which rose through park-like surrounding land with many tree shaded walks, greenery and open lawns.

After catching his breath, Gabe was looking around when he noticed a family strolling along the walkway on the other side of the fountain. The spraying water obscured his view, although a girl, maybe eight or nine, was the exception as she skipped ahead of the rest, coming into Gabe's clear line of sight, then running back to do the same again. She made Gabe smile. She wore a city youth league soccer uniform, hers being dark and light green striped shorts and a light green shirt with a white number and writing on the back. Dried mud caked her arms and legs, and much of her uniform, and Gabe idly thought they must be returning from her game. Her family emerged from behind the water jets and came into clear sight. It was a man and a woman holding the hands of a young child between them. Every few steps they swung the child forward and up into the air. Gabe couldn't hear much over the fountain but could make out the kid screaming with delight on each swing.

Suddenly, Gabe pushed himself forward, his eyes focused intently. The man resembled Justin. Gabe wasn't positive so he rose and walked part way around the fountain. From there he was certain it was Justin. Gabe was caught off guard. Justin hadn't struck him as the family-man type, but, then again in the cell Gabe probably hadn't seemed the corporate lawyer type. *Maybe he could get useful info from Justin*, Gabe thought. He took a step toward them, then stopped. *What if Justin's wife didn't know he'd been arrested?* Uncertain what to do, Gabe hung back and in moments it was too late as they entered one of the apartment buildings. He noted the building number then slowly made his own way home, limping and aching more as he went.

CHAPTER TEN

Jasminn spent early Sunday morning in her apartment, a two-bedroom on the second floor of a four-story walk-up east of First Avenue on the Upper East Side. The building was old but reasonably well maintained. It sat on a side street lined with similar buildings, some with bodegas or other small businesses on the ground floor or in the basement.

Puttering around, Jasminn thought about Gabe and she became more concerned. Knowing he wasn't seriously injured she'd moved past his bruises, but she found his explanation and the way he'd told it strange. It reminded her of their freshman year when he'd continually denied having the hots for a petite blonde in a freshman intro class. He'd ended up dating Janis, the blonde, for most of their first year. Jasminn wanted to know whether he was now telling the truth, which she doubted, and if not, what was really going on.

Leaving her apartment, she made her way to the Q line subway. Trains ran less frequently on the weekends, but eventually one came. She took it and after getting off and another wait, she switched to the Lexington line and took that to Bleecker Street. From there she marched east and south until she was pressing continuously on Gabe's intercom button, seemingly trying to push the button through the intercom panel.

Gabe jumped in response to the buzzer's ring, and he was surprised by Jasminn showing up. He'd only gotten back from his run/walk a few minutes earlier so greeted her in his damp outfit with sweat covering his body. He held open his door.

"Hey, what brings you down here?"

Ignoring the question, she strode past him into the kitchen, grabbed a cold bottle of flavored water, spun to face him and with flashing eyes proclaimed, "You're pulling a Janis on me."

He was confused and he shifted back onto his heels, opening and closing his mouth, first puzzled then unsure what to say.

"What're you talking about? I'm not seeing Janis or anyone. Last I heard she's in Omaha and's married with kids."

She stepped toward him. "I'm not talking about you seeing anyone. Why would I care about that?"

For a moment Gabe's eyes dropped.

"I'm talking about you lying about your bruises and you being at that protest and everything about it."

Gabe raised his head and looked her directly in the face, knowing that after all this time she could read him like the proverbial book. Nevertheless, his immediate response was to deny, deny, deny. Telling her the truth might only put her in more danger.

"I don't know what you're talking about. Have all those elbows to the head from playing ball finally caught up with you?"

"Don't give me that crap." She took another step toward him. They now stood barely a foot apart, she looking up slightly into his eyes and he looking down slightly into hers.

He thought, *She's my closest friend. I can't lie to her and maybe she'll be safer if she knows the truth. Anyway, it's clear I'm not going to be able to keep anything from her. Sorry, Smith and fuck you too.*

Breaking eye contact, Gabe moved to the sofa, his back to her.

"Alright. I'll tell you. Everything."

As she joined him he asked, "What do you mean you don't care if I'm seeing anyone?"

She ignored the question, unwilling to be distracted from her quest or confront that issue, and resumed her stare. It took awhile, but Gabe eventually told her the whole story, including Smith and Jones' threats about what would happen to her. When he was done he said in a low voice, "I don't want anything to happen to you."

Jasminn leaned over, whispered "I know," and kissed him. Her lips felt so soft against his. It was a short kiss, but its feel lingered on the stunned Gabe's lips.

She sat back, then said, "We need a game plan."

"Are you crazy?" he burst out. "After everything I just told you? You should go hide somewhere until this is all over."

She crossed her arms and sighed but said nothing.

"Don't go to your parents'. That's too obvious." He was talking rapidly, not paying attention to her. "Go somewhere you've never been and where you don't know anybody. That's best."

She shook her head. "Not happening. When have you ever seen me back off?"

"We're not talking about taking on an opposing player in a game," Gabe yelled, losing control. "We're talking about fucking Homeland Security."

She shook her head again. "Doesn't matter. You're prepared to do whatever you have to to protect me, and I'm going to do the same for you. We're in this together."

Pulling her to him, Gabe gave her a long tight hug. Neither of them was sure whether it was a hug of thanks or another type of hug all together. When they broke apart neither of them said anything about it.

After a long pause he said, "At least don't go to any protests. Who knows what Smith and Jones might do to you at one."

She agreed, then asked, "Should we tell Matt?"

"It was his text which got me down there. I think he feels bad enough that I was knocked around. Also, he's not going to any protests unless you push him. Let's leave him out of this."

Later, sitting across the kitchen counter from Gabe, the two of them looking at their phones, Jasminn wanted to smash hers, but restrained herself.

"Can you believe this shit?"

Gabe took this outcry in stride. For many years he'd been the designated listener of her venting, or as he thought of it, being her 'ventee'. Sometimes she got worked up over matters he considered trivial and that would amuse him, but he knew from experience, including punches she'd thrown at him, not to let her see that. Instead, he looked at her, eyebrows raised, and asked, "What shit?"

"All this stuff from the scum bags on the right."

Gabe didn't know which stuff she was referring to.

"I've been following this trail of posts for several days and it's driving me crazy. If I didn't believe in non-violence this would make me very violent."

"Calm down, Jaz. I'm sure it's not that bad. What is it?"

"The other day I was reading an article on *The New Patriots' Rights* site…"

He cut her off, issuing a loud sigh and shaking his head in exasperation. "Why do you read that far right material? You know it drives you crazy."

She lowered her voice, calming down some. "As some famous general said, 'Know thine enemy'. I read them occasionally to see what they're saying and to know what they're up to."

Gabe looked away so she wouldn't see him roll his eyes.

"Amazingly, ignoring all evidence, they're still claiming the Capital invasion was a false flag operation. It's insane. And that's one of their least crazy comments."

"Why's that bother you so much? That's nothing new."

Her mouth tightened and she threw up her arms in frustration. "I know, but there are all these likes to this article and tweets and blogs adding on to it. They're still demanding that the sentences of the people convicted in the capital attack be reversed, and for the government to go after the left. And they're threatening more actions."

"It's the same lines."

"Well this rouses their nut cases all the more. Plus it puts more pressure on weak-ass politicians to act to keep their people happy, especially in the extreme states. Look at what they've dragged you into."

He couldn't disagree with her last point. In the meantime, he'd moved around behind her and started massaging her shoulders, hearing her moan quietly in pleasure, and wondering how such strong shoulders could be so hot.

CHAPTER ELEVEN

Gabe tilted back his office desk chair, wireless keyboard in his lap and feet up on the HVAC unit. Even though he was a star, his office was the same as the other associates of his seniority. Shelves and drawers lined half of one wall near the window. Two visitors' chairs sat in front of his desk.

Unable to concentrate on a document which normally would have interested him, Gabe gazed out the window and thought about his situation and about Jasminn. His office was on the forty-second floor and faced uptown with a great view of Central Park. Gabe's cell phone buzzed, interrupting his musings. The caller announced himself with a laugh as 'your cellmate Justin' and proposed they get together. Gabe might have accepted anyhow, but the lurking specters of Smith and Jones compelled him to do so. They decided on dinner the next night.

The meeting place was a pub in Murray Hill—once a sleepy out of the way part of town which had since become a popular neighborhood for recent college grads with an active bar scene and street life.

Inside the pub the next evening, Gabe worked his way through the noisy bar section already busy with former frat and sorority young professionals. He spotted Justin seated at a table in the back and let out a slight sigh of relief after finally making his way there. While they chatted, Gabe looked Justin over again. He confirmed to himself that Justin was medium height, medium build, had an angular face with thick black hair covering his ears, and brown eyes under almost nonexistent eyebrows—definitely whom Gabe had seen in Stuyvesant Town. This time Gabe noticed a feature he'd missed before--a jagged scar running about four inches from just below Justin's right ear down the side of his neck. Gabe didn't want to be rude, but the scar was too visible to ignore.

"How'd you get that?" he asked, pointing generally in the scar's direction.

"Shrapnel."

Justin added nothing, so Gabe dropped it.

Justin had one hand wrapped around a mug of half-way downed beer. When their waiter appeared, Justin ordered a burger for himself and Gabe ordered a beer and a burger. The conversation was stilted. They only knew each other from the jail and the air that night had been rife with suspicion and tension. They each talked some about themselves.

"Yeah," Justin said, "I work in film production at a studio in Queens. What I really want though is to get to direct or produce someday, the same as everyone who works there."

Gabe listened while looking around, mainly watching for Smith and Jones.

Keeping the conversation going, Justin said, "I live in Queens. Our apartment is near the studio and it's much cheaper living out there than here, especially since my wife and I have two kids."

Gabe's head snapped to face him.

"You live in Queens?"

Justin nodded.

Not thinking, Gabe said, "But I thought ...."

With a sudden edge in his voice and leaning toward Gabe slightly, Justin asked, "You thought what?"

Gabe was at a loss. He was certain it was Justin in Stuyvesant Town. It was possible they'd been visiting, but it hadn't struck Gabe that way. To him it had looked exactly as if they'd been going home, especially since they had a soccer playing daughter who'd needed a bath.

"You thought what Gabe?" Justin repeated, his voice hardening as he leaned forward more.

Recovering, Gabe waved one hand., "Oh, I assumed you're a Manhattanite. You seem like it."

Justin sat back. "I'll take that as a compliment, but I'm part of the Bridge and Tunnel Crowd."

Gabe looked down at the table to hide his confusion. He'd been so sure it was Justin he'd seen in Stuy Town and that he lived there. Gabe banked his sense that Justin was lying and dropped the subject.

They made more small talk and sipped their beers until Justin leaned toward Gabe again. He said quietly, "Thanks again for coming, Gabe." He paused before adding, "You know we were lucky that night."

Inwardly, Gabe disagreed, not recalling any moments of good fortune. "How so?"

At that moment, the waiter delivered their burgers. They both took a moment to garnish the burgers and take a first bite. Justin had ordered his rare and juice ran down his chin and onto his beige shirt. Grabbing some napkins he wiped his face and tried to save the shirt. Gabe signaled the waiter for a glass of seltzer to aid in the clean-up.

Once order was restored Justin said with a smile, "You can't take me anywhere. Anyway, as I said, I think we were fortunate. In fact, I think somebody purposely put us together to see if we'd say anything important."

Gabe tried to hide his nervousness.

"I can't buy that, at least in my case, since I'm irrelevant to all this. Nevertheless, assuming you're right, how would whoever this was know what we said."

Justin eased back and grinned in amusement. "You don't know much about how the prison system works or criminal justice law, do you?"

Taking another bite of his burger, and doing so without any spillage, Gabe replied, "No, my specialty is acquisition deals."

"That's not what I meant. I meant personal experience from being on the inside."

"If you're asking had I been in jail before that night and do I know how jails generally operate, the answer on both counts is 'No'."

"That's what I meant." Justin continued, "I'm sure you're knowledgeable though about the Fourth Amendment's right of privacy."

Justin sounded condescending, but figuring he might learn something Gabe replied dryly, "Yes, I'm familiar with it, but go ahead."

If Justin picked up Gabe's hint of annoyance he didn't react. Instead, while eating French fries with one hand and holding a napkin at the ready with the other, he took Gabe through an analysis similar to Smith's and finished by saying, "Anyway, legal or not, I'm positive they intended to tape us."

"And we were fortunate because why?"

"They can't bug every cell. Much too expensive, especially for cameras small enough so they're not easy to spot."

Gabe waited on Justin to continue. As he did so, he caught sight of a cute blonde sitting with a man at a nearby table. She kept looking over at him. Ever so slightly, Gabe shook his head, passing on her, while feeling bad for her date. She's cold, he thought.

Justin drew his attention back. "A cell next to ours had a setup recording its occupants."

Gabe acted surprised. "How do you know? Why'd they do that?"

"Remember I work in film production—I spotted it easily," he boasted, taking a slug of his beer then laughing. "However, three drunks sleeping it off and a junkie were in there. No reason to record them." He paused for emphasis. "Someone screwed up, mixing up where to put us and those guys. They would have recorded them rather than us." He laughed again at the screw-up.

Gabe was impressed by Justin's right-on reading of the situation, but he remained wary of him. "Are you sure about this?"

"Absolutely. So you know, I haven't told our cell mates. I'm confident I can trust you, but don't know about them."

"Well if you're right about the taping that's pretty sharp. As to whom you trust, that's up to you." Gabe felt a twinge about lying but continued with a straight face. "I don't know why anyone shouldn't trust me. I don't know anything about the others beyond what they said that night, and don't have any reason why I should or shouldn't trust them, or why I should care." After a moment he added, "Or whether I should or shouldn't trust you."

Justin ordered them another round of beers from a passing waiter and ignored Gabe's last comment.

"When you got thrown in with us, I was suspicious of you. So was Tall Alex. Since he was all over you from the start I left it to him."

"I don't get it, why should anyone be suspicious of me? I take it you're done with that or we wouldn't be here," he smiled, "unless you're testing me. If you do trust me now, what changed your mind?" He stopped and thought before saying, "Anyhow, what's it matter whether or not you're suspicions of anyone?"

"You raised my antenna for a few reasons. You got thrown in a after the rest of us. I wondered whether it was to be sure you ended up with the right people, meaning the rest of us. Moreover, I saw your bruises. Yeah, you'd been hit a bunch of times, and I'm sure they hurt. But they seemed strategically placed, as if meant to look bad but not do much damage. Am I right? You incur any serious injuries?"

Gabe was curious how Justin would know this and why he'd care about Gabe or the others. Gabe couldn't tell this by looking at the bruises. Nor could Jasminn or Matt.

"You're right that I'm OK. How'd you know?" Half joking he went on, "You a doctor on the side?"

"From my time overseas. I saw a lot of bad things. Now the only blood I deal with is movie blood, but that's how I knew."

Gabe wasn't sure of what to make of Justin's explanation, but shelved that and asked, "So why trust me now?"

"Some friends of mine are good at collecting information about people. And, no offense, but they watched you for the last two days."

Gabe stared at him for several long seconds then shouted, "You got some fuckin' nerve." He jumped to his feet, knocking back his chair and bumping the waiter who was returning with their beers. The bottles fell, breaking and splashing beer all over. Throwing down his napkin he cried, "I don't like the idea of someone checking into me." His jaw tightened and his hands clenched. "I'm leaving before we end up back in jail. This time for public brawling when I beat the crap out of you."

Gabe stormed upfront, pushing his way through the crowd and receiving nasty looks and several elbows in response. Meanwhile, Justin frantically searched his pockets, found he had no choice but to slap two Fifties on the table, then shoved through the crowd after Gabe, spilling drinks and knocking people aside.

On Third Avenue Gabe started south along the busy sidewalk. Justin ran to catch up, pushing more people aside.

"Hold on Gabe. Let me explain."

Gabe whirled and with both hands grabbed the man by his shirt, pulling him up to his toes.

"What's to explain? You had me followed and investigated me?" He lowered Justin so his feet again rested solidly on the sidewalk. "Find any good stuff?"

"Calm down!" Justin chopped down hard on Gabe's arms, freeing himself, then straightened his own shirt. "This all relates to the leaders issue."

The mention of 'leaders' caught Gabe's attention, and despite his anger he thought of Smith and Jones' orders.

"What do you mean?" he demanded, the throbbing veins in his neck visible in the light from an ice cream shop by them.

"Let me explain."

"Whatever you've got to say, make it fast."

Justin gently, but with surprising strength, took Gabe by one sleeve of his sports coat and steered him closer to the storefront where on the other side of the plate glass window a family was sharing sundaes. He moved closer to Gabe, so the latter could hear him over the street sounds. "I'm working to find out who runs things. I need to know and I don't trust anyone. People may try to stop me or maybe they're spying on me to see what I learn."

Gabe backed a step away from Justin and blinked, then looked around, thinking Justin was crazy. A purple light from the shop's neon sign darkened Justin's face preventing Gabe from making it out clearly.

"You must be bullshitting me."

"Why would I do that?" Justin thought for a second. "Please, let's walk up a few blocks to a spot I know. Hopefully, we'll find a place there where we can talk."

Gabe tapped one foot rapidly, feeling nervous and uncertain. He wanted to get away. However, he knew Smith and Jones would be angry if he did so, and they might be watching him now. Feeling besieged on all fronts, Gabe let Justin rest a hand lightly on his shoulder, turn him around and guide him north. They flowed along with the crowd for two blocks then went up a cross street to a plaza surrounding a high rise. A restaurant was centered in the plaza and large planters with stunted bushes and cement benches were scattered about. Justin led them to a bench off to one side and coaxed Gabe to sit.

Gabe didn't look at Justin. Instead, he gazed through a large plate glass window at the restaurant's crowded bar. *Everyone's partying and having a good time but me*, he thought.

"So?" Gabe asked

Justin was bent forward, a forearm atop each thigh, and staring straight ahead. "One thing I've learned is that on the far left orders aren't given directly. They're passed along via drops and other maneuvers. The purpose is to hide the leaders' identities. Apparently, most of them are worried about government infiltration or the alt-right attacking them, maybe even trying to kill them."

He waited for Gabe's response. When Gabe remained silent, Justin continued. "I understand them. I really do," he insisted in a strained voice. "I don't trust the government and understand fearing fringe nut jobs. I'm not objecting to their decisions—what brings us to the streets and where and how we protest. Not knowing who's running things doesn't work for me though. In the Army, not knowing which officer up the chain of command called the shots and whether they knew what they were doing, but my knowing they could get us grunts killed, freaked me out. An Army shrink considered discharging me. The same sort of thing gets to me here. I admit it's become like an obsession."

Justin paused again to give Gabe another chance to speak, but Gabe maintained his silence, making Justin work. Justin sighed.

"Listening to what you said that night I figured you felt the same. Aren't I right?"

Gabe tried to think quickly. *What's the best way to satisfy Smith and Jones while avoiding getting in deeper than necessary?*

He finally spoke. "Sure, I'd like to know who runs things." Justin nodded before Gabe asked, "Have you done anything about this?"

Justin flung a stone he'd plucked from the planter next to him. His laugh was sarcastic. "I've tried plenty, but except for that one piece of info I just shared, I've gotten nowhere. Flat out no-go. And you?"

Once again Gabe tried to figure the right course of action. He stood, Justin rising with him, and Gabe paced near the bench, trying to give the impression he was thinking about this leadership issue. Finally, employing the same piercing unblinking cold look and flat steel voice he used when work negotiations got difficult, Gabe said, "Let me be clear. I am not one of these leaders you are talking about, nor do I know any of them. In any case I see no reason why I should tell you anything."

Justin's face screwed up in shock at Gabe's manner. Gabe intentionally lightened his tone somewhat. "I admit I don't like not knowing who calls the shots. I'm going to take some time to think about this. I mean how hard I want to pursue answers and whether I'd do this with you. I'll get back to you in a few days. We clear?"

Justin had not adjusted to seeing this side of Gabe and was slow to respond. He replied, almost apologetically, "Fine. Hey, I'm sorry. I didn't mean to get you worked up. What you said is fine."

"Good. I'm heading downtown to go home. You should head home … to Queens."

Justin nodded and they parted ways.

CHAPTER TWELVE

Gabe put off thinking about Justin on his way home. Once there he sat at the kitchen counter. He munched a granola bar since he hadn't gotten to eat much of his burger and thought *Now what do I do?* No answer readily coming to him, from a cabinet above the kitchen sink Gabe took an unopened bottle of fine aged Scotch. His uncle had sent this to him when Gabe had first come to New York. Gabe was not a Scotch drinker, but he finally cracked the seal, poured himself two fingers worth and headed to bed, counting on the drink to quickly put him under. It didn't.

At his office the next morning Gabe finished prepping for a negotiating session on a new deal. He flipped through the lengthy document they'd be discussing. He wore a suit, but feeling this was becoming the new old normal he didn't do it up as he had for his last meeting. He had to get his head in the game and off of Smith and Jones and off of this Justin development. He was tired and the Scotch had left him with a headache. With the aid of three aspirins, an energy drink and two cups of coffee he pulled himself together. The meeting went smoothly, and they were done much sooner than Gabe had expected.

Afterwards, back in his office Gabe shut his door and put his office phone on Do Not Disturb. The diligent course of action would be for him to revise an agreement based on the meeting. Gabe had lost his focus though and instead thought about Smith and Jones and last night's strange meeting with Justin. He decided to see what he could learn about Justin. From exchanging numbers, Gabe knew his full name was Justin Fairlawn. Gabe searched that name together with film studios in Queens but came up empty. Then he searched Justin's name alone and the only hit was for InDepth, a leading business information site.

Gabe brought up Justin's InDepth profile and immediately was struck by the picture. Gabe brought his face closer to the screen to see the details better. It was in partial profile, shielding Justin's scar from view. He had much longer hair and a beard and the picture was blurry, all told making it hard to recognize him. After studying Justin's profile, Gabe realized it was odd in other respects. It named a production studio as his employer, but there was only a one-line mention of this studio on InDepth, and nothing elsewhere. *Why would a studio want to be so low profile? It should be just the opposite.*

Gabe's InDepth membership enabled deep data dives and he took full advantage of this. Justin's contacts list was short, and Gabe clicked on a few of them, InDepth taking him to their profiles. After looking at several of Justin's contacts' profiles, he randomly clicked on a contact of one of Justin's contacts. However, instead of being taken to that person's profile, he got an error message. He tried another of this contact's contacts and the same thing happened. Gabe returned to Justin's profile and did the same with several more of his contacts. Each time the link to the contact's contacts was a dead end.

Gabe sat back and scratched his chin. He was no computer expert, and certainly no computer fraud expert, but he thought Justin's profile must be fake. He stared at the screen, then swiveled and looked out the window. He guessed that Justin's supposed contacts' profiles existed for cover, but whoever had set this up hadn't expected anyone to bother clicking on these contacts' contacts. *Why do this if Justin was who he said he was?* Gabe couldn't think of any good reason. His feet thudded to the floor in triumph as he concluded that Justin must not be whom he said he was. *In that case, who was he really and what was that whole story he told Gabe?*

Gabe came up with one half-baked explanation as to why Justin could be for real despite this InDepth conundrum, but he didn't buy it. Instead, he came up with several other theories as to whom Justin could be. *Maybe Justin was a leader on the left and used a false identity to protect himself.* Or *maybe he was on the extreme right and was infiltrating the left.* Or *maybe he was a government spy. Or maybe he really was crazy. But how to find out?*

Gabe mulled over the situation, chewing on a pen. He acknowledged that he was out of his league. He needed a top notch online hunter to track down Justin Fairlawn or the Justin he saw in Stuyvesant Town, or whoever this guy really was. Luckily for Gabe, he had a top notch hunter.

/////

Leaving the office early by lawyer's standards, Gabe went uptown to Jasminn's apartment. He'd WhatsApp'ed her, saying he needed her help, but saying nothing else. Entering her apartment, Gabe looked at Jasminn. *Here's my hunter, or if it's not politically incorrect, my huntress.* Right then though, she wasn't dressed like a hunter or a huntress. She was wearing oversized faded sweatpants with their college logo, a worn grey oversized tee shirt with small rips around the collar and a bandana tied as a turban with a few tufts of hair sticking out.

Gabe was about to explain about Justin when Jasminn's roommate emerged from her bedroom. Kate was a bright, attractive woman who was making a name for herself in product branding. From day one though it had been clear she wasn't fond of Gabe. He made a point of acting nicely toward her but would barely get a civil response.

Jasminn told her, "Gabe and I have something to discuss so, not to be rude, but we're gonna go into my room."

"Go right ahead and discuss things," Kate replied, putting air quotes around the word discuss. "I'll crank up my music so I don't hear the bed shaking from your discussion." Once again with the air quotes.

Jasminn rolled her eyes and pulled Gabe into her room, shutting the door behind them. Within moments Kate's music was coming through the wall.

"She is a piece of work," Gabe said.

"That's because she's got the hots for you." Smirking, Jasminn added, "For some odd reason she thinks you're cute."

"Yeah, right,"

For the apartment's size, the room was large. However, computer equipment took up most of the space not taken up by her bed and dresser. Extra sturdy shelves were mounted on two walls to hold some of the hardware, there being so much of it. Although Jasminn had left her high-paying tech job, she kept up with the latest and greatest in the computer world. With her current job she couldn't afford any of the newer equipment, but her mother hoped at some point Jasminn would return to the upper echelon of the tech world, so without telling her husband, she covered the equipment costs and Jasminn's large monthly internet bills. Most everything else in the room related to basketball. Numerous trophies and medals for tournaments won and MVPs earned sat atop the equipment and her dresser. Several WNBA posters hung on the walls as well as a photo of Jasminn and Charles Barkley and a photo of her playing for their college team. Despite all the expensive computer equipment, the décor reminded Gabe that she'd gladly trade everything to be a WNBA bench warmer. On the narrow nightstand wedged in the corner sat a small photo of her and Gabe during practice. Gabe particularly liked it because it showed him airborne tipping in the ball while she stood flat footed below watching him.

"What do you need help with? Your jumper worse than usual?"

Gabe laughed slightly, humoring her. They both knew he had a better shot. He moved some clothes and sat on her bed while she faced him, relaxing in her ergonomic computer chair—another contribution by her mother. He told her all he knew about Justin, including basically being an online ghost, what he'd found on InDepth and being sure it was Justin he'd seen in Stuytown. He didn't have to go through the Smith and Jones or jail parts since she'd already gotten that out of him. When he was done they sat silently, Jasminn rocking her chair back and forth as she thought. The movements under her shirt as she did so revealed she was braless and distracted him, while also reminding him how she accused men of being infantile. He agreed but was still distracted.

She asked, "Who do you think he is?"

He walked her through his theories.

When he was done, she said, "And I assume you want me to find out the truth about him."

"If it's not too hard for you, Jaz." He smirked, knowing comments like that spurred her on.

She spun her chair around to face one of her several keyboards. "Just watch me boy."

She spent the next two hours working feverishly but from the noises she made and the droop in her shoulders Gabe knew she was getting nowhere. Eventually he ordered a pizza. The timing was good. The pie arrived as she hit some keys with disgust and spun back around. They grabbed Lite beers from the fridge and ate sitting on her bed.

Although Gabe knew the answer, he asked, "No luck?"

She shook her head.

"I guess whoever handled this did an excellent job hiding him."

Jasminn looked up from her second slice, saved a mushroom from falling off its edge with her free hand, and explained, "That's not it. It's not that Justin Fairlawn has been so well hidden that he can't be traced. It's that there is no Justin Fairlawn. It's a manufactured identity."

He froze with a mouthful of pizza and the remainder of the slice hanging from his unmoving hand. Then he hurriedly half-chewed the piece in his mouth and forced it down.

"How can that be? Who is he then?"

She shrugged, distracting him again. "I've no idea and with only the little information you've given me I've got no way to find out."

"What about facial recognition software?"

She waved him off. "I don't have it. Regardless man, even if I did, I doubt we'd get a match using the InDepth photo. I'm sure that crappy photo is not accidental. It's to make sure he can't be tracked through it. You happen to have any other pictures of him? Maybe his mugshot?"

Gabe shook his head. "Very funny."

"Any other information which could help?"

Gabe shook his head again and lay back, resting his head on her pillow and staring at her ceiling. Neither of them spoke for some time.

"Wait a sec," Gabe said, sitting up. "I do have an idea, Jaz. It's a long shot and I don't know if it could work, but anything's worth a try.

"What is it?"

"I told you I'm positive I saw him with his family in Stuytown. The girl was wearing one of those uniforms from the kids' soccer leagues. Maybe we can trace him through that."

"You're crazy. Thousands of kids play in those leagues. Plus, you're talking about hacking and you know I don't hack."

Gabe ignored her objections, his voice rising with excitement. "We can narrow it down. First, I'm sure the girl was around eight or nine so that narrows it a bit."

"Assuming you're any judge of that, which I question."

"I can't be far off. We know more though. The team has green colors. . ."

"That's a big help," she jumped in sarcastically, rolling her eyes.

"As usual you didn't let me finish." He smiled to show he didn't mean anything by the comment. "The way the leagues work, each team has a sponsor and its name is written on the back of the shirt. I couldn't see the entire name and wasn't giving it any attention, but I'm pretty sure it started 'MOCI,' or something like that, in all caps."

"It might be possible to find the team if we got lucky and if I hacked, but I don't."

"Come on. With your killer skills you're going to tell me you've never done any hacking?"

She remained quiet then leaned back, locked her fingers behind her head and stretched her back. "Yeah, I've done some, just to keep up on my skills."

Trying to stay focused on the subject, rather than the sights, he said, "Please, Jaz. This is important. We're being threatened by Homeland Security and who knows what danger Justin might pose."

"Reminding me that's whom we're dealing with is supposed to make me want to do this?"

"It's supposed to make you acknowledge how high the stakes are. Anyway, we're only talking about hacking a kiddie soccer league. It's not an important or supersecret site."

Wavering, she said, "What if we do find the right team? What then?"

"The girl's uniform number was either One or Seven so we look for that. And if a girl with one of those numbers on the right team lives in Stuyvesant Town she's got to be his daughter. I'm even sure I know their building number. Come on, Jaz."

He gave her the building number.

Giving in, she said, "OK, you know I've got your back. I'll do it."

She slid back onto her chair and turned back to the computer. Once more her fingers started flying across the keyboard. About five minutes later she abruptly stopped and slowly spun around to face him.

"We overlooked a key point," she said.

"What?"

"A children's league is a perfect target for pedophiles. The site is well protected."

"Oh shit, you're right. We didn't think of that." He looked at her with a smile. "But you can get through that, right?"

"Jesus, Gabriel Bentley! You really don't know anything about computers, do you?"

"What now?" he moaned.

"This is serious security. Plus, I see it tracks anyone trying to get through. It's like a direct line to the police. 'Hello Mr. Policeman, please go and arrest that sexual predator. Here's the address.' Christ, Gabe."

"OK, so maybe it's a drop harder than we imagined."

"A drop?"

He sat silently, then rose, put his hands on her shoulders and said, "You're right. Forget it Jaz. There's no way you should mess with that. I'm sorry I suggested it. I'll figure out some other way. Thanks though."

He kissed her lightly on the top of her head and left.

///

Gabe was asleep when his cell buzzed. It was after 3:00 am. Jasminn was calling.

He sat up and grabbed the phone.

"Hey, you OK?"

"I'm fine Mr. Sleepyhead. I've got the information you wanted, and more."

"What! But what you said .... and I told you not to."

"Since when do I listen to you? Anyway, while I said it was serious and would be difficult, that's only for mere mortals. Yours truly didn't even break a sweat. It was as easy as taking you down low."

After a pause he asked, "Are you certain they can't track you?"

"Positive. The trail dead ends at a rural internet café in Kazakhstan. However, I don't want any bad guy figuring out how to crack their security, so I sent the site master a message warning them and telling them how to fix it." Gabe smiled at that. "Listen, I don't want to email the info to you so will give you a hard copy. Go back to sleep, Gabe, and remember you owe me big time."

CHAPTER THIRTEEN

Gabe was anxious to get Jasminn's information first thing the next morning, but he needed to handle the document he'd ignored the day before. He rushed through it, knowing it wasn't his best work, but decided it was good enough. He could now spare several hours from work so rushed to Jasminn's office where she'd promised to step out and give him the information.

Gabe bought them fresh fruit shakes from a food truck and they headed to a public seating area in the atrium of a neighboring high rise. The atrium was starting to fill up but it was early enough for Gabe and Jasminn to beat the heart of the lunch crowd and get a table.

Smiling, she told him, "You know, a fruit shake doesn't cut it as my reward for this info."

"I know and I promise you dinner at the restaurant of your choice." He pressed her, "Now, please tell me what you learned."

"Don't you want to know how I did it?"

Gabe actually didn't care about the 'how' and if Jasminn had worked for him he might have insisted she go right to the 'what'. However, she didn't work for him and would be annoyed if she didn't get to boast at least some about how she prevailed in her quest.

"Yes, definitely tell me how you did it. It must've been incredibly difficult."

Jasminn proceeded, speaking quietly, but smiling and gesturing throughout. Gabe tried to follow, but only understood bits and assumed that the blank look on his face gave this away. He believed she said, but he couldn't be sure, that she'd first laid an online path ending in that café in Kazakhstan. Then, working backwards, by means he absolutely did not follow, she penetrated the leagues' computer system at a surface level, staying above the security system. There she looked around, somehow locating information, but not accessing it. She told him she'd located the data for the leagues, eventually isolating the seven through ten year old girls' leagues and their teams and rosters, all without triggering the security. He thought, but couldn't swear, that she said she manipulated the system so without extracting data and setting off alarms she could browse through it.

"Then I found the team we wanted," she said in triumph, raising her voice before looking around, chagrined, and lowering it again. "It was for ten year olds. You'd said you couldn't see the sponsor's full name on the girl's shirt but that the first four letters looked like 'MOCI.' I've no idea what you imagined that would spell, but it turns out the first four letters were 'MCGL' and the sponsor's name is McGlenn."

Gabe was impressed.

"On the McGlenn team only one girl lives at the Stuyvesant address you gave me. It had to be her. Also, her uniform number is seven, so at least you got that right," she said with a smile.

Gabe put his hands on hers, holding them briefly before patting them and saying, "You are spectacular! That's great! So now I just have to work back through her and see if the so-called 'Justin' is her father and then I'll have him."

"Relax, Gabe. I've lots more—his real name, background, pictures and a guess about whose side he's really on."

She pulled an envelope from a pocket in her dress, holding it up next to her forehead. Back in college she and Gabe had discovered old clips of Johnny Carson's Carnac the Magnificent and had loved the bits. Paraphrasing Carson and his sidekick she intoned, "I have here in my hand a sealed envelope…."

Gabe laughed, trying to grab it. "Enough already. Tell me."

She pushed his hand away, slit open the envelope and used her notes to fill him in.

"His real name is Michael Yang. He grew up in, you'll love this, Fair Lawn, New Jersey."

"Thus the 'Fairlawn' last name I gather."

"You gather correctly. Here's his high school yearbook picture."

Gabe was not good at telling if people looked alike but thought the pimply teenager in the picture might be a younger scarless Justin.

"From there he went to Rutgers, got his degree, then enlisted in the Marines. He did two tours overseas. Here's his picture from the local Fair Lawn paper when he returned home after his second stint."

She handed him a copy of the newspaper clipping. This time Gabe could definitely tell it was Justin, scar and all.

"What else?" he asked, anxious for more.

Jasminn put the papers back in the envelope. "Very little. I found his marriage announcement and his mother's obituary, but that's it. Not a single word about what he's done since leaving the Corps."

"That's weird. What do you think it means?" Gabe scratched the back of his neck.

"To me it screams that he does something covert. At some point someone must have deleted his online presence from the time he left the Marines and keeps it dark. My bet is he's with the government."

"Like a secret agent, eh?" Gabe asked, this making some sense.

"Seems like the best possibility to me."

Jasminn noticed two women looking over at them, silently asking if they could share the table. Jasminn gave them her 'Don't mess with me' look. They hurriedly looked away, grabbed chairs away from any table and ate with their food wrappers across their laps while complaining about her.

Gabe had one elbow resting on the table and a hand holding his chin. "If he does work for the government I doubt it's with Homeland Security since Smith and Jones are interested in him," He added, "Unless that's an intentional fake. You know, Homeland Security saying they suspect him to prove his bona fides."

"Maybe, 'though that strikes me as pretty extreme. I think it'd probably be more like 'the right hand doesn't know what the left hand is doing.' As I understand it," she continued, "the CIA can't legally engage in domestic activities, so that should rule them out."

"That's right, but who knows if that's correct in all cases, or if they observe that if it is. It could be the FBI. Does the NSA do this sort of thing? Or maybe the Bureau of Firearms and whatever they're called."

"Does it really matter which one? Anyway, the point is he's probably with the government and is trying to use you, so you should stay away from him."

"If I can."

"Yeah, if you can."

They looked around, looking for anyone suspicious.

Jasminn went on, "Maybe he's with the far right trying to infiltrate the left."

"Possible, I guess, but you make a strong argument as to why he's government."

"Well," she said, "whichever it is, this is not good. It was best when you thought he was just some guy on the left, or a nut job."

They sat in silence, people watching, thinking about the situation. Gabe reached over and hugged her and they both grinned. "This is great Jaz. If you dig further do you think there's any chance of finding out who he really works for."

She shrugged, "I'm not sure, but I'll try. Whomever he's with I can make things harder for him," she stated, glee creeping into her voice.

"How?"

"I'll tell some of the protest people I work with about him. We'll spread the word. Soon people will know not to trust him. He can't do much spying then, no matter who it's for."

"Very nice. Very sneaky too. I like it. Let me know if you find anything more."

Jasminn nodded, saying, "We should give up our table. There's lots of people looking for free tables who're giving us dirty looks."

With that they rose and watched the race for their table.

CHAPTER FOURTEEN

That evening Gabe had dinner with a woman he'd met through an online dating site. These sites were definitely not his thing, but he used one this one time after Matt kept pushing him. Gabe and his date, Alice, dined at a trendy restaurant. Reservations normally had to be made months in advance, but a connection of Alice's had gotten them one only a week out. They'd made the date pre Smith and Jones. Gabe had not been keen on setting up a date this way before them, and felt much less so now, but didn't want to be rude so didn't cancel on her.

She was a lawyer, giving them something in common, although they practiced in different fields--she primarily defended companies in EPA proceedings. She was attractive--a striking angular face, short blond hair worn swept back and a lean body. She was into fitness, which gave them something else in common, although her thing was cycling and she knew little about basketball.

Gabe had a hard time holding up his end of the conversation or giving her his full attention. Instead, his mind kept wandering back over the last few days. He tried to pay more attention to her, but even before they'd finished their main courses he knew this was going nowhere. On the job, many lawyers conduct themselves as Type A personalities. Gabe turned it off when not "lawyering," as he put it. Alice was apparently Type A all the time, which didn't appeal to him.

For Gabe, dinner dragged on much too long, although apparently she perceived it differently. Finishing her espresso she invited him back to her place. Gabe's first thought was '*Why not?*', but then he thought about Jasminn and made an excuse about an early morning meeting. After splitting the check and before going their separate ways she gave him a deep kiss.

Gabe grabbed a cab and headed downtown. *At least dinner was some distraction.* During the cab ride he decided that since Matt got him into this date, Matt would have to get him out of any further dates without offending Alice. He had the cab drop him two blocks from his apartment at his local Korean grocery. He picked up a few necessities before heading the rest of his way.

Half a block from his building, he suddenly felt an intense pain just behind his right ear—he'd been hit. He fell, landing partially on the sidewalk and partially in the street, and his groceries spilled. Temporarily confused, Gabe looked up. A man in dark clothes with a brimmed hat pulled low stood over him.

The man shouted, "Stop," kicked Gabe in the midsection, shouted, "Nosing," kicked him in the mid-section again, shouted "Around," and kicked him there a third time. On the third kick, although shook up and in pain, Gabe kicked out, catching his assailant on the outside of his left knee. The man stumbled slightly and grabbed his knee. Gabe caught him off guard by standing part way and then diving at him, knocking him over. Gabe leaped on top of him and started throwing punches, landing some before the other got his arms up to ward off the blows. The man shifted his weight onto his shoulders and drove his good knee hard into Gabe's stomach, throwing Gabe off balance and enabling the man to push Gabe off him. They both lay for a moment, winded and in pain and staring at each other, until the attacker pulled himself up and fled, limping away. Gabe wasn't up to giving chase. Instead, he caught his breath, picked up those groceries which hadn't been ruined and gingerly made it the rest of the way to his apartment.

At home Gabe saw that his suit was ruined, then removed his jacket and shirt to see how much he'd been bruised. The original beatings' marks had faded to a mix of pale red spots and black and blue marks draining into a sickly yellow. He saw the beginning of three new black and blue marks on his front. He didn't do anything for these, but he wrapped several ice cubes in a paper towel and held the wet cold towel to the back of his head. Resting his head on one arm stretched out on the kitchen counter, he wondered who'd unleashed this on him. It only made sense for it to be one of his cell mates. Based on his meeting with Justin, Gabe didn't think it was him. That left Peter, Tall Alex and Short Alex, but no clues as to which one.

////

In his office the next day, sitting through a long conference call in which his role was mainly to listen, Gabe received a text from Jasminn. "It's who I bet it was. Proof when see you."

Shit, he thought. *Now both Homeland Security and the FBI have got me in their sights.*

Gabe paid little attention to the rest of his call, too involved in his own situation. After the call, Gabe took a few minutes to review the approach he'd finally decided on. Looking at the card with Smith's and Jones' numbers, he took a deep breath and called Smith.

The phone buzzed twice before Smith said, "Yes Gabriel?"

"I've got some information for you."

"Good. What is it?"

"Is it safe to talk over the phone?"

"Yes. We've secured your phone." He paused for a second then chuckled. "Other than from us of course. Now please give me all the details."

"That Justin guy. He called me and we met the other night."

"Yes, we know. We had the meeting under surveillance."

The other night Gabe had considered this possibility but hadn't put much stock in it. Now, in response he immediately started sweating and choked for a moment.

"Gabriel?"

"I'm here. Just got something in my throat."

If they'd recorded that meeting his plan was dead. Thinking fast he asked, "Since you heard us, why do you need me to tell you anything? You've already got it."

For the first time since Smith forced his way into Gabe's world, Gabe detected a note of less than complete confidence in Smith's voice.

"I do need it. Surveillance was only visual. I'm sure you remember the blonde-haired woman in the restaurant who kept making eyes at you. She's one of ours. She pretended to flirt so she could openly watch you. She and her companion, another agent, later followed you two to the plaza."

Gabe thought Smith sounded as if he were telling the truth, but Gabe didn't know whether to believe him and felt a twinge of disappointment that the blonde really hadn't been flirting with him. Not having a back-up strategy, Gabe proceeded as planned. He adopted an authoritative, confident tone and tried not to sound nervous.

"It seems you were probably right to arrest Justin that night."

"How so?"

We'll soon see if this works, Gabe thought. "Justin was careful. Feeling me out. I can't be sure but I think he might be an Antifa leader. One of those you're looking for."

Gabe paused, waiting tensely. Smith's end was silent for a long time. *Was Smith trying to sweat him out?*

Finally Smith asked, "What's your basis for this?"

Gabe felt this was moving in the right direction, like one of his negotiating sessions.

"Correction Smith, I didn't say it was my opinion. I said, 'I can't be sure but I think he might be'." The pitch of Gabe's voice rose. "There's a world of difference between what I said and even an opinion, much less a fact. I'm just giving you my sense of him. Don't blame me if it turns out he's not. Especially since you're much more capable of determining this than I am."

"Relax counselor. Don't be so lawyerly. I'll rephrase. What did Justin say that, although you cannot be certain, you think might perhaps indicate that he could possibly be a far-left leader?"

Gabe laughed inwardly at Smith's overabundance of qualifiers. "He didn't come right out and say it, but he seemed to imply that he gives directions about protests. While he was vague, he knew a lot about how things operate, including connections between the non-violent protestors and the extremists. I don't see how he could know all this without being deeply involved with them."

Gabe broke off, staring ahead and waiting to see if Smith would challenge any of these lies Gabe had fed him. Smith was silent so Gabe pushed forward, continuing to throw the b.s. "He must've been locked up before, and I think it might've been under different aliases. He'd spotted the camera in the next cell and told me he thought that the police meant to tape us but, as you'd told me, screwed up and got the drunks next door instead. I told him that he struck me as really knowing the system, and his response was 'Know your enemy'.

"Another thing. That scar of his? He said he got it in Afghanistan. We talked for a while about his time there and things he saw and he was very bitter. He insisted we were wrong to be there and did much more harm than good. Got quite worked up over that.

"Finally, I'm sure he lied to me. He told me he worked for a film production studio in Queens. I tried to check it out online but couldn't find it. It must be bogus. Why would he lie if he wasn't hiding something?"

"That's a good deal of information, Gabriel. This may prove helpful. What did he want from you?"

"He didn't get specific. He may have been feeling me out about spying for him, but he didn't say on whom. I could be completely off base about this though."

"Our challenge here is for the most part we only have the same information you have, that his name is Justin Fairlawn and he lives in

Queens. We'll have to do some digging, but if any of that is false we'll find it out."

"Aren't we now done? I got you what you wanted. You can take it from here."

"Gabriel, you're a very smart fellow, and I suspect dealing with us is making you shrewder by the day. You know you're not done."

Gabe hadn't expected this to get him out of their grasp. Nevertheless, he couldn't help feeling disappointed.

"One other question, Gabriel. Why'd you wait to call me? You should have done so when he first called you."

Gabe had prepared for this question. "First of all, I have to do my job and that takes time. I didn't think of calling you in advance. Since he didn't come right out and admit anything I was thinking about it and putting it all together and finally came out where I did this morning. So once I had, I called you right away."

"Hmmm," Smith muttered then he said, "You're proving useful. As for Justin, stay away from him and don't take his calls unless I tell you to. For the other three, give them another few days then reach out."

Smith disconnected. Gabe sighed and shook his phone in frustration. The one positive aspect he saw was Smith had not mentioned last night's attack on Gabe. That should mean that Smith's people weren't watching him last night. Then again, Smith could be testing Gabe. And what happens if Smith discovers he lied about Justin? He thought, *Oh what a tangled web we weave...*

CHAPTER FIFTEEN

Not long after his call with Smith, Gabe's cell phone buzzed. He recognized Smith's number and had no desire to speak to him again, but felt he had no choice and took the call. "Tell me you've arrested Justin and now we're done."

Smith chuckled. "Gabriel, you have such an excellent sense of humor. But no, and in fact we require additional help regarding him."

"You're supposed to be handling this now," Gabe yelled, surprising them both.

"Calm down Gabriel. We're not asking for much, and I'm sorry to have to say this, but don't forget Jasminn and Matt."

Gabe pounded his desk.

"What do I have to do now?"

"It's quite easy. Set up a meeting with him for later this afternoon at the same plaza as before. Anytime from three on works. Our people will be set by then. We'll start covering him from there."

"What am I supposed to say to him?"

"Tell him you're interested but can't do anything now. Say your firm learned about your arrest. Tell him they're deciding whether to fire you now or later if you get arrested again and whether to permit your continued protesting, even if you don't get arrested again. Say until they decide you need to be very careful and not further upset those senior partners who want to toss you right now."

With no alternative, Gabe reached Justin and set up the meeting, explaining he didn't want to talk over the phone. Next, he called Matt.

////

A light rain was falling when Gabe arrived at the plaza a few minutes before four thirty. Justin was already there, sitting on the same bench as the other night, holding up a small umbrella and reading *The Hollywood Reporter.* Gabe joined him, the seat of his pants getting wet from the bench. Gabe kept his own umbrella overhead and launched into the story Smith had given him. Gabe expanded on it, explaining it was a matter of whether the firm wanted to take a chance on adverse publicity if it infringed on his first amendment rights versus how some clients might react to his actions. Justin slammed down the *Reporter* and started talking rapidly and waving his arms, making drops fly from his umbrella and his umbrella just miss striking Gabe. Throughout this, Smith's team, the two from the restaurant the other night and an agent named Boucher, were nearby, watching and recording them.

Justin leaped to his feet, almost screaming at Gabe while raising his umbrella as if he might strike Gabe.

Just then, a voice yelled, "Gabe."

Justin stopped and he and Gabe turned toward the voice. Matt, wearing a big smile, was rapidly approaching from the restaurant.

"Gabe, what a coincidence! What're you doing here?" Matt asked in a booming voice, holding one hand overhead in a futile effort to block the rain.

Justin looked Matt up and down, grasped the situation.

"Gabe, I'm sorry. I got upset and lost it. You know how strongly I feel about this."

"Uh huh."

"OK. Let me know what happens with your firm."

Justin shook Gabe's hand, glanced warily at Matt, nodded and headed off.

Matt kept his eyes on Justin until he was gone then said, "How about we go back inside and you buy me a beer or two?"

"You're on." Once inside the restaurant, Gabe said, "By the way, you're one shitty actor."

////

It's rarely difficult for surveillance professionals to covertly tail someone who's untrained in counter-surveillance. However, depending upon the surroundings, it can be extremely difficult for less than a full team to successfully follow someone trained in these techniques. Smith's team soon discovered that Justin was the latter type, rather than the former.

Leaving Gabe, Justin, or Suspect J as the DHS had designated him, circled around the building to the north side of the plaza, casually walked west to Lexington then continued north. The man from the restaurant stayed behind with their equipment, while the woman and Boucher set off to follow Justin. The woman tailed him, half a block behind, and Boucher scrambled to get even with him, but across the street. On the northwest corner of Forty-First Street, Justin strolled through a side entrance of an old Art Deco style office building. The woman and Boucher both started running. The building had an underground entrance leading into Grand Central Station and then many choices for escape – multiple subway and train lines plus several exits in most directions. Once in Grand Central, Justin started walking rapidly, seeming to be a part of the commuter crowd. He headed west toward the cross-town shuttle then broke into a trot. Boucher was far behind but had an eye on him and started running to catch up, fitting in with several others running for the shuttle. However, Justin had a Metro Card at the ready and hopped into a departing Shuttle as its doors closed, stranding Boucher at the toll entrance. He had to wait five minutes for the next shuttle to arrive, empty out, take on a new load of passengers and then head back to Times Square. By the time Boucher arrived there Justin was long gone.

CHAPTER SIXTEEN

I can't get a friggin' break, Gabe thought as Short Alex and Peter headed toward him. After the Justin scenes he felt entitled to a respite from all things Smith and Jones, and his former cellmates. It was Saturday morning, and he would have been content to sleep late then lay around doing nothing other than nursing his bruises. Instead, he was in Central Park at another rally—Jasminn had *utzed* him to join her. He agreed because it was Jasminn and it was for a cause no one could object to; another well-deserved celebration of medical workers for their efforts during the Covid crisis. He was sure there wouldn't be any violence at this, but he insisted they stay in the back of the crowd, away from where any action would likely take place if any fighting did break out.

Short Alex and Peter continued toward him. Attempting to be subtle, Gabe whispered, "Jaz, don't look, but two guys from my jail cell are headed over. Don't say anything about what's been happening. Especially about Smith and Jones or Justin."

She responded with a *How dumb do you think I am?* look.

Once Peter and Short Alex reached them, Gabe introduced Jasminn as a 'school friend' and Short Alex and Peter as 'lifers on the lam' while remembering to call Short Alex just Alex.

"Isn't this a beautiful day? What clean air. Much better than how the jail smelled," Alex said, making the others laugh slightly.

Noting that Short Alex was wearing tan slacks and a red polo shirt, Gabe said, "You're dressed very differently today. Nice look."

"These are my work clothes. In a little while I've got to get up to the store I manage. I always have to make sure everything runs smoothly," Alex replied while thinking, *and especially check the status of our special order*.

The four of them ambled over to a rocky outcrop, seated themselves on top, and looked over the crowd. It was a mix of people. Young kids sat on the shoulders of their parents, applauding while hanging on. People from the alt-right, several flags flying above them, applauded and joined in. A roped off area on one side was filled with elderly people and their attendants. Some sat in wheelchairs, others had walkers with folding seats while a few stood proudly on their own.

Jasminn pointed to them and whispered to Gabe, "They're the lucky survivors." Gabe gave her a comforting squeeze, knowing how sad she was over losing a grandmother early in the pandemic.

Peter, who had missed this byplay, said to Jasminn, "Be careful with this guy. He's a dangerous criminal."

Discretely wiping her eyes, she gave him a small grin. "It's alright. I'm also his parole officer. If he acts up, I'll put him back to jail."

Ignoring this repartee, Gabe asked the other two, "So what's with you guys? I didn't think you knew each other on the outside."

Alex replied, "We didn't, but jail makes for strange bedfellows, or something like that. We discovered we share many views." Changing the topic, he asked, "Have you seen Tall Alex or Justin since then."

"No." Gabe was confident they couldn't read him. He thought, *I should try to get info out of them for Smith and Jones*. "What views do you share?"

Peter had been giving Jasminn the once over but received only a dirty look. Shrugging, he shifted his attention. "We both think the left must become more assertive and stand up more forcefully for what we believe. I'm not talking about violence. We're against that of course."

"Of course," Gabe said.

"But we have to make our voices heard by more people and convince them to join us."

"Sounds good," Gabe observed, "but how's that any different from what others have been saying for years?"

Peter launched into a lengthy discourse, often punctuating a point by waving his hands or thrusting a finger at Gabe. Initially Gabe paid close attention, but soon decided Peter was saying nothing new so just let the words flow past him. Meantime, Gabe studied him. Peter looked no different than before except, if anything, his hair was even greasier. Gabe noticed that the broken stem on his glasses was fixed.

As Peter continued talking, Jasminn shifted restlessly. Gabe pulled her closer and she rested her head against his shoulder.

Peter finally wound up, "I was set to go when we saw you Gabe and wanted to say 'Hello'." He stared at Gabe without smiling. "You should be careful. As you said that night, this isn't your thing. You should definitely keep away from trouble."

"Good advice, but getting worked over makes me mad," Gabe replied, his lips drawn up slightly and his eyes narrowed as he stared back, wondering whether Peter was offering advice or issuing a warning.

Peter shrugged, gave Alex a complicated handshake then left. Once he was out of hearing range Gabe asked Alex, "Do you buy that spiel of his?"

Alex smiled. He'd been sitting with his legs dangling off the rock. Now he shifted to sit cross legged and angled his body toward them. "There's nothing wrong with what he said."

Jasminn responded, "No, but there's nothing new in it either."

"True. It might depend upon how you go about things."

"How so?" she asked.

"We're working on that." He studied her. "When you're not being this guy's parole officer," pointing at Gabe, "what do you do?"

Jasminn and Alex chatted, ignoring Gabe. He sat there, a bump on a rock. *Was Short Alex hitting on Jasminn? Was she interested?* Gabe had no claim on her; there was nothing romantic going on between them. But this flirting in front of him bothered him. He remembered how his thoughts had turned to Jasminn when Alice had invited him back to her place. He was thinking about this when Alex interrupted his reverie.

"What? Sorry, I didn't hear you. Guess I was daydreaming."

"Or maybe getting knocked around has messed up your brain," Jasminn suggested with her sly smile.

Gabe gave her a slight smile and shook his head while Alex replied, "I said Gabe, I'd like to discuss with you and Jasminn where things are headed and what we can do. What do you think?"

"Sure," Jasminn replied.

"No," Gabe shouted, then realizing how strongly he'd reacted, and that he'd stunned the other two, he said. "What I mean is, you and I can talk, but not Jasminn. I don't want her involved."

"Who the hell are you Gabriel Bentley to say what I do or don't do?" She glared at him.

Gabe took a moment to make sure he replied exactly right. He held up his hands in front of him in apology. "I'm sorry, Jaz, I didn't mean to come across that way. Of course I don't tell you what to do, but this is different." He looked around, half expecting to see Jones peeking out from behind a tree. "Alex and I are marked by the authorities. You know that. If you get involved with us they'll take an interest in you too." Trying to placate her, he went on, "Hey, for all we know they're watching us now and saying, 'Who's that hot woman with those two radicals? Let's bring her in for intensive questioning'."

Jasminn considered what Gabe said, what he'd gone through and was caught up in. She decided he was right and she could be more useful if she stayed below the radar. With both hands she clutched Gabe's arm and looked up at him adoringly, a damsel worshipping her hero. In a sweet dulcet voice she simpered, "Oh Gabe, you're right. Please forgive me for doubting you. I'll do whatever you say."

The three of them cracked up at her performance, and Gabe was relieved she'd listen to him, at least this one time.

"Alex," he said, "how about you and I meet up soon?"

"We'll see," Alex replied. He uncrossed his legs and shimmied off the rock. "Pleasure meeting you Jasminn. Gabe, be seeing you."

////

Shortly afterwards Jasminn took off for her gym and then to meet some girlfriends. Gabe had less fun as he spent the afternoon and much of the evening in his office handling work he'd ignored over the last few days. He realized his frustration and anger over what was happening was affecting his work—he was taking unnecessarily aggressive positions and being less reasonable on behalf of clients who didn't like that approach. *Too bad. If people don't like it, we can argue about it,* he thought. Finally, caught up enough, at the client's expense he took a car service home to avoid being the victim of another attack.

The next day he, Matt and Jasminn played in a three-on-three tournament. It was a warm-up for the citywide invitational tournament. The games were half court matches. No referees, no pros or ex-pros and each team had to have at least one woman playing at all times. Most teams had five or six players so they could make substitutions, but theirs was just the three of them. Unless a team had a player near Matt's level, a rare occurrence, Matt didn't take over and just reel off points. Instead, he'd play defense, but on offense mainly would set up Gabe for an outside jumper or feed Jasminn down low, only occasionally making a spectacular dunk to keep the spectators happy.

They won their first three games despite Gabe's jumper being off. His bruises prevented him from straightening fully when he shot, and body contact hurt. Trouble broke out in their fourth game. Gabe was being guarded by a man in his mid-forties who had a large gut and didn't move well. Even as battered as Gabe was, he easily went around and over his opponent. After Gabe scored on him for the fourth straight time, the guy started playing dirty, holding Gabe, jabbing him in the ribs, and finally shoving him hard in the back, knocking Gabe to the ground. Gabe came to his feet fast, ready to fight, but Matt restrained him.

They took a time out to calm Gabe down. Back on the court, Gabe saw that his man had taken off his sweatshirt, revealing a QAnon tee shirt. That did it. Gabe called for the ball. Once he had it, he made a ball fake, swinging the ball rapidly from right to left, except he smashed it into QAnon's face, knocking him down. Gabe leaped on him and began hitting. An opposing player struggled to pull Gabe off QAnon while Matt and Jasminn kept anyone else from getting involved. After the fight was broken up, the tournament officials disqualified both teams.

Jasminn dragged Gabe off to the side as Matt kept watch for any attempted reprisals. They'd never seen Gabe act that way. Normally, it was him restraining Jasminn. She consoled Gabe. "I understand you're frustrated. You've been put through shit and that guy started playing like a punk. But QAnon's got nothing to do with this." She went on. "If he'd been wearing a DHS shirt then I'd understand."

He looked at her, confused.

She sighed and her frown showed her disappointment in him. "Come on, Gabe. Department of Homeland Security?"

CHAPTER SEVENTEEN

That evening, still sore and out of sorts, Gabe arrived at his uncle Steven's home. Steven Bentley, Gabe had stopped calling him 'Uncle Steve' around the start of high school, lived with his wife and three daughters in his four-story townhouse in the West Village. Monthly Sunday night dinners at the Bentleys' were a tradition and Gabe thought that explaining to Steve why he failed to show would be more trouble than attending and acting as if nothing out of the ordinary was happening.

Steve was a senior partner at another large law firm. The firm had a strict no-nepotism policy, but when Gabe was in law school Steve had gladly offered to break it for him. Gabe had declined, in part not wanting to put Steve in an awkward position, but mainly not wanting anyone to think he couldn't make it on his own.

Steve and Gabe's father grew up poor in a rundown fringe urban neighborhood, and while Steve was now a big shot lawyer, physically he didn't fit the image. He was short with a massive bear chest above a waist kept from spilling over only by arduous exercise. As if his torso wasn't enough challenge for his expensive tailor, his arms added to it. They were extremely long for a man of his height, requiring extra work on the sleeves. Topping it off, he had an unusually large head stocked with frizzy hair which had bested many of New York's best barbers.

Steve greeted Gabe at the door, right hand extended in greeting, and the left one handing Gabe his first glass of the evening's special cocktail, a Perfect Manhattan. Bypassing the slow-moving elevator, they climbed the one flight to the living room. Gabe made his hellos to the other guests, received air kisses from the women, then he and Steve made their way to a corner to catch up. Gabe described his confrontation with the obnoxious lawyer the other day, it already seeming like ages ago to him. After Gabe finished, Steve slapped him on the back for a job well done, making Gabe wince. Steve didn't notice though as the doorbell rang and he rushed off to grab a drink for the latest arrival.

Gabe remained off to the side, watching the other guests. Perhaps because of his recent experience with untrustworthy and suspect people, one of his favorite Steve stories came to mind. In Steve's first year as a lawyer, he and his officemate had been working on Christmas Eve. He hadn't minded since back then he wasn't married and had no family in the city, and his officemate didn't care since he was Jewish. As Steve told it, the hallway's floor was wood so they heard everyone's footsteps as they headed to the exit, passing their open office door. That evening they'd heard a distinct set of footsteps. "Step, clump. Step, clump," was how Steve described them. The footfalls were made by an elderly partner, Mr. Strun. The younger lawyers considered him one of the few nice senior partners and among themselves they referred to him as "Kindly old Mr. Strun." Supposedly, Mr. Strun got the "clump" while serving in the OSS during World War II, but no one knew for sure. Right before Mr. Strun had reached their office both Steve and his officemate had looked down at their papers, showing they were hard at work. They'd heard Mr. Strun pass by, then, several steps later, return. Both lawyers looked up. Mr. Strun had looked at them from the doorway and cackled, "Merry Christmas, slaves," then went on his way. Gabe knew that of course no partner would use the word "slaves" these days, but he didn't think that the underlying attitude had changed much.

Gabe took another swallow of his drink and forced himself to mingle.

After dinner Steve was with several guests in the library, drinking brandy and smoking cigars. Gabe didn't care for brandy and he'd never smoked, but nevertheless he joined them. The room resembled an old English library, complete with walls of books with a sliding ladder along a railing up top, several deep chairs and a sofa, heavy drapes, a stand with a large globe and a snooker table. The only part of the décor that didn't fit was a Rothko hanging above a *faux* mantelpiece. As Steve said, "The law has been very very good to me."

Gabe got Steve alone in a corner between snooker games.

"Steve," Gabe asked, "do you know much about the Department of Homeland Security?"

Steve's eyebrows raised. "Why? You've a matter with them?"

Gabe hesitated then replied, "No, it's just that its rules may be relevant to something I'm working on."

"No," Steve replied, "I've never dealt with the Department and don't know anything about it beyond what one reads. Sorry."

"No biggie."

"Good, now excuse me, my victim for my next snooker game is getting impatient."

CHAPTER EIGHTEEN

It had been a good week so far. Gabe hadn't heard from any of his cellmates or Smith or Jones. He did his job and hoped the nightmare was over, although he didn't believe that Smith and Jones were done with him. It was about eight on Wednesday night and he was home, doing drills. He flipped a basketball off the fingertips of his right hand, the ball rising a few inches then coming down, resting on his fingertips again, his palm bent back almost parallel to the ceiling and his left hand steadying the ball. A proper shooting position. He kept repeating this motion, each time a tad harder, tossing the ball a little higher. The apartment had a twelve foot ceiling—not high enough for a real jump shot, but high enough for Gabe to jump and get good rotation on the ball. His ribs no longer hurt and the motion was smooth. By the weekend he'd have no problems with his shot and could make up for his recent pathetic performance.

Landing softly after the last shot of fifteen fast reps, he imitated a famous broadcaster and cried out, "Yes! And it counts!"

His cell phone rang. No incoming number showed. *Shit. It's them.*

Having no choice, he hit 'Talk' and grunted, "Yeah?"

"Kid, didn't your parents teach you manners?"

"What do you want, Jones?"

Gabe could hear the snickering. "Why you Kid, of course."

"What now?"

"You haven't been watching the news? Throw on some good protest march clothes and wear work boots or something else sturdy. Then get downstairs. A car will be there in five minutes for you."

Gabe didn't argue or say anything, he simply sighed.

"By the way, Kid, your right elbow is sliding out to the side on your shot. Keep it tucked in."

Gabe was livid as Jones clicked off. Now the bastards were spying on him in his own apartment!

////

Gabe got into the back seat of the dark gray sedan which was double-parked out front. The driver said nothing and Gabe responded in kind. Pulling out his phone, he looked for what Jones was talking about. It was easy to find—an article about it was at the top of the news page. Early that afternoon in her home a woman had shot and killed an unarmed burglar. The article said the woman lived in a castle doctrine state which included protection of property. Gabe was familiar with this doctrine, and the article explained it meant that on their own property a person could shoot an intruder under certain circumstances even if the shooter wasn't in fear for his or her own life. In this case the burglar was a high school student who'd been busy shoving the woman's good silverware into a pillowcase when she shot and killed him. Later she told the police "I wasn't afraid of that white trailer trash." The article made a point of noting the woman was in her late 60's, was black, was a devoted member of her local Baptist church and was an NRA member.

Gabe considered who'd protest about what. Clearly the anti-gun people would come out in force—serving pieces, forks and spoons not being a reason to kill someone. The woman would also make an excellent symbol for Second Amendment advocates. Their people would likely demonstrate in force, viewing her being elderly and black as a plus. Gabe assumed that anyone who'd protested against the armed couple recorded on their front porch back in 2020 should certainly protest this. All of this left Gabe wondering what Homeland Security in the persons of Smith and Jones had in mind for him now.

The car drove over a bump, disrupting his thoughts. He realized that foolishly he hadn't paid attention to where they'd driven, and it was too late to find out; they were now in an underground garage. At the bottom of the ramp stood Jones, leaning against a pillar.

Gabe glared at Jones who smirked in return then mimed a jumper, keeping his elbow tucked. Taking Gabe by an arm, Jones led him to an elevator which brought them to the same large open space as last time.

Baring his teeth slightly, Gabe yanked free and edged away from Jones. "I'm not going back in that cell."

From the far end of the room Smith shouted with a chuckle, "Of course not, Gabriel. You're part of the team. You're going with us."

Reluctantly, Gabe let Jones steer him in Smith's direction. Passing the cell, Gabe peered in. *Same as it was*, he thought. Smith was waiting with three others. They, Smith and Jones all wore the same black bloc type jumpsuits Smith and Jones had worn the night they'd grabbed him. The other three had on helmets with lowered visors shielding their faces. These men, they had to be men from their height and physiques, ignored Gabe and spoke to each other in whispers.

"What's going on Smith?"

"I trust on your way you read about the shooting over that woman's cutlery."

Gabe nodded.

"Many groups have already hit the streets. All across the country. Some protesting against the castle doctrine laws and the killing. Others supporting gun owners' rights and, kind'a bizarrely, claiming this fits in with the BLM movement. Here, the police are steering each side's main group and they'll collide soon at Herald Square. There, presumably, fighting will break out." He continued facetiously, "Despite the police's best efforts of course."

Gabe felt a mix of bewilderment and disgust which Smith saw in the frown furrowing Gabe's forehead and nose and the tightening of his lips.

"Why bring them together? That's crazy!"

Once again, as if tutoring a slow student, Smith replied, "They'd find each other anyhow. It always plays out that way. This way the police can control the situation better."

"Bullshit."

Smith shrugged. "Think what you want. The alternative is factions splitting off along the way and all over the city there's fighting, property is destroyed and there's always looting. Is that better?"

Gabe didn't have a ready answer.

"Alright, enough. We need to get moving. We've got a suit for you the same as ours. Put it on."

"No."

From behind Gabe, Jones dragged out a warning, "Kiiid…"

Smith held up a jumpsuit. "This is designed to provide excellent protection. It goes over your clothes. Don't make a production, Gabriel. Please just put it on." His voice rose as he asked, only partly kidding, "You don't want my colleagues here to have to put it on you, do you?"

Mad at Smith and at the situation, but once again in dealing with Smith seeing no alternative, Gabe donned the jumpsuit. He felt pads attached to the inside in several places, including over his kidneys and in the groin, and some type of light flexible metal in interior pouches across the chest and back. It looked like an Antifa's black bloc outfit, but with its hidden features it reminded him of a bad superhero costume. Smith squirted a greasy gel from a tube and lathered it on Gabe's face, rubbing it in well and explaining that the gel's slipperiness would make punches slide somewhat if he got hit. Gabe let himself be moved along with the rest as they went to the garage and exited in the windowless back of a van. Smith and Jones put on helmets.

"Where's mine?" Gabe asked, pointing at Smith's helmet.

The helmet's visor slightly muffled Smith's voice, forcing Gabe to strain to make out what he said. "You don't get one. You're the star of the show. Your public has to be able to see you."

"What the hell do you mean?"

Smith raised his visor so Gabe could hear him better. "Simple. We'll join the anti-gun march in the front, and when fighting breaks out, which it will, the world will see you courageously fighting for the far left. You'll be an Antifa hero."

"This is crazy. Who's gonna believe this?"

"Oh, everyone will believe it Gabriel."

"I take it you don't care what happens to me."

"In truth, we gave serious consideration to making sure you got hurt. Not seriously hurt, of course, but an injury would make you a sympathetic character. We decided it was better for you to be a victorious hero. My colleagues," he waved at the three silent figures, "are among DHS's best, and our job is to protect you. Don't worry, you'll be perfectly safe."

Gabe listened in disbelief, then cried, "You bastards are insane."

In response, from Gabe's other side Jones elbowed him hard in the ribs, inadvertently showing Gabe how well the padding worked.

Smith switched to his soothing voice. "Don't worry, Gabriel. Nothing will happen to you. You've got five pros here to protect you."

"And despite that, if someone gets past you?"

"Then in that case I guess you'd better fight," Smith replied with a shrug and a small grin.

The van's occupants were silent for the next few minutes. Presumably, Gabe thought, the others were calm and this was a walk in the park for them. He, however, was terrified. He was being set up by a bunch of lunatics as a target at the frontline in a street battle. He had no protection for his head, no weapon and almost no real fighting experience. He was sweating, which the outfit only made worse, and pressure on his bladder forced him to strain not to wet himself. The van lurched to a halt and the driver rapped on the divider.

"This is our stop," Jones said gaily.

The others lightly hopped down then helped Gabe out. Gabe saw that they were on Fifth Avenue, one block south of Herald Square. Smith said, "Here" and handed Gabe a plexiglass shield which was missing a pie shaped section but might give him some protection.

Gabe briefly considered making a run for it, but the others closely surrounded him; being as much guards as protectors. They headed west.

In Herald Square the police had set up metal barricades between the two groups, with Horace Greeley's statue at the mid-point between them. The anti-gun protestors stood penned in on the west side. With help from several policeman recruited for this purpose, Smith's team came north and made their way to the front of the troops on the west end. Right in front of them was where the main action would be.

The men forced Gabe up onto a flat cement block about a foot high. Gabe was lit up but partly blinded by powerful overhead lights. Standing on his pedestal, one man firmly holding one leg to make sure he didn't run off, Gabe experienced a sensation he'd often seen in movies and read in stories, but which he hadn't believed was real. Suddenly, time seemed to move slowly, as if in a slo-mo camera pan. As he looked around, shielding his eyes from the lights, Gabe saw that the front ranks of the gun rights crowd were almost all white men. Many wore tee shirts with pictures of rifles or the symbols of different alt-right groups. A few had flak jackets. Some still wore lettered red hats. Various flags rose above them – mainly the Confederate Battle Flag and the yellow Gasden "Don't Tread on Me" one. He couldn't make out what they were yelling, but their rage was palpable. Swiveling around, the world still in slo-mo, Gabe surveyed the people in that direction. They were a mixed group in gender, race and clothing, although many wore black bloc with one type of head cover or another. Most of the rest had bandanas covering their faces. One thing they had in common with each other and with the alt-right was their screaming and rage. People on both sides stood ready to fight. Faces were twisted in rage, lips were curled and fists were being shaken. Some on the left carried cut-open plastic garbage cans as shields, some on the right had bats and sticks but almost all on either side carried some weapon. Gabe spotted gas masks atop the heads of people on both sides, ready to be pulled into place if needed.

Time snapped back to normal. Gabe looked again to his west, searching for anyone he knew and hoping Jasminn had kept her promise and wasn't there.

On both sides the crowds in front were being shoved tighter against the barricades, these being all that separated the two mobs. A large contingent of police in riot gear stood off to one side, watching but taking no action. Satellite trucks sat parked behind the police, ready to give their audiences a ringside seat for the impending mayhem.

Gabe was scared. He was breathing hard, his hands were shaking, and his legs felt weak, straining to hold him up. *Come on*, he thought, *get ahold of yourself. Don't be a wuss. If Antifa members can do this, you can. Yeah, but they believe in fighting. So force yourself to believe too.* To Gabe's surprise, he was able to slow his breathing and calm down, getting control of himself. He thought, if I must fight, I'll fight.

A cherry bomb went off, making people recoil. A small gap in the crowd opened and Gabe tried to escape through it,. As he started to move, three of them reached out and stopped him as an unfamiliar voice warned, "Don't try it."

The barricades on both sides started to tip. The pressure from the crowds finally toppled them and both sides surged forward, closing in on each other. Gabe stood between them, pinned on his podium as the DHS crew held their positions. The demonstrators came to within five feet of each other, then halted, staring across the narrow divide. No one had attacked yet. Then, a garbage can full of rotten food flew from the anti-gun side across the narrow space, hitting several Second Amendmenters and spewing spoiled food over others. Yelling, the two sides rushed each other, and the battle was on.

From his raised block Gabe had an excellent view of the action. Watching it, he thought the combatants were following some unwritten rules. No guns were fired, not even from the pro-gun side; no Molotov cocktails or other incendiaries were thrown; and he saw no knives. Otherwise, the fighting was fierce, full of kicking, wild punching, bats and clubs swinging and dangerous objects flying. It was ruthless—he saw several men beating a woman, and a man get hit on the head with a fire extinguisher then crumple to the ground. But, when someone was down, while they received brutal kicks and blows, no one went in for the kill—Gabe didn't see anyone carrying out the *coup de gras*. Meanwhile the roaring was mixed with cries of victory and screams of agony.

At first Gabe didn't need to protect himself as the five DHS men kept him safe. Then a projectile from the alt-right side struck him in his ribs. It wasn't a direct hit, and the suit did its job, absorbing much of the impact. Gabe looked at the alt-right and saw two large men rushing directly toward him, one slightly trailing the other. Gabe's protectors must not have seen them or been otherwise engaged, because the two came on unhindered. By reflex, Gabe swung the plexiglass shield, edge first, at his lead attacker. He thought he'd only grazed the man's shoulder; however, the attacker grabbed the side of his neck with one hand. He kept coming, so Gabe swung again. This time the shield's flat surface caught the assailant on the side of his face. He fell backwards, knocking into his fellow attacker. Still standing, but appearing disoriented, the man raised one hand to his face and staggered off, wobbling his way through the oncoming ranks.

The second man was armed with a cricket bat and was cagier. He didn't rush headlong into range of Gabe's shield. Instead, he reached out and at arm's length swung the bat at Gabe. Gabe got the shield up partway. It deflected the blow, but one end of the plexiglass cracked. The man took a second swing, missing Gabe but grazing the helmet of one of his guards. The defender fell and the impact caused the bat to fly from the attacker's hands and he lost his balance. Someone shoved Gabe forward. He raised the shield further and it poked his teetering foe in the ribs. The man clutched himself where he'd been hit then made his own retreat. Gabe looked around for any other attackers, but suddenly he was tackled from the side. He and his tackler went down, the man on top. Without thinking Gabe struck the man with a flat hand strike into the front of the throat. The man rolled off Gabe, grabbing his neck and choking while Gabe stared in amazement at what he'd done.

So far, the police had stayed outside the fighting, pummeling anyone who got within range of their batons, but not intervening. Now a riot squad, supported by gas canisters and hoses blasting powerful water jets, drove a wedge into the struggling mass. The police struck out with their batons and hard polycarbonate shields and fired rubber bullets and tasers. Members of both groups started fleeing. The police continued striking and firing.

Two of Gabe's defenders grabbed him and pulled him along as they started to make their own escape. The DHS men made a wedge with Gabe in the middle and shoved their way through the crowd. They ran down a flight of stairs into a subway station and jumped the turnstile, helping Gabe over. Along with protestors from both sides, they continued the length of the subway platform, fleeing the riot squad. They resurfaced south of the action where their van was waiting for them. One of them shoved Gabe into the back, and the rest scrambled in behind, the last man barely getting the door closed before the van took off, speeding down Broadway.

Smith pulled a bucket from beneath a bench and placed it in front of Gabe. "Just in case," he said. At the same time, Jones brought an oxygen mask to Gabe's face and told him to breathe deeply.

As they approached Twenty-Fifth Street the van slowed and pulled to the side but didn't come to a complete stop. The three helmeted figures opened a rear door, jumped out, slammed the door and ran off. The van continued downtown, the driver now observing the speed limit. They took a circuitous route so Gabe once again had no idea where they were when the van finally pulled into the underground garage.

Once inside, Gabe rushed to the bathroom. There he repeatedly threw cold water on his face and hair. Looking in the mirror above the sink he saw his face still glistened from the gel but was unmarked. He was ghost white, his lips were purple and his eyes had a manic look and, drying his hands, he saw that his hands were shaking.

Waiting for Gabe, Jones said to Smith, "Those two guys did a good job. It really looked as if the Kid beat them off."

"Yeah, well don't let him know. It's important he believe he really did do that."

"Understood, but I have to give the Kid credit. That third guy was for real and Gabe took him out with that strike like a pro," Jones said.

Gabe emerged from the bathroom, his gait still unsteady, and with a little help from Smith and Jones he made his way to what he thought of as 'The Big Room'. Seated on folding chairs, they stripped off their padded jumpsuits.

"You guys didn't arrange that shooting which started all of this, did you?" Gabe asked as he bent over, his head near his knees.

"My word may not count for much with you Gabriel, but I promise you we wouldn't do that and we didn't. We've simply been waiting for the right opportunity and took advantage of it when it occurred."

From a nearby small refrigerator, Smith grabbed three beers, flipping one can to Jones and opening Gabe's before handing it to him, uncertain whether Gabe's shaking hands could manage it.

"See Kid," Jones said, "you've now established yourself as a fighter for the left and not just a marching and chanting wimp."

Sitting up, Gabe took a deep drink. Feeling better, he said, "What good does that do, other than perhaps getting me arrested since I must be easy for the police to identify?"

"The point is, Kid, members of the far left who were there should have seen you and higher-ups on the left should want to meet you. Or at least that's the plan. Better hope it works or you'll have to do this again." Jones smiled, the notion clearly appealing to him.

"Actually," Smith explained, "don't worry about being arrested. We've covered that. Plus, the TV images of your face are blurred."

"What about you guys? How would I explain you?"

"We weren't the ones heroically standing above the crowd. No one would spot us in that mess, and certainly not figure out we were protecting you rather than fighting."

"Speaking of which, what happened to you protecting me when those guys attacked?"

Gabe was looking at Smith so could not see Jones' grin. Smith said, "You're right. We messed up. Luckily, you handled them on your own. Great job. Especially the guy with the bat. He looked really tough."

"Yeah, well...." He took another large swallow.

"Gabriel, give yourself credit. You handled yourself well."

A trash can sat about ten feet away. With a flick of his wrist Gabe tossed his empty beer can into it. Turning to Jones he gloated, "All net."

Jones pursed his thin lips but said nothing.

"And next?" Gabe asked.

"We wait," Smith replied.

////

Police, FBI agents and Homeland Security agents were monitoring both groups. Some marched along undercover, chanting and waving banners, while others watched from above. The agencies were mainly looking to expand their activist databases on both sides. They would have benefitted by coordinating their efforts, but interagency turf disputes prevented that.

As the crowd grew in Herald Square, a Homeland Security spotter assigned to the anti-gun marchers was using a high-powered lens to scan them grid by grid when he spotted a possible target. He doublechecked the database, then certain, announced over a scrambled channel, "Alert! Suspect J located. Thirtieth street ten yards west of Sixth. South side. Wearing white nylon-type pullover. Scramble Surveillance Team One."

In response Team One rushed into action, ready to follow wherever Suspect J went; positioning their vehicles in all directions, covering subway stations and street agents moving to holding spots at various distances from Suspect J. He'd escaped the Department once, but they wouldn't let that happen again.

Although the fighting broke out further east, the spotter ignored the action, kept Suspect J centered in his lens and issued reports to Team One. As the demonstrators dispersed, Suspect J moved with them. For a few blocks he stayed in the middle of the crowd, then he broke off. He spent almost two hours roaming the city, taking the Seven subway to Hunters Point in Queens, there switching to an eastbound LIRR train, reversing directions at Forest Hills, and taking a westbound train to Atlantic Avenue in Brooklyn. From there he took several cabs between long walks, ending up on the West Side, walked some then took another taxi followed by a gypsy cab before walking the last stage to his home.

Suspect J, as the DHS called Justin, had eluded Homeland Security's unequipped two-person team last time, but the Department had been ready this time. As he entered his building in Stuyvesant Town, despite his steps to lose what to him was purely hypothetical surveillance, Surveillance Team One was right with him. They established a perimeter around his building and another around Stuyvesant Town and Peter Cooper Village. Suspect J didn't know it, but he was trapped. Less than an hour later, after going through Stuyvesant Town's computers, they identified Justin Fairlawn as Michael Yang. It took another hour, then Smith and Jones learned that Yang was with the FBI's Anti-Terrorist Division.

CHAPTER NINETEEN

Smith and Jones crashed for the night at the Department's New York headquarters. They shared a small room where their cots sagged, the blankets scratched and outside their window an old neon sign buzzed all night. Smith got little sleep although, unbothered, Jones slept soundly through the night.

Early the next morning, while Jones showered and shaved, Smith reached Einner and explained the Justin situation. Interagency case disputes often became heated as no agency wants to relinquish a case. The only exception is if its agents believe the case will probably go nowhere, in which event they'll gladly let the other agency take the case and the blame when it crashes. Smith didn't believe that was going to happen here and made the argument that they should cut Justin out. Einner trusted Smith and said he'd take it up the chain, but since it would take time to work his way through the necessary channels, he authorized Smith to contact Justin in the meantime and assert the Department's position.

After the call, Smith showered quickly, cringing under the spray since Jones had used up the meager hot water supply. Smith's cringing was followed by his drawing up his nostrils and grimacing while putting on yesterday's clothes. Jones watched with amusement as sweat and other bodily fluids did not bother him.

Justin had not yet left his building when Smith and Jones reached the inner perimeter of watchers. There they happened to take up position on the same bench Gabe had been sitting on when he'd seen Justin.

Smith sent a young agent to get them coffee and bagels. Jones scarfed down his bagel and Smith was about halfway through his when Justin exited through the building's main entrance. They left their remaining food and coffee and hastily headed around the fountain toward him.

Justin stood a few steps outside the building entrance, stretching and enjoying the morning air. He wore jeans which were recut to be looser to cover the pistol strapped to his right ankle, and a white tee shirt with a picture of Abbie Hoffman in handcuffs on the front, and on the back it said, 'DON'T THINK OF STEALING THIS SHIRT'. He got only a few steps before he saw Smith and Jones heading in his direction. Justin's face showed nothing, but he was immediately suspicious of them and he slowed, then halted and looked them over. Their slacks and sports coats were wrinkled, and their shirts were creased. More importantly to Justin, both men carried themselves purposefully and Justin thought one of them, the man with a thin pointed face, looked primed, as if ready to strike. Justin had no doubt they were aiming for him and had serious intentions. What he didn't know was what those intentions were and who they were, although he suspected they were alt-right. He decided not to make a move for his pistol right away, although his muscles tensed and he was ready if need be.

About fifteen feet from Justin, one man stopped and extended an arm signaling the thin faced man to halt. He offered a hint of a smile and said loudly enough to be heard over the fountain's splashing, "Good morning, Justin. We mean you no harm. We're on the same side. May we approach?"

Justin's eyes flicked back and forth between the two of them and through tight lips answered in a cold voice, "Have that guy stay where he is. You come forward, slowly, but don't block my line of sight." Pointing to Jones he added, "I want him in view at all times."

Smith nodded and slowly approached. Once close enough so Justin could hear him while he spoke softly, Smith said, "We're Homeland Security, Michael. I'm going to reach into my pocket and pull out my badge and ID to show you. OK?"

Justin's eyes widened upon being called "Michael" then he nodded, watching Smith closely while at the same time his eyes kept flicking back to Jones. Using a two finger grip, Smith slowly pulled his badge and ID from his breast pocket. Justin waved him closer and studied them.

Satisfied, his muscles relaxed and he said, "You can't be too careful."

"No, you can't. May my partner join us?"

Justin peered over at Jones. Justin didn't know what it was, but despite working for Homeland Security, something about Jones bothered Justin. Nevertheless, he nodded and Smith waved Jones forward. Upon reaching Justin, Jones showed Justin his badge and ID, using the same two finger grip.

"Can we talk somewhere private?" Smith asked. "In your apartment?"

Justin shook his head. "No, my family's upstairs." After a second he added, "I've got a place though."

They followed him around to the building's rear and down a short flight of chipped cement steps to a weathered battered door. Justin took out a set of keys, fiddled to find the right one then unlocked the door. They followed him into the building's boiler room, stopping on a metal grill platform with a metal railing sitting about fifteen feet above the floor. The room's machines were loud and the room was uncomfortably hot with the smell of oil permeating the air. Smith and Jones both looked around carefully.

Justin advanced to one end of the platform, faced them and leaned back against the railing. He spread his arms wide—his body language suggesting either he was relaxed and being friendly and open or he was prepared to fight.

"What makes you think my name's Michael?"

As usual, Smith did most of the talking for him and Jones.

"We know you're Michael Yang and are with the Bureau's Anti-Terrorist Division working to infiltrate the left here in New York under the name Justin Fairlawn. Before we learned who you really were, we spotted you at last night's demonstration and tailed you here."

Justin scowled in anger and just for a moment his eyes dropped at Smith's last statement.

"Don't take it hard. You're very good but we had a full crew watching you starting from Herald Square. You didn't have a chance."

"But why'd you tail me?"

Smith employed his smooth voice. "You've done an excellent job working your way in with the left. So good we believed you were one of them and perhaps a higher-up."

Justin rolled his eyes at Smith's line. He felt like he was being bs'ed and he didn't like it. He looked up briefly at the ceiling and gathering what likely had happened, he asked, "Were you responsible for my being picked up recently? The night I was put in the cell which should have had the camera?"

Smith smiled and tilted his head slightly in acknowledgement. "We'll take responsibility for everything except putting you all in the wrong cell. The NYPD gets the, ahem, credit for that."

Justin looked Smith directly in the eyes. "Exactly what are you gentlemen involved with?" he asked.

"Same as you. Looking for the bad guys."

"These overlapping assignments rarely work out well," Justin said, shaking his head.

"I agree," Smith replied. "I've notified my supervisor, and I'm sure now you'll notify yours. We'll let the higherups sort this out."

Justin's hands closed tightly around the top rail and he came fully erect. "I've been on this a long time. I'm not backing off."

Jones smirked in response, staking out the contrary position.

"You got something to say, Jones?" Justin demanded, staring at him and shifting his weight to be ready in case Jones came at him. "We can have your friend here step aside and work things out just between you and me."

Jones smiled. His tongue momentarily visible as he licked his lips. A crocodile ready for dinner.

Smith held out his arms to stop both of them.

"Cut it out. Let's settle down. To resolve this, D.C. will want to know what we're both doing and where we stand. It would help if we shared some basic information."

The other two stood silently, still maintaining eye contact with the other, but fortunately, Smith thought, at least neither was moving in.

Smith continued. "I'll start. Do I call you Justin or Michael?"

Justin listened to Smith but kept an eye on Jones. "In here, doesn't matter. Out there, I'm Justin."

"OK, Justin. First thing, Gabriel Bentley. You know, Gabe? He's ours."

Justin smacked his right palm down hard on the metal railing, the sound reverberating through the large room.

"Shit." He exhaled through pursed lips and accused Smith, "I take it you purposely threw him in that cell with the rest of us."

Smith nodded.

"And our meetings? You monitored them?"

Smith nodded again.

"Did you record our conversations?" he demanded, staring angrily at Smith.

"No, only visual," Smith lied. "We do though have Gabriel's description of your first meeting and his thoughts about you." Surprising Jones, Smith asked, "Do you want to hear them?"

Now it was Justin who nodded. Smith replayed the call from his phone. When it ended Smith said, "See, he thinks you may be involved at a high level on the extreme left."

Justin tilted his head, perplexed by what Gabe had said, but he maintained a straight face. He was now certain, regardless of how anything else played out, that Smith and Jones would get to hold onto Gabe. He stroked his chin and looked away for a moment, considering keeping his mouth shut, and knowing Gabe would not only be their asset but their problem as well. They were all with the government so Justin decided he should let them know to be suspicious of Gabe. He moved off the railing, chuckled and said, "He lied to you, Smith."

Jones' upper lip curled slightly but Smith showed no reaction. "How so?"

"He was clearly trying to get you to focus on me. What I told him was that I was merely a foot soldier who wanted to find out about these leaders." His voice got harsher. "I didn't do or say anything which could give him any reason not to believe me." Enjoying this part, he sneered at Smith and more broadly at Jones. "Actually he told you lots of lies. He lied about my military service. I didn't say any of that. The only thing I said about my serving was that I hated not knowing who gave us our orders and whether they were competent and informed. If you served you'd understand. The point is, he lied to you. You may want to consider why he did that and tread carefully."

"Thanks. We'll speak to him about that," Smith replied, not sounding concerned or appreciative. "Have you had any contact with any of the other men from your cell?"

"No. Gabe was my initial target."

"Well we're using Gabe in part to get to them. You should steer clear of them as well." Smith said this nonchalantly, knowing it would upset Justin.

Justin took a deep breath and exhaled, then as Smith expected, he replied angrily, "I'm not giving all this up and you don't get to decide matters, Smith. That's above both our pay grades." They exchanged cold looks. "I assume your surveillance team is still out there. Get rid of them and keep your people away from me so they don't give me away, if they haven't already."

"Understood. Give us five minutes and the area will be clear."

After they left, Justin stared after them then picked up a wrench lying on the grating and smashed it against the railing several times. He knew he'd have to report in, then wait to hear how the bureaucrats decided matters. He wasn't optimistic.

Surprisingly quickly, by the end of the day Washington had settled matters. Homeland Security got Gabe, the two Alex's and anywhere that led them. They both received permission to pursue Peter. The FBI otherwise had free rein to continue its investigation. Finally, they were ordered to cooperate and share relevant information, although upon reading this last directive Smith and Jones both laughed, then Jones spat and muttered, "Yeah, like that'll happen."

CHAPTER TWENTY

After her smoothies with Gabe, Jasminn picked out who among her fellow organizers she'd first let in on Justin, figuring she'd expand from there. Her picks were Rosie and Rebecca, two women she often worked with, mainly in logistics for demonstrations.

Later that day, Jasminn, Rosie and Rebecca were sitting in a cramped back room of a small textile manufacturer's plant in Queens, south of the Midtown Tunnel. The owner who let them use the space was an old man whose grandfather had been forced to flee Mussolini's Brown Shirts, and whose son was active in various causes.

They sat perched on rickety chairs around a rickety table engaged in the tedious task of reconciling lists of online volunteer contact information. Some volunteers provided text or What's App contact info, others their Facebook pages, others various other apps and a few their email addresses. Another list consisted of older people, generally donors, for whom their only contact information was land lines.

Anyone seeing the women wouldn't imagine they'd be involved with anything of concern to the government. Rosie was a heavy Latino woman in her late thirties with two junior high school girls. She'd been born in Latin America and grown up in a mid-west city where racist slurs and harsh mistreatment had been a part of everyday life. New York City was no paradise, but she felt safer there being surrounded by its mix of people and cultures. She always seemed happy and had a smile and would help anyone needing her. Rebecca was quite different. She was in her early thirties, from an upper-middle class town on Long Island. Her parents were Jewish, but she said she was not and that "this whole religion thing is crazy." She was so thin Jasminn assumed she was anorexic, and had short glossy black hair except where it was dyed. Her normal style of dress was combinations of black leather clothing and boots, this day being no exception as she wore a black leather bustier, tight black leather shorts and high black boots with stiletto heels. Numerous tattoos in bright reds and blues were set off by her light skin.

Calling for a break and sipping from a bottle of energy water, Jasminn asked, "Do either of you know Justin Fairlawn?"

Rosie and Rebecca both thought, then Rosie nodded, her chin rising and falling in the deep folds of her neck. "*Si*. He is here some."

"What do you think of him?"

Rosie shrugged, one strap of her dress sliding off her shoulder. Pulling it back up, she said, "He is a nice man. He always offers to help."

Jasminn shifted her gaze to Rebecca. "You know him too?"

"I know who he is, but I don't know him," she replied, sneering slightly, shaking her head and emphasizing the latter 'know'. "Definitely not my type."

"Why're you asking, Jaz?" Rosie asked.

Jasminn still avoided making eye contact. "A friend of a friend warned me about him."

This got Rebecca's attention. Her right hand slid toward her right boot where Jasminn knew a long knife was sheathed. Rebecca asked loudly, "What's the problem? He a rapist?"

"No, nothing like that," Jasminn replied, amazed at how Rebecca's mind worked. "The word is he's undercover for some group. Either the government or the alt-right."

Rebecca was instantly enraged and sprang to her feet. "A spy?"

"That's what I'm told."

Shaking her head, Rosie argued, "No, no. I can't believe that. He's clean, works hard and is always polite."

"Does he ask you questions about what's going on and things? Such as who calls the shots?"

Rosie bit her lower lip and with her colored handkerchief wiped the sweat off her forehead. "*Si*. But maybe he's just curious."

"We should cut him," Rebecca spat out.

Briefly concerned, Jasminn looked wide-eyed at her, then laughed. "Come on Becca. You like to seem tough, but you're no more going to stab anybody than I am. Even less, and I don't carry a blade."

"Jasminn, this is serious for you to say this." Sniffling slightly, Rosie asked quietly, "How sure are you about this."

"I'm absolutely positive. I swear to you." Looking over at Rebecca she added, "And I affirm to you."

Rebecca laugh and sat back down.

"So do you want to do something?" asked Rebecca.

"I want to spread the word. It'll be our own internal doxxing. I think he's mainly trying to find out who are the key decision makers. No one should tell him anything. We should exclude him from actions."

Rosie asked, "You think others will believe us? I believe you Jaz because I love you and I trust you. But I don't know about others."

"You're right, Rosie," Jasminn nodded. "However, my friend's friend showed me proof. Tell any doubters to talk to me."

Rebecca's brows were furrowed, and she cautioned, "Someone will tell him what's going on, or he'll smell something and find out one way or another. If you're right, this could be dangerous. Mainly for you."

Jasminn said quietly. "This has to be done."

"OK," Rebecca said, making eye contact with Jasminn and holding her look. "We'll do it." She looked at Rosie who nodded her assent, her chins wobbling. "And Jaz, maybe you're right and I wouldn't cut him, but I've got brass knuckles and I affirm I would use them."

The three of them broke up laughing then returned to their mind-numbing task.

////

Justin sat slouched at the counter, his second beer resting in front of him. The bar was a dive in an industrial neighborhood. It was well into the late afternoon, but the day-shift crews weren't off for a little while so hadn't yet filled up the joint. The afternoon sun came through the front window around the bar's name stenciled in large letters. At this hour the only other lighting was the illumination from scattered neon signs for different beers, some of which were no longer brewed. The floor had no sawdust or peanut shells for atmosphere, just liquor stains, some blood stains and dirt.

The place was a block from a leftist group's storefront where Justin frequently helped out. Today though he hadn't stayed long. His perception of how people were acting toward him was confirmed. They talked to him as little as possible and generally declined, politely but firmly, his offers to help. Losing Gabe to Homeland Security, and to Jones in particular, frustrated Justin, but Gabe was just an opportunity who'd fallen into Justin's lap. These people cutting him off went to the heart of his assignment and made him strongly suspect that somehow his cover was blown and his months of work wasted.

Justin gazed at the mirror over the liquor bottles lined up on the wall behind the bar. In it he saw Lars, a man from the storefront with whom he'd been friendly, rush by, making tracks for the men's room. Seeing him, Justin decided to try to get some answers. He proceeded to the restroom where he confirmed that Lars was its only occupant. Lars was at the lone urinal, crammed between a wall and a modesty panel. Justin reached back and quietly locked the door.

"What's doing, Lars?"

Lars twisted his head and shifted some, turning any further being risky, and replied, "Justin. How're you?"

Justin regretted what he was about to do, but it was necessary. He took two steps and stopped directly behind Lars; not touching him, but close enough to pen Lars in.

Lars felt his presence. "Hey, give me some room here." When Justin didn't move, Lars said, "If you're that desperate, use the stall."

Ignoring what Lars said, Justin leaned forward, bringing his mouth close to Lars's left ear. "I said, 'What's doing, Lars?' I mean, why are you and everybody treating me like this?"

Lars didn't move other than to roll his shoulders forward, hunching deeper into the narrow space and away from Justin. "I don't know what you're talking about. Come on, back up. This is weird."

"Unfortunately for you it's going to get a lot weirder and unpleasant if you don't answer me." Justin put a hand in the small of Lars' back. "It's interesting how defenseless we feel at a pissoir."

Lars gulped and started breathing faster. Justin's attitude would've bothered him under any circumstances, but Justin trapping him while he had one hand occupied like this, was flat out freaking him. The hand in the small of his back nudged him ever so slightly.

Lars' froze up, unable to finish his business.

"Well?"

Lars surrendered. "The word is you're a spy. We're not supposed to talk to you or have anything to do with you."

Justin maintained his pressure. "Who's saying this?"

"Everybody's saying it."

A harder nudge in the back. Lars' nose was now only an inch from the wall. His free hand flew up and braced against it, trying to stave off being pushed any further.

"Who started this? Tell me, Lars. Who's behind this?"

Lars' body was shaking slightly, and a few drops landed on the floor near his feet, but he was silent.

Justin laughed. "Are you kidding me? You're going to take a stand while standing at a urinal? That'll be quite an epitaph for your tombstone."

Justin wouldn't hurt Lars, much less kill him, but at this point Lars believed he'd do anything.

"Jasminn," he croaked.

"Jasminn?"

"Yeah, you know. The black woman. Really good looking. Former college basketball player. Jasminn."

Justin kept him pinned. "So how'd Jasminn get this wild notion?"

"I heard that some friend told her. People say she's got proof your name isn't even 'Justin'."

Hearing 'college basketball player' and 'some friend told her' Justin immediately thought this must have come from Gabe. Still pinning Lars, he initially thought maybe Smith or Jones had told Gabe to spread this, but this cold shoulder treatment had started before his run in with them. *Gabe must have found out some other way. But how?*

Later, thinking about this, he decided there'd be a bureaucratic shitstorm if he challenged Gabe directly, so decided to try Jasminn first.

He stepped back from Lars then washed his hands. Lars stayed put, zipped up and took deep breaths, calming himself.

"I'm sorry Lars. The way everyone's treating me has really upset me." That much Justin meant. "I mean I'm so committed and then suddenly everyone shuts me out. Including you, and I thought we were friends. I'm going to talk to Jasminn and get this straightened out. I promise I'm not what they're saying."

Now Justin again meant what he said. "You have my word I wouldn't have hurt you."

After Justin left, Lars bent forward, rested his head on the wall, and remained there, thinking about how ridiculed and scared he'd felt. Eventually he shuffled to the sink where he washed, repeatedly threw cold water on his face and used paper towels to wipe the sweat from the back of his neck and under his arms.

////

Justin received a copy of the Bureau file on Jasminn that evening. It was thin, having nothing more than basic information, some details on her playing career and job experience, plus pictures of her at several rallies. He realized that she and Gabe were classmates and saw that she was well-versed with computers, but beyond that he learned nothing useful. Armed only with this knowledge, at a few minutes after seven the next morning he was situated across the street and partway up the block from Jasminn's walkup. He pretended to read *The Post* while waiting for her to show. Jasminn left her building promptly at seven-thirty, heading west and passing Justin on the other side of the street without noticing him. He let her get slightly ahead, then followed her.

She stopped at a nearby shop to get her customary coffee and donut. After she placed her order at the counter, a quiet voice behind her said, "Jasminn, you and I need to talk."

She spun around. Her nostrils flared and she sucked in her breath, but she had enough awareness to grab a metal napkin dispenser to serve as a weapon. A man stood right behind her, too close, even in this post-pandemic era. She hadn't seen Justin in person before, but the man resembled him from the few old pictures online and Gabe's description, and the scar was a give-away. Recovering, she thought *if he expects me to be scared he's going to be very disappointed.* She kept hold of the napkin dispenser, leaned back against the counter creating more distance between them and coldly stared. Her skin tightened above her eyebrows. "Move away from me."

He shuffled back a foot. "Please give me five minutes. Don't worry. I promise I won't do anything to you." At the same time he looked past her and ordered a small coffee.

Thrusting her jaw out, she replied, "I'm not worried. You should be the one worrying. I'm not promising not to do anything to you." He smiled in response.

Jasminn weighed what to do. Here in the donut shop she wasn't afraid of him, and she thought he might tell her things which would help Gabe, so she decided she'd give him his five minutes. She picked up her order and made her way to one of the small tables. Justin hastily paid for his coffee and hurried over, concerned she'd bolt despite her bravado. Seated opposite her he studied her face, looking for signs of nervousness. Instead, her lips were pursed, and her unblinking eyes met his; she was not scared or nervous. He saw for the first time how attractive she was.

"Tip?"

He stared at her blankly, then red-faced and feeling compelled, he returned to the counter and deposited a bill in the college fund tip jar. She watched him to be sure he did so, and he watched her to be sure she didn't leave.

Reseated, he looked at her and said sternly, "I understand you've been spreading false stories about me. Why're you doing that?"

Her eyes widened and the corners of her lips turned up in mock amazement. Taking a bite of her donut, she replied with a small chuckle, "False stories? That's the line you're going with? Lying about lying?"

"I'm not lying. I'm as committed as you are, and I'll bet I've been as involved as you. I was arrested recently at a protest. Have you been locked up?"

She glanced away and gave a small yawn. "Actually, I was pulled in the same night as you."

Justin hadn't known this—apparently it hadn't made her Bureau file yet—and it surprised him. He sat back for a moment and thought about it. *Was the timing a coincidence or had Smith arranged her arrest for some reason, presumably in connection with Gabe?*

They sipped their coffee and she ate her donut while they talked.

"From one jailbird to another, sorry to hear that, but it changes nothing about me."

She rolled her eyes. "You really are quite the bullshitter." After pausing, she sat back as if victorious, and continued in an exasperated voice, "Aren't you, Michael, Mr. FBI agent?"

In turn, he sat back, his mouth slightly agape, and he shook his head. *How does she know my name?* He thought again, *this cold shoulder started before Smith and Jones so it couldn't be due to them. Anyhow, no way they'd reveal my real name. Not even Jones.*

Trying to sound innocent, he said, "My name's Justin, not Michael. Where'd you get those crazy notions that it's Michael and that I'm an FBI agent?"

She said nothing, continuing to stare at him and enjoying herself.

He took a shallow breath then followed up in a menacing tone. "If you were right about me, which you're not, you'd be putting yourself in a lot of trouble. You could be charged with obstruction of justice."

She didn't back off. Instead, she pushed herself forward and asked, "What crime is the FBI investigating which I'm obstructing?"

Not wanting to get into that, he replied, "Alright, ignoring that, who told you I'm with the FBI and my name's Michael?"

"Come on. I've got to get to work. If you want to talk straight, do so. Otherwise, I'm gone. No one told me anything."

Her *chutzpah* both frustrated and impressed Justin. In his experience, most people wilted rapidly when accused by the law of crimes like obstruction of justice. He pushed further. "OK, how'd you come up with this ridiculous information?"

She took a large drink of her coffee and looked directly at him while reciting, "Your real name's Michael Yang. You grew up in Fair Lawn, New Jersey. After college you joined the Army, serving two tours. After becoming a Fed your online profile went black. Or almost black."

Jaw dropping, he looked at her. He debated what to do, while she studiously ignored him and wiped donut crumbs off her top. This woman, presumably with help from Gabe, was ruining months' worth of undercover work and could do even more harm if she spread his real identity. He thought about the safety of his wife and daughters.

"You think you know all that, but you're wrong–everything you just said is fake data which someone posted. However, I'll tell you some things about you I know are correct. You're a gifted geek who gave up a promising career for your do-gooder work. You're a close friend of Gabriel Bentley. He must have entangled you in this, making you a co-conspirator. Since you're the computer whiz, odds are you're the one who dragged up any online data. So, in addition to obstruction of justice, there's probably a criminal hacking charge."

She looked at him, as if offended, then grinned. "Don't be ridiculous. First off, if you're not with the FBI, how could I possibly obstruct anything? Moreover, hacking's illegal and I wouldn't do anything illegal. Let me ask you a question though."

Justin nodded, for one of the few times in his career unsure how to handle a situation.

"Why is the FBI," she purposely omitted Homeland Security, "snooping around us? We're nonviolent protestors. The worst we've ever done is hit the streets without a permit. Plus, the few times we've gotten caught up in violence it's when we've been attacked by the alt-right."

Justin was still denying her claims. He shook his head. "I have no idea what the FBI does or what it's interested in. Even if you're correct about non-violent protestors, shouldn't the government be investigating the Antifa and the dangers created by the extreme left?"

She proceeded to lecture him. "You know as well as I do, Michael," purposely hammering on his real name, "the government's own reports, including the FBI's, warn that the right-wing extremists are far and away a much greater danger than the left. They said this before the attack on the Capitol and they still say it."

"That may be, Jasminn. I wouldn't know. But if I am who you insist I am, I must've been assigned to do what you claim I'm doing, so those reports must not matter. And maybe there's a whole bunch of other undercover agents infiltrating the extreme right. I've no idea. If you're right and I am an agent, blowing my cover would be bad enough, but revealing my identity could endanger my family so you'd better not do that, or whether you're right or wrong I will come after you."

Jasminn had had enough. Neither of them was admitting anything and the conversation was going nowhere. The one comment that struck her was his reference to his family's safety. She had exposed his role and would continue to oppose him, but she told him for the safety of his wife and kids she wouldn't give anyone his real name or enable them to track him down. Before he could say anything more, she dumped her garbage and left him sitting there, pondering what to do.

CHAPTER TWENTY-ONE

Gabe thought of the last two plus weeks as being like riding a terrifying roller-coaster--a rickety old wooden one, but one nevertheless with the speedy ascents, heart-stopping steep descents and sharp hairpin curves used in the most modern metal coasters, but for which his wooden coaster was woefully unfit. The ride had started the night he went to protect Jasminn in response to Matt's text. That night it had risen steeply, almost straight up, then flew down, banking hard on curves to the right and left on the descent, again and again, tossing him from one side of the coaster's car to the other. He had no seat belt and wasn't hurled from the car only by gripping the safety bar so tightly his hands bled. He felt at any moment the car would lose its hold on the tracks and sail off, smashing him to the earth far below. The ups and downs and vicious curves had continued, but after that first night they had not been as high or as treacherous until the night in Herald Square when he'd believed either he or the entire roller coaster would crash. Since then the ride had slowed and ran on a more level track closer to the ground. However, he knew he was not done with Smith and Jones, or more accurately they with him, so the ride was not over and he could do nothing other than prepare himself for the next ascent.

Friday morning Gabe was in his office, juggling several small matters and occasionally tossing a nerf ball from hand to hand when he received a text from Short Alex inviting him to a party that night and suggesting he bring Jasminn. Gabe paused in his work but kept tossing the ball. He was up for a party, having a good time and maybe forgetting about his roller coaster of torture for an evening. Unfortunately, an invite from Short Alex might well mean this wouldn't be a regular party and his roller coaster might start upward once more. *Perhaps, no definitely, even worse,* Gabe thought *Short Alex might have his eyes on Jasminn.* Gabe threw the ball fiercely against the wall, leaving a mark, and snagging it on the rebound, determined not to let Short Alex try for that ride in the Tunnel of Love. *Enough amusement park metaphors.* He considered declining the invite or not telling Jasminn, but felt he was being foolish. He let Jasminn know and they decided they'd go.

Before the party, Gabe and Jasminn had dinner in Long Island City. They went to an old style seafood restaurant someone had recommended. The fish for several dishes came from the Hudson. The river was supposedly clean now after years of pollution, but, regardless, many customers, including Gabe, shied away from those dishes.

They'd barely sat when Jasminn announced, "This place looks nice but there's no way it counts as the fancy dinner you owe me for tracking down that Justin or Michael guy, whatever you want to call him. Especially after he accosted me over my donut."

Gabe said nothing in response or anything else for the next few minutes other than declining the waiter's suggestion of an expensive bottle of sparkling water and ordering a drink. He was too busy pretending to study the menu but actually peering over it at Jasminn. Gabe wore plain grey slacks and a solid navy blue button down shirt. By contrast, Jasmin was all fixed-up. It had been a long time since Gabe had seen her like this. Her dress was in another league. It was tight, extremely short on one side and long on the other; her shoulder and midriff on the short side were bare; and the dress was a shimmering pink and gold. Gabe figured there was a name for this style but had no idea what it was and didn't care. He delighted in how she looked. They were friends, the closest of friends. Yet tonight, as had happened more than once recently, he couldn't stop thinking of her as more than that.

Aware of his covert looks, she smiled, secretly pleased she'd drawn this attention, and rather than calling him a sexist pig as she normally would have, she teased him. "What're you thinking?"

Gabe looked away while sipping his water then fumfered. He felt himself blushing, but the low lighting masked this. Collecting himself, he grinned and said, "I'm thinking how nice you look." His smile became a leer. "Much better than in your game shorts and jersey."

"Nice?"

"Yeah, 'nice'," he replied, not realizing his error.

"That's all?" She extended a long leg out from under the table, the dress' short side facing him and riding up even higher as she turned, all in all a well-planned provocative tableau.

"Let me rephrase that," he said, giving her leg the attention she was seeking and it deserved, "You look beautiful."

An uncomfortable silence followed.

"And how do I look?" he asked.

"Nice," she said facetiously, teasing him. "In your case, I think you look nicer in your basketball shorts. It's especially nice when I back down into you on the court."

After saying that, she lowered her eyes in embarrassment, a rarity for her. Gabe understood what she implied but didn't reply. They both studied the menus and avoided looking at each other or saying anything until their drinks had been served and they'd ordered their meals.

Making up his mind, Gabe caught her attention and while captivated by the sparkles in her aquamarine eyeshadow asked, "How long are we going to continue continuing this?"

"Continue continuing what?"

"Come on," he said in frustration, leaning toward her. "You know perfectly well what I'm talking about. We're together so much. We're best friends." He paused. "Hell, I'm way beyond thinking of you that way and I've never said this, but I think you are so goddamn sexy."

Her eyes opened further as if she was shocked, then she dropped them demurely and replied in a bad fake Southern accent while pretending to fan herself, "Why Mr. Bentley, I do believe you are making advances. You are making me blush. Sir, what are your intentions?"

Instead of answering, he came around the table and whispered in her ear some of the things he'd recently been thinking about them doing.

"Now you're really making me blush," she replied, trying to keep up the demure act, but a broad grin steadily overwhelming her.

Gabe reseated himself. "Now, what do you think?" he asked, a slight quiver in his voice.

To Gabe's amazement and delight she came around the table and whispered what she'd thought about them doing. After she sat back down Gabe gathered himself and slid his chair around next to hers and put his hand on hers, thinking *I'm acting like a schoolboy.*

"Should we go to the party?" he asked.

"I'm debating whether we should even stay for our dinners," she replied. "But yeah, let's eat and then make an appearance."

Gabe knew they should go to the party to see if he could learn anything useful, but he didn't want to. She laughed at his crestfallen face and stroked his arm. The waiter appeared with their entrees. He smiled at their new seating arrangement and returned shortly with glasses of red wine on the house. While they ate, under the table Gabe stroked her leg for the first time, awestruck by how firm but silky smooth she felt. He forgot about Smith and Jones for the longest time since they'd forced their way into his life.

////

The party was at a converted warehouse. No signs announced the club, but two enormous security guards on either side of a metal door served as giveaways. One of the guards added to Jasminn's evening by carding her but merely waving Gabe through. "*Great*," Gabe thought, '*now I'll get cracks from her about her looking young while I look old.*"

The scene inside was what they expected—a large dimly-lit open space with flashing strobes. They checked out the crowd. Some people, in particular women, were all dressed up, while others were dressed down; some in just jeans and tees. Jasminn tapped his shoulder and pointed to a couple wearing full length fishnet body stockings. Gabe couldn't tell if the woman had on a thong or not, but it was clear she wore nothing else. The man only wore a strategically situated bow tie holding him in place.

The dance floor was packed with people gyrating to loud music, or as Gabe yelled to her, as he'd often said, "Sorry, it still ain't music to me." She shrugged. Despite knowing he wouldn't join her, she wormed her way into the dancing throng. Gabe still felt high from dinner and was content to watch the scene as he worked his way around the perimeter toward one of the bars along the walls. He finally reached his destination and decided to toast the two of them even if he had to do so alone. He bought an overpriced glass of champagne and his lips puckered and he shook his head as it proved to be as bad as he should have known it'd be.

"Champagne?" someone yelled. "What're you celebrating?"

Short Alex had snuck up on Gabe unseen and now stood next to him, looking up inquisitively.

"A bright star in a dark sky," Gabe replied off the cuff, but then relishing the description and thinking that he'd share it with Jasminn.

Short Alex was confused, the lines above his eyes deepening accordingly, but Gabe added nothing. Short Alex waved an arm around the room, yelling, "Quite a turnout."

"Yeah. Is this your doing? Organizing parties?"

"No, I've got nothing to do with it. It's a friend's gig, but they treat me well. I manage a combination hardware and army-navy store."

"What?" Gabe yelled. "I can't hear you."

Short Alex started moving away along the wall and waved for Gabe to follow him. As Gabe did so, he felt guilty. He thought Short Alex was a good guy. He didn't relish getting damning information from him or passing it on to Smith and Jones, but one look at Jasminn on the dance floor reminded Gabe he had no choice. Short Alex pushed through the crowd until they reached a roped off area with another large guard. He nodded to the guard, who nodded in response and pulled aside the rope. Short Alex took them through a door and into a dingy hall. A stunning tall woman in a red cocktail dress stood just inside. She obviously knew Short Alex and stooped to give him a big hug then led them to a room. Unlike the rest of the club, the room was well lit with comfortable furniture, neither grungy nor overdone. They sat across from each other and the woman in red took drink orders, Short Alex insisting that Gabe order something better than the club's bad champagne. The woman shut the door on her way out, almost completely shutting out the noise from the main room which caused Gabe to sigh slightly in relief.

"What I said," Short Alex said, "was that I manage a combined hardware and army-navy store. My father owns two stores and I manage one." Laughing, he added, "Someday I will be the king of nuts and bolts and plumbing snakes."

"I get the sense maybe you like it, so that's great."

Gabe assumed Short Alex would turn the conversation to the movement, which Gabe didn't feel like dealing with, so he continued on a different track. "I'm impressed that you knew my law firm. Normally it's only people in large companies or finance who know it."

Short Alex smiled. "It's too well known not to be known even by guys like me who work in a hardware store. By the way, did they find out about your being arrested?"

Gabe nodded.

"How'd they react?"

Gabe sighed. "It's up in the air. Several senior partners want me gone now, and certainly if it happens again, but while others don't care about me, they're saying it'd look bad if it got out that the firm fired someone for exercising their constitutional rights."

"That'd be a bitch, to lose your job over that. Them wanting to can you isn't so surprising I guess, but it's so wrong." He paused, looked closely at Gabe and said, "I guess if they're serious about maybe firing you, you've got to weigh your involvement with the protesters versus your job. What are you going to do?"

Gabe knew Short Alex was fishing, but Gabe wasn't biting. "If they press me, I'll move to another firm as a matter of principle, but then likely stop demonstrating. As I keep saying, I'm not that involved." Gabe changed the conversation. "Although I take it you're very involved."

Short Alex crossed his legs and leaned back, making him look even smaller. "What makes you say that? That night I was just picked up the same way you were. Anyway, even if I were more involved, I'd tell you I wasn't. I don't think either of us know the other well enough to say anything else, regardless of what the truth is."

Gabe's reaction to that was to seriously wonder whether Short Alex was in fact very much involved. "I imagine that's right. Although, I'd think having an army navy store could be very helpful. You could get all sorts of gear the Antifa could use without raising any eyebrows."

Short Alex studied Gabe closely then laughed and changed the subject, saying, "I take it that's not your kind of music out there."

"Definitely not. I used to mainly be into classic rock from my father's era, but I've become a serious blues fan too."

Short Alex straightened up, a huge smile split his face. "So am I. Who're some of your favorites?"

Gabe grinned. He loved talking the blues. "New or old?"

"Both!"

They launched into a joyful discussion, interrupted only by the woman in red returning with their drinks, which she said were on the house. They compared different artists, discovering how much they had in common and toasting their favorites. They agreed that the really old timers, the originals, such as Robert Johnson and Lead Belly deserved the credit for getting it going and they toasted them. However, they agreed that to most modern ears many remakes surpassed the originals, such as *Cream*'s version of *Crossroads* and both Howlin' Wolf's and *Z.Z. Top*'s *Dust My Broom*. Their final toast was to Willie Dixon whom they agreed was the most underappreciated songwriter of all time and the greatest blues composer since World War II.

Their blues tour had taken them through a second round of comped drinks from the woman in red and they could have kept going, but Gabe knew he ought to get back to Jasminn. He eventually found her dancing in a group with two guys and three other women and seemed unaware that he'd vanished. Managing to pull her away, the two of them had a drink with Short Alex, who now had the woman in red clinging to his arm. They had one more round, for which Gabe insisted on paying.

Shortly, Gabe and Jasminn made their excuses. In the back of a green cab crossing the Fifty-Ninth Street bridge and heading to her place,

Jasminn's heart pumped as if she was nearing the end of a long run. They weren't kids and this wasn't near either's first time, but it would be different. She wondered whether this is what maidens had experienced in a different age—the coming culmination of what they'd thought about for a long time. From years of pushing body to body on the court, they knew so much about the other's body. However, they'd always been clothed and, they'd never even seen the other in a swimsuit. It had been like knowing only the broad strokes of a painting or looking at a blurred picture where you only saw the outlines and the proportions. They would now discover the unseen details. Now it would all come into sharp focus—the unknown specifics she'd wondered about would become clear; for the first time solving the unspoken mysteries. They looked at each other. She was sure he thought the same. They smiled and one of his hands reached across his body to caress her thigh and slowly work his way north.

CHAPTER TWENTY-TWO

Gabe woke. He was drowsy and his eyes were still closed, but he knew where he was. The air had her scent. His mind flooded with memories of last night. He remembered her skin moving against his and later nestled up tight against him. He opened his eyes and sat up, a stupid grin on his face. Jasminn wasn't there. A towel lay at the foot of the bed. He wrapped it around his waist and went out to the kitchen living room area.

Jasminn stood facing the sink, her back to him. She was humming a tune he didn't recognize but instantly liked. Kate lay on the couch, reading a section of the Sunday Times.

Seeing him, Kate cried out to Jasminn, "Aha! I figured you were humming 'cuz there was somebody in there." She looked at Gabe and flashed her usual snarky grin. "But him?"

Jasminn ignored Kate, and without turning she fixed Gabe a cup of coffee—black with sweetener.

He took a sip and said in a fake theatrical voice, "Aah, delicious. Just the way I like my women."

Both women groaned.

////

Peter had contacted Tall Alex, and that Sunday morning they met at the base of the Vessel, a large architectural structure or sculpture, depending upon one's point of view, situated in the plaza at Hudson Yards. Shaped similarly to a funnel, an elliptical trough rising about one hundred fifty feet around an open center, it's comprised of staircases, walkways leading in seemingly random directions and connecting platforms, somewhat reminiscent of an Escher drawing. Its open structure provides views from all spots in all directions. Unfortunately, several jumpers had committed suicide off the Vessel, and despite security measures having been taken no one was allowed to go up it.

Peter was waiting when Alex arrived. In contrast to Peter, he was wearing light blue shorts and a violet polo shirt with mustard color deck shoes.

They nodded to each other, and Alex trailed Peter to steps at one side where they sat.

Peter looked over Alex's outfit. "That's quite a look you've got goin' there."

"This is how a lot of guys in my crowd dress." Alex joked, "Think of this as camouflage."

Peter rolled his eyes and shrugged.

"Before its shutdown I'd had to go up the Vessel several times as part of showing out-of-towners the sites," Alex said. "You?"

"Never got around to it. Too late now."

As they talked, Alex studied Peter. Peter was several years older than him, Alex thought, perhaps in his later thirties, and apparently he had little interest in his appearance—he wore a stained windbreaker and his pants had a small rip, but not the fashionable-type rip.

Alex glanced around the plaza. "We got arrested at that same protest that night, but I haven't seen you at any others."

"I can say the same about you."

"I'm always there. However, I stay masked and in the middle of the crowd. That night was my first time getting arrested."

Peter looked him up and down. "I assume you dress more discretely at them."

They exchanged chilly looks.

Peter continued, "Anyway, I'm always there. I mainly hang with the Brighton Beach crowd. Most Russian and other Eastern European immigrants living there keep a low profile. We have vivid memories of our old countries' governments. Some who're now citizens stand up for the America we believe in and for why we came here." He challenged Alex. "Alright?"

"Alright."

They were silent. The only sound was the wind whistling through the Vessel.

They were both suspicious generally and extremely cautious as to whom they spoke openly. However, after some small talk they each concluded they had no basis to believe the other wasn't on the level, and they thought they could work together.

Peter got down to why he'd proposed meeting. He shook his head in amazement. "Those pictures and videos have sure gone viral."

Alex knew what he meant. "Yeah. I've looked at lots of them. It's strange though, unless you know it's Gabe you really can't tell."

"True. I don't know why, but in every picture his face has a glare obscuring it somewhat," Peter responded. "But it was him. I saw him standing up there with my own eyes, as clear as day."

"Do you think the government has identified him?"

"I never trust the government and when it comes to surveillance I assume they can do most anything. In this case, my question is why they'd even bother. Presumably, to them he's merely one more Antifa."

Alex's top lip curled over the lower one as he thought this over. "I'm not so sure. They always wear masks, but he wasn't."

Alex continued. "I was very surprised, no, actually stunned, by him being up there the way he was. Yeah, we only met that one night, but by the end I didn't think Gabe was part of any extremist group, or for that matter had the balls to be on the front lines. Frankly, that first night I'd figured he was either an innocent victim the cops picked up or maybe a government plant."

Peter didn't say anything.

"Do you think he could really be deeply embedded on the extreme left?"

Peter replied, "No, I'm sure he's not. I had some digging done and he's got a complete online history. It wouldn't fit someone like that." He paused briefly. "A neighborhood guy I know does some hacking. For a few bucks he pulled up Gabe's school records. He's a smart fellow; at least book smart. My guy also got the names of several of his suitemates. Pretending to be with their college's alumni office, I reached one of them and got the sap to confirm Gabe was in his suite, so that's real. We couldn't get much from his law firm. Their security's very tight, although my guy was able to confirm he definitely works there. Unless the ex-roommate is a plant and the entire history is a complete fraud, it all matches. He's not much involved, if at all."

Alex had listened closely to Peter's recitation. He whistled softly. "I'm impressed. I take it to you this means he is who he says he is."

"Uh-huh. As I said, I had my doubts about him at first, same as you. He just didn't seem to fit. But I'm satisfied at this point."

"Or at least as satisfied as one can be."

A teenage couple neared them. Alex gave them a friendly nod and a smile, and he and Peter stopped talking while they passed. The couple kept walking away, then started kissing and groping each other.

Alex continued, confident the couple was out of ear shot and, regardless, were much too busy with each other to pay any attention to him and Peter. "Then what was he doing up there the night of that riot? Do you think something's been working him up? First, enough to be interested in leaders the way he was in the cell? And then so much more that by the time of Herald Square it caused him to join in the fighting the way he did?"

Peter shrugged. "My guess is he's like some people, not many, but a few. Shootings and other bad things keep happening; at first people ignore 'em; then at some point they get madder and madder and become determined to resist. Like you and me. Right?"

Alex didn't answer directly. "Sounds plausible."

"Maybe that execution over a bunch of spoons took Gabe past his tipping point."

"Could be." Alex tilted toward Peter. "And the way I see it, if so, maybe we can use Gabe to ferret out some of the Antifa people who really call the shots. I still want to know who they are. Don't you?"

Peter nodded then, despite his windbreaker, he shivered as a strong gust of wind hit them. To his annoyance, Alex appeared unbothered. Trying to ignore that, Peter replied, "Yeah, I want to know. I've tried to meet them but have had no luck. It's as if they're hiding, even from our own side. But we're the ones out on the streets, not only devoting time but maybe getting hurt and maybe ending up serving time. And who knows what their real motives are? Yeah, it pisses me off."

While Peter complained, Alex saw a vein pulsing in his forehead and the cords in his neck tighten. He said, "I'm with you on that."

Once again they were silent, Peter making sure the young lovers were still busy and nobody else was nearby. Although satisfied the area was theirs, he lowered his voice, forcing Alex to lean further. "Do you know Earl Reuben?"

"I know of him of course, but I've never met him."

Earl was a lawyer who'd represented many leftists in rights cases, almost always defeating the government's efforts to convict them. Some in the press had referred to him as the next William Kunstler. However, he'd stopped handling cases and assumed a different role.

"I know him; not well, but we know each other. The word is he's involved and aids protest leaders, plus it's rumored he's got extreme left ties."

"Have you tried to get him to introduce you to these people?"

"Yeah, but he won't. His line is that even if they existed and he knew them, their identities would be secret."

"In that case, what about him?"

"What I was thinking is that the Herald Square scene might make Earl see some value in Gabe. If Gabe gets in with him, maybe Gabe learns stuff and then he tells us. Who knows. Maybe by bringing Gabe to Earl, Earl will open up more to me."

Alex thought about this. "I've got my doubts that this'd work."

"I'm going to do it and thought you'd want to be a part of it. Anyways, what's there to lose?"

"OK. But what's to say Gabe would go along?"

They both considered this, then Alex shrugged, saying "Let's try. You think we can reach Earl? Whatever happens I'd like to meet him."

A cool blast of wind swept over them, making them both shiver. Peter was superstitious and the breeze unsettled him, blowing when it did. He replied, "I know where he often hangs out. It's not far. We can see if he's there."

Heading off, Alex decided he'd probably been wrong to be suspicious of Peter, and thought, depending upon how this went, maybe he'd involve Peter in his main operation.

////

The two men walked south, soon reaching a neighborhood where the streets were still cobblestone and had old-fashioned streetlights, many festooned with brightly colored pennants. They passed ground level art galleries and buildings with open doors leading to galleries on upper floors. Tables for over-priced restaurants with sparkling crystal glasses and wrought iron chairs took up the sidewalks and spilled into the streets. These restaurants had either managed to survive the pandemic or opened since then, but either way they were taking full advantage of New Yorkers' desires to dine out and enjoy the freedom.

In a few short blocks, after tripping over cobblestones and sidestepping piles of horse manure, they reached another gallery. It looked similar to many they'd passed, but Peter stopped in front of it. In the front bay window was a large oil painting of an armored samurai warrior with his head bared and face looking off sideways into the distance. They both studied it, struck by the figure's power and dignity.

Looking at it, Peter said, "Kinda reminds me of Gabe from the other night."

"I see what you mean, but I think you're giving Gabe too much credit." Alex knew art and added, "By the way, don't plan on buying that unless you're an awful lot wealthier than you appear."

Peter shook his head, acknowledging it was beyond his reach. Nevertheless, Peter stepped into the gallery. Explaining back over his shoulder, "Earl's an owner so's often here."

From across the street an elderly Chinese man watched them enter the gallery. The man hit a number on his phone and when his call was answered, he said, "You won't believe whose place they just went into."

CHAPTER TWENTY-THREE

Alex followed Peter to the rear, not having time to look at the art mounted on the walls, or the metal and glass sculptures placed throughout. Peter stopped at a partly open door which he gently opened the rest of the way. The door was to the private viewing space where the gallery's sales generally were finalized—sometimes with long time clients who understood art, but more often with buyers who liked a work's colors or thought it went well with their décor.

The room's sole occupant was a man studying an abstract mixed media work on the far wall. The only light was from a clear beam illuminating the work. The man spun toward the door. He recognized Peter, and while turning on the room's main lights and killing the beam, he pointed to the piece, saying, "This one I don't get at all." He waved them in.

Following Peter, Alex got his first in-person look at Earl. Earl's appearance lived up to its billing. He had curly dirty blonde hair, the back reaching his shoulders and the rest sticking out in various directions, partially covering Obama-type ears. But Alex's attention was drawn to Earl's face. His skin was not one color, instead it had several shades of browns and off-beiges fading into each other. Running in a thin line partway down the bridge of his nose and directly above his eyebrows his skin was a deep rich mahogany. Moving up his forehead it faded to a russet shade and by his hairline faded further to taupe. The portion of his neck protruding from his shirt and his jaw and the sides of his face were a dark cocoa bleeding to a mix of sepia and redwood across his cheek bones. His forehead had thin lines, except for one furrow which was much deeper and its color much darker than the other lines. He had short arcs above each eye which were also deep and dark. His eyes were blue and his nose made a compelling case for Jewish genes in the mix. His lips were thin and as he smiled, Alex saw small yellowish teeth.

Earl's uniqueness was not limited to his appearance. Articles, mainly on social media, often mentioned him and his purported role in the left wing. Law enforcement agencies had open files on Earl, but none had sufficient evidence to make a case. Twice he'd been brought up in front of grand juries, but neither one had served up an indictment.

Earl greeted Peter, who introduced Alex. At first Earl and Peter talked in generalities while Alex sat by. Alex couldn't put his finger on what it was exactly, but he sensed that not only did Earl not know Peter well, but Earl chose his words carefully, as if he didn't fully trust Peter. Of course, Alex thought, Earl's position might make him act that way with most people. It wasn't long before Earl asked why they'd come.

Peter replied, "Have you seen pictures of that unknown fighter at Herald Square."

"I did and thought it was quite interesting. Everyone 's wondering who he is."

Peter said, "We know him."

Earl's eyebrows rose, crinkling the mahogany-colored skin and further deepening the arcs above his eyes and the furrow stretching across his forehead.

"In the pictures there's a glare on his face, but I was there and saw him clearly. The three of us once shared a cell for a night. There's no doubt it's a guy we know."

Earl took this in and thought before asking, "Is he well known?"

"Not at all. Earl, we were shocked to see him up there fighting, especially without a mask." Peter went on eagerly, "Do you think he might be useful? Would you like to meet him?"

Peter reminded Alex of a salesman making his pitch. However, Alex's lingering suspicions made him wonder if Peter had ulterior reasons for ingratiating himself with Earl beyond what they'd discussed.

Earl sat silently, twisting stalks of his hair. Finally, he said, "I'm willing to meet him, but only on my terms. Beyond that, we'll see. To be blunt Peter, this doesn't sit one hundred percent with me. I don't know you well and we haven't worked together. And now you show up here with Alex, who I don't know at all," he briefly looked at Alex, tilting his head and scrunching his face as if in apology, and continued, "and you tell me you two know this mystery man and offer him up to me."

Alex wasn't used to playing second fiddle and he jumped in before Peter could respond. "Earl, what you said makes perfect sense." Alex kept on, not giving either of the others a chance to interrupt him. "I guess you could worry whether he's something else. Maybe for some reason a government agent or secretly a right-winger. Maybe we've been taken in by him or are part of some plot. Even if any of that were the case, so long as you don't say the wrong things, which of course you being you, you wouldn't, what have you got to lose? If there's a problem, you'd smell it out."

Looking Alex over closely for the first time, Earl nodded, and muttered, "Fair points." He thought for a moment further, again playing with his hair. "What's this mystery man's name?"

"Gabriel Bentley," Peter said, reasserting his position.

"Alright. Get ahold of this Mr. Bentley and arrange for him to meet at three. You bring him. I'll text Peter later with the location."

"We'll get him," Peter said as Alex nodded in agreement.

////

The same elderly man who'd watched Peter and Tall Alex go into the gallery watched them leave. He waited several minutes then texted "All clear" to the same number as before.

After Peter and Tall Alex were gone, Earl made himself a cup of herbal tea and was back in the same room, seated with the tea on a table, reviewing their meeting. There was a rap on the door and a voice Earl knew well said, "Hey Earl, how you doin'?"

Earl looked over, his face breaking into a huge grin. He jumped up, rushed to his visitor, lifted him easily and gave him a big hug. "Alex, my boy, so good to see you."

"Would you please put me down. I may be short, but I'm not a kid anymore," Short Alex chided him.

Laughing, Earl put Alex down, seated himself and gestured for Alex to sit next to him.

"My, this has been a busy day," Earl said. "I just had other visitors."

"I know. That's why I'm here."

The deep-set arcs above Earl's eyes rose slightly.

Alex continued. "You met with Peter and a guy named Alex – who by the way several people are calling Tall Alex while calling me Short Alex. Quite offensive. Anyway, I've had people following Tall Alex for several days, and they're still doing so. I was intrigued when I heard that he met Peter this morning, and then quite surprised when I learned they came here." He paused. "What's going on?"

Earl and Alex had no secrets from each other, so Earl proceeded to tell Alex everything.

/////

A little earlier, after exiting the gallery, Peter and Tall Alex walked aimlessly for a few blocks, thinking about the meeting and what to do next.

Alex patted Peter on the back. "Your idea of meeting with Earl worked. But now how do we get Gabe to go along? We don't even know if he's around."

They continued walking, saying nothing until Peter said, "From the jail we know he wants to know who's leading on the left. We don't know the story behind Herald Square. Whatever his reasons, it's hard to see how he wouldn't want to get in deeper." He shrugged. "I think we call him and say this is his chance."

Alex nodded, having no better idea.

They took seats outdoors at a small café, ordered espressos and then Peter called Gabe.

CHAPTER TWENTY-FOUR

While Alex and Peter were busy with their meetings, although it was Sunday Gabe was in his office working, and Jasminn was hanging out with him. Several other lawyers were there as well, the day of the week not relevant to keeping the work flowing. Occasionally, someone taking a break would pass by and say "Hi." Inevitably, out of curiosity and for the firm's gossip mill, they'd try to get the story about Gabe and Jasminn.

When Peter called, Gabe pretended it was a work call to expel their latest visitor. Peter gave him a lengthy spiel about Earl wanting to meet Gabe, and why Gabe should meet him. Gabe knew enough about Earl from the media to instantly grasp the potential value of this. Meeting Earl might go a long way in helping his Smith and Jones problem. He hadn't done as much work as he should have, but decided he'd done enough to get by, so he agreed. Throughout the call, Jasminn remained slouched in one of Gabe's visitors' chairs, her feet up on a corner of his desk. However, she'd stopped reading a review of a new computer security program on her phone, and instead listened to Gabe's end of the call. Once he was off, she demanded the full particulars.

As he filled her in, her feet came off his desk, she put down her phone and sat up straight. When he finished she said, "Earl's a big name. Despite what Peter said it's strange he'd want to meet you. More importantly, I don't know whether you should meet him. You'd be digging yourself in deeper."

"There's an old proverb. 'Sometimes to dig yourself out, you must first dig in deeper'."

Her eyes screwed up in annoyance. "That's about the stupidest thing I've ever heard. Clearly a Gabe original."

"Then again," he said, "I've never understood how you dig yourself out of a hole. It seems a contradiction in terms to me." He started to straighten up the papers spread across his desk. "Anyway, the key is that I'll tell my Homeland Security bastards about this to show I tried. I can use this to help get done with them."

She was skeptical and told him so.

"I've an idea but it requires your help," he said. After a second he shook his head and said, "On second thought this might dig you into a hole as well. Forget it."

She leaned over the desk toward him. "Come on. What is it?"

"I know Homeland Security logs my calls, and worse they're probably recording them. I think it's unlikely that they're monitoring your phone though. I think I could use it undetected."

"I'm not worried. Use it." She gave him a lecherous look. "For a price."

Acting innocently, he asked, "What's the price?"

She ran her tongue across the outside of her lips, making the price clear. He grinned, then agreed in a fake begrudging voice. She unlocked her phone and he called Peter, saying, "It's me. Do as I say. Right after I hang up call me back on my phone, not this one, and say you'll pick me up in five minutes. Then pick me up as soon as you can. After that, all contact will be by this phone, not mine. Understood?"

Peter was confused. "I hear you, but what're you worried about?"

"After all those pictures and videos posted online, I'm entitled to be worried about everyone and everything." Gabe banged his fist on his desk and yelled, "Look, for all I know, some alt-right guys are hunting me right now."

"You're overreacting man, but fine, I'll do what you asked., I'm with Alex, uhm Tall Alex, and there's no way we'll get to you before about forty-five minutes."

"That's alright. Just do as I said."

Gabe hung up, followed by Peter calling back on Gabe's phone.

Gabe called Smith. "Your plan worked. I've attracted attention. Peter's picking me up in five minutes to go meet Earl Reuben."

He listened, amused by Smith's excitement over Earl coming into the picture, then replied, "I'm sorry you can't get here that fast. Not my fault. I can't say to Peter, 'Peter, we have to wait until my Homeland Security watchdogs get here'." After a long silence at Gabe's end he said, "I'll do what I can" then hung up, still smiling.

"I got them this time."

Jasminn gave him a low wolf whistle then said, "You're very good at this wheeling and dealing. I guess that's why they pay you the big bucks. Now for my payment."

"Here?"

She stood and closed the door behind her. "See, the door's closed. Now come here."

Doing as she said, Gabe wondered who this wild woman was he hadn't seen before and regretted he hadn't known her earlier.

////

By the time Peter was to call, Gabe and Jasminn were dressed.

"I'm leaving now so please give me your phone," Gabe said.

She put a hand on one hip. "I'm going with you."

"No, using your phone's enough exposure."

"You like it when I'm exposed."

He shook his head, frowned and reached for her phone. "Not that way."

She stepped back, placing her other hand on her other hip and jutting out her jaw. "Regardless, I'm coming," she insisted.

By the time Peter called to say they were almost there, Gabe had conceded.

On the street, a white four-door came to a stop in front of them with Alex driving and Peter riding shotgun. Gabe held the rear door open for Jasminn, but as she started to get in Alex said, "Hold it Gabe. Whoever this is, she can't come."

Gabe answered, "This is my girlfriend, Jasminn." This was the first time he'd said this and he liked its sound. "She's coming."

Jasminn slid across the back seat and said, "Hey, Peter."

Alex asked Peter, "You know her?"

"We've met."

Now in the car, Gabe closed the door but kept a grip on the handle. "Your choice, Alex," he said, "either she comes or we both get out and forget this. I don't care either way." He and Alex locked eyes through the rearview mirror. Gabe held the stare, unblinking, his mouth set in a firm line.

After a moment of silence Peter nudged Alex. "It's fine, Alex. Let it go."

Alex disliked not having his way. He hesitated for a few more seconds, his shoulders sagged, then with a slight sigh he drove them off.

"Where we going?" Gabe asked.

"We don't know," Peter answered, twisting around to look at them. "Earl'll call to tell us where. That's how he wants it and he's calling the shots. About our calls, I guess you don't trust your phone's security."

"No, I do, I'm just being careful because of those images."

Jasminn spoke up. "Anyhow, it's taken care of. The phone can't be tracked. It's in my backpack. The SIM card and battery are out and wrapped in aluminum foil, and they're inside a cigar box with a fancy lead exterior which I borrowed from some senior partner's office."

"How do you know that stops anyone from tracking it?" Alex asked.

"I'm a geek. I know."

No one had anything else to say on the topic, so they dropped it and drove mostly in silence. Not knowing where they'd be meeting Earl, Alex stayed in midtown, driving loops down Park Avenue and up Madison. After several laps Peter got a call. Done listening he said, "OK, I know it. We'll be there as soon as we can."

Peter announced, "The Riverside Park skate park . It's around one hundred eighth street on the Park's lower level."

Alex drove them uptown then across the top of Central Park, showing a pronounced disinterest in yellow lights. On Riverside Drive they got lucky. Jasminn spotted someone pulling out of a parking spot and Alex squeezed into the spot.

They'd been somber and to lighten the mood Jasminn said, "A spot opens up when you need it. Just like in the movies."

Gabe asked, "What now?"

Peter replied, "You and I will go down to the skate park to meet Earl. Jasminn and Alex can go part way or wait with the car."

Neither Jasminn nor Alex liked being excluded, but Peter said that Earl had insisted that only he and Gabe should show up, so they let it go. Instead, they accompanied the other two to a spot on the upper level from where they could make out one side of the skate park.

////

At the lower level, Peter led Gabe along the grass bordering the cement skate area, while watching out for out-of-control skateboarders. Partway, Peter pointed and said, "That must be him. That's where he said." Gabe followed Peter's finger and could see a man across the way standing in shadows between the tallest half pipe and a raised tunnel. He'd picked a strategic spot -- he wasn't visible from anywhere but straight on, and even from where Peter and Gabe stood they couldn't tell who he was.

They trotted the rest of the way around the perimeter. Facing Earl, who remained in the shadows about ten feet from them, Peter introduced Gabe and Earl. Throughout their car ride, while waiting for Earl's summons, Gabe had thought about the situation. He'd decided he was not beholden to Peter or Alex; he didn't have to follow their directions; and he wasn't sure he trusted either of them.

"Hello, Earl," Gabe said. "Peter, I want to speak with Earl alone."

Peter's head spun toward Gabe and his mouth opened. He'd arranged this meeting and wanted to be part of it.

"What are you talking about. I'm the one who arranged this."

Peter argued, but Gabe held firm.

Earl then resolved it. "I agree. It should be just the two of us."

Making no attempt to hide his anger, Peter stormed off. Kicking up dirt, he went past the skate park's west side and flopped down on a shaded grassy area. From there he watched the skateboarders while wondering why Gabe had insisted on this, fuming and considering how he'd get his revenge against Gabe. Pebbles lay strewn near him and he fingered some, contemplating throwing them on the cement to see if he could bring down a skateboarder, or tossing some at cars on the West Side Highway behind him. Ultimately, but only with a great amount of self-control, he didn't do either.

Speaking across the distance between them, Gabe said, "Two people can talk more openly than three."

"I agree."

Gabe walked the rest of the way to where Earl stood between the two skating structures. Following Peter's directions he made a concerted effort not to stare at Earl's face—his face, neck and hands being his only uncovered parts.

Gabe said, "Interesting place you picked."

"I'm always careful. The authorities watch me sometimes." Earl continued, "I take it you're the celebrity fighter," the way he spoke sounding like a confirmation of fact rather than a question.

Gabe shook his head once and briefly looked away. "I wouldn't use the word 'celebrity'," he replied, shucking off Earl's comment. Ignoring the fact that he still wore last night's clothes, Gabe eased himself to the ground, and seated himself against the side of the tunnel.

"I guess you're right since your face wasn't visible. How'd that happen?" Earl asked, focusing on reading Gabe throughout their talk.

After watching himself online and seeing this effect, Gabe had prepared a stock answer. "Someone gave me a cream which was supposed to make blows slide. It worked, at least somewhat. We weren't thinking about my picture being taken or how I'd look. I was there to fight. That crazy castle dominion shit put me over the edge."

Instead of following right up, Earl looked at him for several seconds. While they'd been talking, clouds had passed and the sun now shone more brightly down on them.

Earl's head tilted. "Why weren't you wearing a mask like most leftist fighters?"

Gabe had no doubt Earl was extremely difficult to fool, but Gabe had to convince him. "I'd had a cap and a bandana but lost them in a scuffle before the main action. Perhaps I could've melted back into the crowd but the fighting broke out. Making it worse, I'd gotten jammed in and forced up onto a block. There was no way to retreat even if I'd wanted to."

Earl pressed, the former litigator in him resurfacing more and more. "Why be up front in the first place? Obviously, that's the most dangerous area. Peter and Alex hadn't pegged you for that sort of guy."

Gabe's voice hardened. "I guess they were wrong, weren't they?"

"How'd you feel up there, being exposed that way? Were you scared? Excited?"

Gabe looked up at Earl. *Enough. It was time to push back.*

"Hold on. You're interrogating me as if I'm on the witness stand. I'm only here because those two begged me. What's your interest in what I did or didn't do or why, and why should I tell you anything?"

Before Earl answered, Gabe heard a scraping sound above him. He looked up. A skateboarder was riding her board on the top of the tunnel rather than through it and was tipping over toward Gabe. As she started to fall, Gabe pushed himself up and caught her, breaking her fall and knocking Gabe back down. The girl, Gabe guessed she was about thirteen or fourteen, nodded to him, put one foot back on her board and pushed off with the other, heading back into the action.

"You're welcome," Gabe yelled after her.

"Nice catch," Earl said. He spryly lowered himself to the ground and sat cross-legged opposite Gabe. "You're right," he said. "I owe you an apology. I didn't mean to come off that way, but I am interested."

The thread-like lines on Gabe's brow creased and he raised his voice, almost shouting. "That's what it's about? I let those guys drag me here, supposedly for the 'good of the cause,' but for all I know the cops might be watching us because of you, and now they'll see me. And all this is because you're 'interested'? Thanks for nothing."

He started to rise, pushing his back against the tunnel's side for leverage.

"No Gabe, please sit. I'm not talking about my personal curiosity. Let me explain."

Gabe paused halfway to his feet, steadying himself with one arm against the tunnel, then grudgingly and starting to feel sore, slowly eased himself back down.

Earl had been concentrating on Gabe's face, and now his own face broke into a grin. "I see it. I think that bit of outrage just now was an act. A good one, but a performance piece. You want something from me and that's why you're here."

Gabe ignored Earl's explanation and neither spoke, it being clear each would be cautious about what he said to the other.

Gabe shifted his head around, looking at Earl from several angles, and asked, "All those skin tones on your face. Is it vitiligo? Is it all over you?"

Earl jerked back as his jaw clenched, the tendons in his thin neck stuck out all the more and his fingers on one hand raked the dirt. Several long moments passed then he relaxed, grinned and gave a hearty laugh.

"I've got to give you credit. Everyone's curious about my skin, but few have the nerve to ask. Do you want to know about my hair or eyes or nose as well?"

Gabe's hands rested in his lap and he turned his palms up, making it clear Earl was free to say whatever he wished.

Ignoring Gabe's questions, Earl said, "I'll explain why I agreed to meet. Some background though, to make sure you understand where I'm coming from. Know that, despite the government's efforts to jail me and their monitoring me, I'm a bad target. I'm not a member of any extremist group, much less a leader like the government suspects. And believe me, I'd certainly never get out there on the front lines and fight like you did.

"I do however believe strongly that the left must aggressively oppose the extreme right and on more occasions than I'd like, the government. By 'aggressively,' I do include violence when necessary—but only when absolutely necessary. I'm a political philosopher or strategist, call it what you will, and an advisor. I'm close to some people who could be called leaders and others who play influential roles, but I don't aid and abet, to quote the law. I only serve as a big picture guy, never specifics. Whether people listen to me or not is up to them."

He grinned. "As an extreme example, I would never even hint to people that they do something such as storm the Capital, but after I spoke they might decide to do so." Despite himself, Gabe laughed. "I also connect people and provide other lawful assistance from time to time and serve as a spokesperson occasionally. But everything is legal."

Gabe continued sitting, saying nothing and letting Earl go on.

"As to the movement itself, let's talk about the extreme left. You may know a lot of this, but I want to be sure. I'll use a term the media loves and label those who do fight as Antifa even though there really isn't any significant coalesced group as such, like there are on the right. The Antifa, but not leftist demonstrators as a whole, serve primarily as oppositionists—meaning generally those people act in response to events and circumstances, as versus primarily being initiators. For example, the so-called Antifa has fought Neo-Nazis and other alt-right groups many times and, incorrectly in my opinion, way too often against the police. Don't get me wrong. I fully acknowledge that in some cases what starts out as defensive in intent can change, and in those cases they've become the aggressor. Many point to the Portland courthouse takeover and other actions there and in other cities as proof. That may be right, but it's a small aspect of the overall situation.

"In my opinion, one of the left's biggest problems as an effective movement is that there are few true leaders, especially on the extreme left. Plus, of those, almost none are out there on the streets publicly leading, or even speaking publicly on the left's behalf. And note, I don't consider politicians as being relevant in this regard."

Earl waited for Gabe to speak, but Gabe remained silent, once again forcing Earl to continue.

"Who today is a modern Martin, Stokely, Malcolm X, Abbie or, in his younger days, Jerry? Who today on the left is not only formulating theory but also directing actions and putting themselves out there on the streets and inspiring others to act? Way too few, and none are rallying figures. Confusing all this is that one of the tenets of many people who might be labeled Antifa is that there shouldn't be leaders—instead, they favor a collective approach. They say that movements should be about ideas and political and social beliefs, and not about leaders or their charisma. As a result, oppose the notion of leaders. That may sound nice, but it's not practical.

"Compare all that to the right, where many of their groups have leaders who are vocal and openly out there. Easy examples are the Proud Boys and the Oath Takers, and I could name many more."

Earl paused for a moment and looked around to be sure there was no one nearby.

"This may sound odd, but while I hate almost every word that comes out of those men's mouths and what's in their minds, I give them credit for stepping forward."

"I take it that you want more people to accept leadership roles, and you're saying the leaders of the left, especially the far left, should reveal themselves and lead in the open, and not from the shadows?"

Earl gave a slight nod and picked at some blades of grass. "Basically. Adding to the problem, some fear that either the government or the extreme right will take down visible leaders, whether by locking them up or killing them. And yes, those risks shouldn't be ignored."

Gabe lost Earl's thread for a moment as he thought with disgust about what Smith and Jones were making him do.

"On top of that, even when any people who might be considered Antifa leaders do fight, they wear masks, which makes sense in terms of the dangers, but doesn't demonstrate their leadership."

Gabe chuckled. "Sounds to me that they're mostly chicken shit and shouldn't be leading anything. Makes you wonder about following them or having anything to do with their groups."

"I wouldn't put it that way. In my opinion, more people do need to act openly as leaders or key figures or whatever you want to call them. Such as when you think of the Yippies, you think of Abbie and Jerry, and vice versa, even though while they were founders, they were supposedly anti-leadership.

"Sadly, the left has many victims and martyrs—way too many. I'm not betting this philosophy on leadership or how leaders function will change anytime soon.

"One thing the Antifa, or anarchists, or whatever label is assigned to the extreme left…another thing it lacks are icons, maybe even heroes; people admired for their courage and determination in the face of danger and whom others want to emulate. You might be such a person."

Gabe looked at him as if he was crazy. "Exactly what do you mean by that?"

"Based on that night at Herald Square and ideally future actions, you could play that role."

"Let me get this straight. You want me to play Superman and inspire others by risking my life?"

Earl chuckled. "I wouldn't say Superman. At most, more like Batman, and I think you're overstating the risks."

Gabe shook his head and said, "I don't know why you think I'd do this to help your notion of what should be done." He thought, *this is my lead in.* "Anyway, this is a complete non-starter unless I meet some of these leaders or so-called key figures or whatever you're calling them and buy into them or at least into their ideas and commitment."

"That's understandable. It may not be doable, but it's understandable. I'll let you know." Earl studied Gabe. "I thought you wanted something. Meeting them is what you wanted, isn't it?"

Instead of answering, Gabe said, "There's no reason for us to be in touch through Peter." He handed Earl one of his cards. "In fact, I see no reason to share this conversation with him," he added.

Earl knew Gabe hadn't answered his question, but he let that go and said, "I agree on both counts," while pulling a pen and a piece of paper from a pants pocket.

Gabe held up a hand, saying, "I don't want your contact info. If the government's watching you and so later questions me, I want to be able to truthfully say I've got no way of reaching you. You can contact me, and if you do I assume it would be from a burner phone or some other secure means. Right?"

"You're quite careful for a man who fought as you did." He looked at Gabe's card. "I should've figured. You're a lawyer too. What's your field?"

"Corporate. I do deals."

Earl nodded, understanding that in its own way their meeting had been a negotiation.

Gabe made his way to his feet, slowly. Grabbing the falling skater had reawakened some of the aches from his multiple beatings.

Earl lightly sprang to his feet. "I'll put your contact info in a secure file and destroy this card to give you more distance." Wiping the dirt from his pants, Earl added, "I want you and Peter to wait here for a few minutes until I'm gone."

Earl took off. Gabe was left to fend off first Peter's then Alex's and Jasminn's questions about what he and Earl discussed, but Gabe refused to say anything other than "Earl insisted that I don't share anything. All I can say is that it was productive. We each need to think, and Earl may or may not get back to me."

CHAPTER TWENTY-FIVE

Gabe thought Peter and Tall Alex were so mad for not filling them in on the Earl meeting that they might leave him and Jasminn to make their own way from Riverside Park, but Alex drove them to the Upper East Side. Not wanting to reveal where Jasminn lived, Gabe had Alex drop them several blocks from her apartment. They sat at the Marx Brothers Playground, watching a pick-up soccer game on the nearby field as Gabe filled her in on his talk with Earl.

When he was done he asked, "And, did you and Alex have a nice time?"

"Hardly. We got into an argument. I was tempted to hit him. I got kinda suspicious of him. I wonder a bit what side he's on."

"That's crazy," Gabe said.

"I can't repeat it word for word, but I don't think he's into peaceful protesting—I think he's got no problem resorting to violence. Besides, he shared his views on assorted topics, and while he was careful in what he said, I really do think he might be on the right."

Gabe's eyes had widened as Jasminn spoke.

"I can't believe it." He thought briefly. "Could he be in the same position as me or be an agent like Justin and trying to get you to talk?"

"I guess that's possible."

"You're the computer whiz. Why don't you do some digging on him online?"

She replied, "I was already planning on that. What about the DHS? What're you going to do about them?"

"I'm not sure. One thing I am sure of though is that my buddies probably have their phones in hand, waiting to hear from me and, in Jones' case, anxious to knock me around again."

She pulled out the cigar case from her backpack. "Here. Fix it then go ahead and call them."

In the nearby soccer game, a small player dribbled half the field, dodging much larger defenders and drilling a shot into a lower corner of the net. Gabe watched the shifty player while thinking how Smith and Jones knew about Jasminn and manipulated him by using her as leverage, and how he didn't want to make that worse.

"I'll take the case, but I'm not going to do that here. Assuming they track the call, I don't want to have to explain why I was up here. I won't mention you."

She pointed out that they knew all about her, so he could say they'd been hanging out, but Gabe held firm. They sat for a few more minutes, Gabe watching the same player make another excellent run before walking Jasminn to her apartment. He took a cab downtown to his place and considered what to tell Smith and Jones. Once home, he took the phone from the cigar case and reconnected it. He'd intended to relax for a while and think more before calling them, but the phone rang as soon as he'd put in the chip and battery and turned it on.

Wearily, certain who it was, Gabe swiped the Talk icon. "Yeah?"

It was Smith. "Where have you been, Gabriel? We were worried about you."

Jones was on too and he added in a mocking tone, "Yeah, we were worried."

"I was meeting with that Earl guy, like I told you."

"What happened to your phone?" Smith asked.

With one hand holding his now infamous phone, Gabe opened the refrigerator, started to take a soda then grabbed a beer instead. "I met Peter and Tall Alex and before we drove off they demanded it. They popped out the card and battery, wrapped them up and put them in a metal case."

"Playing junior secret agent?" Jones snorted.

"Not me," Gabe replied, looking out a window with one foot tapping nervously. "That was all their doing. I take it you've been using it to track me, but they disconnected you." He took a slug of the beer and sat on a kitchen stool.

Smith was impatient. "Enough with the phone. Were you with Earl all this time?"

"No. The three of us drove around for a long time, killing time while waiting for his call. I don't wear a watch but don't think we met until around four or so. As soon as I got home, I reconnected it, and before I could even get a beer, here you be."

Smith and Jones were silent, then Smith said in a stern voice familiar to Gabe, "We'll send a car for you, then go over in detail your meeting with Earl . . . and other things."

Gabe jumped to his feet, spilling beer on himself and the floor. Somewhat to his surprise and very much to theirs, he barked, "No!"

"No?"

Gabe rushed on, not thinking. "No. I'm tired and I've got another contract I have to revise tonight. I'm not going anywhere."

Smith's voice was calm, but Gabe detected an underlying threat. "Gabriel, I thought you understood how this works."

Gabe was nervous but argued back. "Yeah, I do, but you've got to understand something as well. I've a job which takes up a huge amount of time. Being your slave can't be a second full time job."

"Come on, Kid, cut the crap," Jones yelled.

"No, it's alright, I understand," Smith said. "We'll meet tomorrow and let Gabriel get his work done and get a good night's sleep. That sound good, Gabriel?"

Gabe was busy wiping up the beer and Smith's response relieved him. However, he saw through Smith's bullshit. Grateful nevertheless for the respite, but still tense, he made his way to the sofa and sat on its arm, kneading one knee with his free hand. "Fine. Yeah." Thinking fast, he said, "How about we meet in the lobby of the InterContinental Hotel? It's around the corner from my office and we can talk there."

"I'd rather we met in private, Gabriel. Our place is better."

Gabe didn't know how far he could push, but he tried. "Smith, I don't have time to be driven all around the city the way your people always do to me. Plus, I don't want Jones hitting me again."

He collapsed onto the sofa, his shoulders sinking into it. Either Smith would let him have this relatively small token or his efforts might make matters worse.

"Alright. The InterContinental. Be there at eleven-thirty."

"Kid?"

"Yeah, Jones?"

"Just so you know, if I need to work you over, meeting there won't save you."

////

Upon Gabe entering the InterContinental, an arm slid through his right arm. It was Jones, who then pulled him along.

"Morning, Kid."

To anyone paying attention, they would have resembled two friends or lovers walking with arms intertwined, but Jones' grip on Gabe's arm was painfully firm. Jones took them up to the balcony circling the main lobby. In a corner, obscured from view by a pillar and several plants, three chairs sat arrayed. Smith sat in the one tucked into the corner and pointed Gabe to one across from him. Jones took the seat catty-corner from Smith.

"Good morning, Gabriel."

A waiter came over and Smith and Jones ordered coffee. Gabe shook his head.

Smith looked at Gabe's outfit and nodded in appreciation. As an attempt at a statement, Gabe wore one of his best tailored suits with an expensive shirt and a designer tie. Smith was impressed, especially since he and Jones wore off-the-rack sports coats and slacks and no-iron shirts.

"Nice clothes. Clearly being a lawyer pays a lot better than working for the government." Smith leaned forward and spoke slowly, stressing each word. "However, it doesn't change our relationship."

It wasn't easy, but Gabe ignored Smith's comment and asked, "Do you want to hear about my meeting with Earl?"

"Certainly," Smith replied, relaxing back in his seat.

"But first, Kid. Why'd you lie to us? We don't appreciate that and it's stupid."

Gabe's head swiveled to Jones. He thought, *Which lie?*

"What're you talking about?" he asked, positive his guilt was written across his face.

Jones slid forward in his chair, he curled his right hand into a fist and with his left one he grabbed the chair's edge. Seeing this, Gabe thought that despite being in public, Jones was going to attack him.

"You lied to us about Justin. I really really hate being lied to. Smith says I shouldn't get nasty about it," Jones gave a quick smile, "but sometimes I just can't help myself." Still seated, Jones shifted his weight onto the balls of his feet and his eyes and lips narrowed to tight slits.

Gabe looked at Jones, then at Smith, counting on him for protection, but Smith sat unmoving. Caught off guard, Gabe desperately tried to recall what he'd told them about Justin. His muscles tensed and he could feel sweat beginning to trickle down the back of his neck and his throat tightening. He remembered parts of what he'd said but knew that his biggest lie was not in what he'd said, but in what he hadn't said. He replied, "I don't know what you're talking about."

While saying this, Gabe cringed, expecting Jones' attack. Instead, Smith held up his phone which had been out of sight. He then played back the part of the call in which Gabe told them about Justin.

The replay finished, Smith asked sarcastically, "Remember that?"

Gabe nodded, his face partly turned away. He was trying, so far unsuccessfully, to regain his composure. At the same time, he tried to pay attention to Smith while watching for any move by Jones.

Smith said, "We spoke to Justin. He said that's not how it went."

He stopped, catching Gabe's eyes looking around and a few beads of sweat appearing above his upper lip. None of them said anything, and the only sounds were the muzak playing in the background and the voices of people in the lobby.

Seeing no easy way out, Gabe almost whispered, "I didn't lie. Maybe I exaggerated a bit. Justin definitely made me suspicious of him." Gabe didn't tell them that Justin was with the FBI or his real name, afraid doing that would only make matters worse. "And, I was scared. Shit, the way Jones is sitting there scares me now."

Jones smiled, taking that as a compliment, but not relaxing his pose.

"You wanted answers, so I gave you answers. I wanted out of this then, and I still want out. That's all there is to it."

They sat silently, Smith's right ankle resting across his left knee, his foot moving to the muzak. He was studying Gabe closely, and Gabe thought of him as a human lie detector. Meanwhile Jones stayed poised with his nasty grin. Gabe didn't know what would happen.

Smith had previously decided not to tell Gabe about Justin being with the FBI, and Gabe's explanation didn't alter his thinking. He said, "I'm going to let this pass this one time, Gabriel, but do not make the same mistake and lie to us again. I will not be tolerant if you do. that I've warned Justin to stay away from you, and I'm warning you to stay away from him. Got me?"

Staring down at a faded coffee stain on the carpet, Gabe muttered, "Yeah."

Smith's posture relaxed and he gave Gabe a friendly smile. Jones didn't offer a friendly smile, but he did unclench his fist and sit back.

"OK. Now tell us about Earl, and Gabriel, the truth."

Gabe had planned what he'd say. Getting caught lying would be dangerous, especially now, but telling the complete truth was not going to help him. He'd decided to blend what he'd say now with what he'd told them last night and weave in and out from there.

"They, Peter and Tall Alex, picked me up then took my phone. I assume it was Alex's car since he drove, although I guess it could've been a rental or borrowed. Anyway, it was a white sedan with a black interior, but I'm not a car guy and don't know the make. Whether because we weren't supposed to meet Earl until later or they felt concerned about being followed, we drove around at first. We stayed in Manhattan, perhaps because they wanted to avoid any E-Z Pass locations. For a while we did loops up Madison and down Park. Maybe to spot anyone tailing us. Or shake anyone. I've no idea.

"Eventually Peter received a message. From the sound it seemed like WeChat. After that we drove up to Riverside Park. Peter and I went down to the skate park while Alex stayed behind. Once we found Earl, he insisted on the two of us talking alone.

"Earl started by questioning me, mainly about Herald Square. His focus was why I was upfront and standing on something that made me so prominent, as he put it, but especially without a mask." Gabe rolled his eyeballs at Smith. "I think he was debating whether I was incredibly brave, a fool, a combination of the two or something else, such as a plant." Still eyeing Smith, he said, "He seemed suspicious of the glare on my face in the images. Was the lotion supposed to do that?"

Smith nodded with a narrow smile. The waiter returned with their drinks. Jones paid then waved the receipt, saying to Gabe in a rare non-belligerent tone, "Government bookkeepers are sticklers for these."

Gabe continued. "He wants me to publicly reveal my identity and become an extreme left figurehead or something. I assume he's including being visibly active in the future in a way that motivates people."

"Why?" Smith interrupted.

"He's got a whole philosophy about the leftist movement and feels it lacks leaders who are out front visibly leading, plus that there's a need for what I think he called 'personification of the cause'. He stressed that the left needs more than just beliefs or victims."

"Sorry, but it's not our job to help the left. What'd you tell him?"

"That I'd have to think about it, but I wouldn't agree until I'd met some leaders and decided what I thought of them. He said he'd have to speak to them. I mainly said it because I figured if it worked out you'd love it."

"And is he arranging this?" Smith asked.

"Undetermined. He's going to talk to them."

Smith went on. "How long do you have to wait before you follow up with him?"

"I can't follow up. I've got to wait for him. I gave him my contact info but he refused to give me his. He was adamant about that. I guess that's part of his playing safe."

In a rare display of frustration, Smith smacked his hand against the arm of his chair. "Do either of the other two have his contact info? Maybe you could get it from them."

"I'm sure Alex doesn't, but Peter must since he and Earl communicated back and forth while we drove around. Assuming Earl was using his own phone. And Peter's a strange guy. Since Earl insisted we talk without Peter and made me promise not to tell Peter or Alex what we spoke about, Peter may have written me off. My guess is, the most he'd do is reach out to Earl for me."

Smith said, "We'll give Earl a few days. If you haven't heard by then we'll push matters." Smith uncrossed his legs and sat up, preparing to leave.

"There are two other things," Gabe said.

"What're those?" Smith replied, caught off guard.

"First, are you tracking me with my phone or listening to my calls? I won't accept that."

"Gabriel be realistic. It's not what 'you'll accept', it's what we decide to do."

Gabe glared at him.

"The other matter?"

Gabe blurted, "God damn you people."

Gabe hadn't planned on saying that and instantly raised his arms in self-defense against any attack by Jones. However, only the corners of Jones' mouth turned up slightly.

Smith ignored Gabe's outburst and repeated, "What's the other matter, Gabriel?"

"You seem to have forgotten I'm not employed by you. Plus, my real job is more than full time and you're messing with it."

That morning, a partner had summoned Gabe to her office and rebuked him for being late in preparing documents for a deal. This was the first time a partner had ever chastised Gabe and he'd intensely disliked it. Gabe told this to Smith and Jones.

"This only happened because I spent yesterday afternoon doing your crap. Am I as valuable to you if I'm fired?"

Smith appeared truly sorry to hear this and apologized to Gabe. "We'll figure something out, Gabriel."

CHAPTER TWENTY-SIX

Back at his firm's offices, Gabe ducked into an empty conference room and called the main number for Jasminn's office. The receptionist was annoyed with him as he kept insisting that she get Jasminn to come to reception to take the call on that line rather than transferring it to Jasminn's line.

Jasminn finally picked up after Gabe had waited a few minutes. "What's going on Gabe?" she whispered, "Lauren's pissed about hiking around to get me. Why didn't you call me directly?"

"Tell her I'm sorry." His voice quieted. "Listen, I just met with S and J, you know who I mean, and I'm positive they're tracking my phone and probably tapping it. It occurred to me that maybe they've also tapped the phone in my office. Then I thought maybe they're doing the same to your phones."

She let out a long breath into the phone. "Are you sure you're not being paranoid?"

He snapped back, "Yes, I'm sure." Realizing he'd been sharp, he tried to mollify her. "Maybe I am, but remember what Heller said about being paranoid."

She laughed, remembering it well. "Yes, I understand it doesn't mean they're not really after you. I assume you didn't call just to tell me about your paranoia."

"Right. I want you to see if you can get some prepaid phones, you know burners, maybe two for each of us. I'd do it, but don't want to risk being followed."

"More paranoia."

"Just playing safe. You know, let's get two for Matt also."

"Where do I get these? I don't know how to do this."

He thought for a second. "Talk to the staff at one of the electronics stores you go to. Someone must know. Make sure you don't leave a trail. Pay cash. I'll pay you back."

"Gabe, I've got to go, Lauren's giving me nasty looks. Don't you think S and J will be suspicious if you stop using your phone?"

"We'll still use our regular phones. Just not for calls we don't want them to hear. Thanks Jaz."

Jasminn hung up and while walking back to her cubicle she considered which phone to use for sexting.

////

That evening, on her way home Jasminn stopped at an electronics store and asked a saleswoman how to go about buying burners, teasing about her boyfriend becoming paranoid. To Jasminn's surprise, the clerk was nonplussed, simply asked how many, and went to the back room, returning shortly with the phones. As Jasminn paid, the women told her that the store bought them from someone else so they were not easy to trace back to the store, much less to Jasminn. The clerk didn't ring up the sale or make any record with Jasminn's name on it.

Jasminn was thinking about the phones as she walked when, half a block from her building, Justin stepped out in front of her from behind a parked car. He held his hands up, open palms facing her.

"Jasminn, I come in peace. I need to talk to you."

She kept walking directly toward him, forcing him to move aside, and replied, "But why do I need to talk to you?"

He started to reach out to grab her arm but stopped himself. "Because Gabe's in danger."

She halted, squaring her shoulders and turned back to him. Her lips drew tight and lines appeared at the corners of her eyes.

"You threatening him?"

"No, I'm trying to protect him. And I'm risking a great deal in doing so."

His face was drawn and he held out his hands, seemingly beseeching her. She decided to hear him out.

"What's this danger?"

He quickly looked up and down the block. "We can't talk out in the open. It must be somewhere private. Can we go to your apartment?"

Her eyes shot up and she shifted her grip on the bag with the phones, preparing to use it as a weapon. "Either you're crazy or you must think I'm incredibly stupid if you think I'm letting you up there."

"OK, how about someplace nearby, say a bar or a restaurant?"

She studied him. She knew he was FBI, but he looked around while they talked and seemed nervous, contrary to how she expected an FBI agent to act. She decided to hear him out though.

"There's a bar back up at the corner. See it?"

"The one with the purple awning?"

"Uh-huh. Give me five minutes then meet me in there."

Without waiting for him to reply, she circled around him then continued back up the block.

Justin entered the bar exactly five minutes later. It wasn't crowded, mainly a couple of old people nursing their drinks. As he stood by the entrance looking for Jasminn, two men approached him. One was a hefty white man with a bushy beard and typical bouncer looks. The other was a thin Latin man. Neither looked friendly.

The Latin man said, "Hey! You look lost. You in the right place?"

Justin tried to walk by them but the large fellow blocked his path.

Justin shook his head, "Guys, what's going on? I'm just here to meet a friend and have a drink."

The white guy said, "We know everybody here. What's your friend's name?"

He looked the men over, puzzled by their behavior. He was confident of the outcome if he had to take them on, but it'd be a nuisance if the police showed. Hoping to avoid a messy situation, he said quietly, "Her name's Jasminn. OK?"

The Latin man edged closer and in the same unfriendly voice asked, "And your name?"

Still looking to avoid a confrontation, Justin examined both men. Under the Latin man's jeans, near his ankle, there was a barely perceptible bulge. Gabe could tell it was a knife. If need be, he could pull the gun strapped to his own ankle, but that would only heighten any problem with the police. Instead, he said, "Justin or Michael. She knows both names."

"Why didn't you say that sooner?" the white dude asked, exposing dirty yellow teeth as he grinned without looking any friendlier.

The two men escorted him to the back, the Latin one leading the way and the white guy bringing up and blocking the rear. They ushered him to a booth where Jasminn sat facing the front of the room.

"This the guy, Jaz?" the leader of the procession asked.

She nodded. The men let Justin sit but before leaving the Latin man said, "We're right here if you need anything, Jaz."

"Thanks guys. It makes a lady feel good knowing you're around," she said with a big smile.

Justin twisted his head around the back of the booth and took one more look at the two of them as they slowly walked away. He turned to Jasminn. "Are you serious?"

"You're the one who said Gabe could be in danger and who looked so nervous. This is my neighborhood place and the guys want to make sure nothing happens to me."

He paused. "Nice to have friends like that."

She nodded and at the same time the waitress showed up.

"Hi Pam," Jasminn said. "A beer please, and water for him."

He said, "Make that a beer Pam. Whatever's on tap."

Pam headed back to the bar while Jasminn said, "I didn't think you guys were allowed to drink on duty."

"True, but I am very much not on duty."

Jasminn looked more closely at him, her head tilted. "I don't get it. If you're not on duty, why do you want to talk to me?"

"Because I'm under orders not to talk to Gabe."

Her face scrunched as she tried to follow him and said, "More importantly, what's this about Gabe being in danger?"

Justin sighed, took a long swallow of his beer, and leaned toward Jasminn. "I don't know how much Gabe's told you, but I'm guessing it's a fair amount. Has he mentioned either of the two guys named Alex or a guy named Peter from our night in jail?"

"He's not only mentioned them, but I've met them all," she replied, causing him to sit back against the back of the booth.

"How'd that happen?"

She ignored his question. "What's this have to do with Gabe being in danger?"

"I'll explain, but please answer my question first."

Jasminn shrugged. "We hung out at a club the other night with the fellow you guys call 'Short Alex' and then on Sunday for a while with 'Tall Alex' and Peter." She purposely omitted Earl.

"With Tall Alex and Peter, together. Interesting. You're a smart woman. What do you think of them?"

"Correction, I'm a very smart woman. Now, I'm not saying another word until you explain. Or should I ask my two friends who escorted you in to escort you out?"

He rolled his eyes. "You are tough, aren't you?" He shook his head but gave in. "The key thing is that Gabe should stay away from Peter. Have nothing to do with him. And definitely do nothing with him that might constitute 'collaborating' or 'aiding and abetting'."

"You make Peter sound like serious trouble. What's the story?"

He looked her square in the eyes. "I'm going to disclose some information that I shouldn't."

She was speechless.

"I'd never heard of Peter or any of them before we ended up in jail together. Afterwards though I accessed their Bureau files—I know I'm admitting to working for the FBI."

She gave him a big grin and clenched a fist in victory. He ignored this and went on. "Tall Alex's file is empty, and I've asked about that. The file for Short Alex was thin and uninteresting. That wasn't so in Peter's case. Although he came to the United States when he was young and is now a citizen, he's a suspected foreign agent."

Now she was surprised. "For whom? What's he done?"

Justin shook his head. "I've said as much as I'm going to, except that there's nothing in his file about being involved with the left wing. I don't know what he's up to, but I can assure you, having read his file, he's not a great believer in human rights or other left wing causes, or non-violence for that matter."

She said nothing, and quickly finished her beer. Stunned by what she was hearing, she waved two fingers in the air, catching Pam's attention. While she thought more about what Justin had told her, he downed his drink. Neither of them said anything until Pam returned with their second round plus a basket of shelled peanuts.

Pam gone, Jasminn asked, "If what you say is true, why'd you tell me? Isn't that a violation of a whole bunch of FBI rules?"

"It is a violation and I'd get into serious trouble if it got out. From our past conversation I'm sure that you know I have a wife and kids, and I'm asking you not to tell anyone that I said anything, but I had no choice." He looked at her, seeking her sympathy. "The Bureau and another organization …

She interrupted him. "You mean Homeland Security?"

He nodded. "Yes. Both organizations are actively focusing on Peter now. I'm not allowed to be involved with Gabe, not that I want to be at this point, so watching Peter is now my main task. If Gabe gets caught doing anything with him, even if Gabe thinks they're acting for the left, it'll be a race to see which agency arrests him first and he'll be in a lot of trouble. I like Gabe. He's got a future ahead of him, and I'd hate to see it ruined. It's bad enough what DHS is doing to him now."

Jasminn thought about what he'd said, and she looked everywhere but at him. *Could this be a ploy by Justin?* she wondered, unshelling a few peanuts. *If so, what's the play? After all, Justin was only telling her that Gabe should avoid Peter. Gabe should be fine doing that, although it might prove difficult while satisfying Homeland Security. What about Earl though? Did he pose a danger as well?*

Justin's hand was resting on the table in front of him. She reached across and lightly touched his hand. "I'll make you a deal." He looked at her while she swallowed then she said, "Does Earl Reuben pose a danger?"

Justin was shocked by her mention of Earl and started to pull back his hand, then stopped and phrased his answer very carefully. "I didn't know that Earl had anything to do with this. I'd love to hear how he's involved, but I'm pretty sure you aren't going to tell me. I'll say this, it's not smart to be around Earl either because everyone's looking to nail him. But I don't know of anything specific that would pose a threat to Gabe. Does that answer your question?"

"It does." She patted his hand then drew back her own. "You've impressed me. Telling me about Peter was a big risk." She smiled. "You actually seem like a decent guy," her smile broadened, "for a G-Man that is. And you have my word, so long as you don't double-cross Gabe or cause him any trouble, no one will ever know about our conversation and your wife's and kids' husband and father won't be in jail because of me."

Justin rose, gulping the rest of his beer. "One more thing, have Gabe be extremely careful with the DHS guys. He shouldn't trust them."

He started toward the exit then looked back at her. "Be careful on whom you sic those two bodyguards of yours. Odds are they would've ended up pretty banged up." He strode out, passing the two men while giving them a big smile and leaving Jasminn to figure out what to do.

CHAPTER TWENTY-SEVEN

Trying to catch up on his work, Gabe stayed at the office until after nine. Having had enough, he wanted to go home, but Matt had wanted to get together so they'd agreed to meet for a quick drink at one of the few decent bars in Gabe's neighborhood. Due to a UN special session, lining up a car service or getting a cab was impossible. As a result, Gabe took the subway down to Astor Place and started walking from there.

With everything that had happened to him, Gabe was becoming more and more cautious and keeping an eye out. Suddenly, he stopped and ducked under the awning of a used record store. Gabe's attacker from the night of his date with Alice was standing across the street under a streetlight. At least Gabe thought it was him. The man was lighting a cigarette and absorbed in getting his lighter to work. Gabe dashed across the street and hid in the shadows up against a building about twenty feet away. The man's back was to Gabe, but before he bent his head to light his cigarette, he turned in Gabe's direction and the streetlight shone directly on his face. Now Gabe had no doubt it was his attacker.

Gabe was unsure what to do, but before he decided, the man went into a storefront behind him. Gabe waited several minutes, but when he hadn't come out Gabe made his way over, keeping his back against the buildings. A curtain inside covered the window and in front of it hung a sign reading "Massage" and below that "Russian, Ukrainian and Korean Girls." *A dingy looking 'rub and tug' joint.* Now Gabe was more unsure what to do. He rejected going in after the man. Gabe didn't know how long a wait there'd be before his attacker came out, especially since the sign listed the prices by the amount of time spent there.

Just then Gabe received a text from Matt asking for his ETA. Gabe texted back, giving Matt the address where he was and telling Matt to get there ASAP. Matt showed up about ten minutes later, and Gabe filled him in on the attack and his attacker being in the massage parlor. Matt was in favor of rushing in, arguing that a guy couldn't be more vulnerable than if they caught him naked with some woman working on him. Gabe agreed that the man would feel exposed so more likely to talk, but said they'd probably end up in a big argument, if not a fight, with whoever ran the place. Grudgingly, Matt agreed, and they waited.

Matt had read the sign in the window, and half-sitting on a nearby standpipe, but out of the streetlamp's light, he said with a laugh, "Hopefully he's either cheap or quick so we don't have to wait too long."

Gabe laughed and shortly, as if summoned by Matt's wish, the man exited the parlor, still tucking in his shirt. He started walking in the opposite direction from Matt and Gabe and didn't notice them. They set off after him with Matt leading the way, and as the man was passing an alley, Matt grabbed him and shoved him into it. The man was taken unawares and started struggling. He got nowhere, and soon gave up. Matt held him pinned to the wall with one arm. The man was shaking.

"What do we do now?" Matt asked, looking partway to his right.

The man looked in the same direction. At first he saw only a dark figure, then Gabe stepped closer and he made out Gabe's face. He tried to slide away from Gabe, but Matt held him tight, and they could see the whites of his eyes in the dim light. Gabe thought, *He's afraid we're going to beat him like he tried to beat me.*

Gabe said something he'd never imagined he'd actually say. "Hold him while I frisk him."

Matt shifted his grip to the man's arms. Gabe only knew how to frisk someone from the movies. He pulled a wallet from the man's back pants' pocket but found nothing else of interest, although he could have missed a small weapon if the man had been carrying one. One thing he didn't do, was pat down the man's crotch.

Trying to sound confident and aggressive, Gabe demanded, "Why'd you jump me that night?"

The man had recovered some. "What're you talking about? I've never seen you before. Let me go. You've got my wallet."

In response Matt pushed the man harder, jamming his back into the uneven pointy edges of the bricks behind him.

"Let's not bother with that bullshit. We both know it was you. Now tell me before my friend gets nasty," Gabe ordered, thinking he was stealing dialogue from old movies.

"Alright," the man whimpered. "Have him take it easy. My back's getting all cut up."

Matt lightened the pressure, but only slightly.

"Well?" Gabe asked.

"I was hired to do it; to give you that warning. But I promise, I wasn't trying to kill you or hurt you badly."

"Yeah, kind of you," Gabe responded. "Now, who hired you? And don't give me those 'You can't tell me or they'll kill you,' or 'You don't know his name' lines. My friend will be mad if you do."

The man sagged against the wall and stared down. "Honestly. I don't remember his name. I swear. Maybe I heard it once a long time ago. It's the truth!" Matt started pressing the man harder against the wall, the bricks digging in deeper. "But I can give you some information," the man rushed on, his mouth contorted in pain.

Matt let up again and the man quickly spat out what he knew. "He's a guy I see around my neighborhood. About average height, black hair. Big clunky glasses."

While his attacker was talking Gabe had been looking through the wallet. His eyebrows rose. Gabe said, "Tell me about his hair."

The man looked at Gabe, his face screwed up quizzically for a moment, then he said, "I get it. His hair always falls on his face and it always looks dirty. I don't know why he doesn't wash it more."

Gabe nodded, held up the man's driver's license, and said "Dimitri of Brighton Beach. . . is the man's name Peter or Pietrov?"

"Yes. That's it," Dimitri exclaimed.

"Did Pietrov tell you why you were to deliver this message?"

"No, and I didn't care. I just wanted the money." He looked at Gabe with a hint of anger. "I made him pay extra for my pain and my doctor's bill from my knee you hurt."

Gabe shook his head. "No sympathy for either of you." He paused while thinking. "Now Dimitri of Brighton Beach, I'm going to give you back your wallet and we're going to let you go, but I'm keeping your license. If anything happens to me or any of my friends, this goes to the police and they'll pick up you and Pietrov. Is that clear?"

"Yeah," Dimitri nodded rapidly, his head bobbing up and down.

Gabe flipped Dimitri's wallet down by the latter's feet and Matt released him. Dimitri grabbed the wallet and looked at them both with a mixture of hatred and fear before running off.

After he was gone, Gabe realized Matt's arms were shaking.

"I can't do that again, Gabe," Matt said, "Self-defense is one thing, but not this."

Gabe nodded, patted Matt on his back and pocketed Dimitri's license as they headed to the bar for their now greatly needed drinks. As they walked, out of the corner of his eye Matt looked at Gabe and asked, "Gabe, that day outside the Mexican restaurant and now this. . .what's going on? Are you somehow involved with the government?"

Gabe gave his best smile, "Don't be ridiculous. What would the government want with me? These guys are just fanatics. On both sides."

Matt hesitated as if about to say something, then shook his head as they entered the bar.

CHAPTER TWENTY-EIGHT

While Gabe worked late and he and Matt had their run-in with Dimitri, Jasminn thought about what Justin had told her and what she should do. The whole thing was getting to her. For a while she'd stayed in the bar where she felt safe. Eventually, after having a cheeseburger with fries, she had to go less than a block to her apartment, and, to the amazement of her two bouncer buddies, she asked if one of them would walk her home. They'd never seen her shaken up, so they both walked her, pleased to do so and counting on the bar not to be destroyed in the few minutes they were gone.

She knew she had to tell Gabe everything Justin had said as soon as possible, but they couldn't use their new burners since he didn't have one yet, and she didn't trust Gabe's phone and had strong doubts about the security of her own. Having no other option, she used her phone to send Gabe a text: "AVOID GREASY HAIR. MEET TOMORROW."

That done, Jasminn prepared to dig into Tall Alex. The more she thought about their conversation in Riverside Park, the angrier and more baffled she became. She also thought his empty FBI file seemed too convenient. She'd find out whatever there was to find out about this bastard.

She expected a long night so got comfortable, changing into her favorite oversized tee, and making herself a cup of strong tea. With these necessary tools she took her seat and started her hunt.

Her first problem was that searching 'Tall Alex' wasn't going to work and she didn't know Alex's last name, have his phone number or a picture of him. She knew all of that sat on the NYPD's computers from the night he'd been arrested, but there was no way she'd try to hack those computers—that'd be worlds beyond hacking a kiddie soccer league. Instead, she searched articles about the left and images of left wing protesters, but for a long time had no luck. Eventually she found a blurred picture from a rally in which one face might be Alex's, but she wasn't sure and the quality wasn't good enough for an image search.

Jasminn took a break to stretch and get more tea. She was waiting on the microwave when Kate came home, looking a bit worse for wear, but nowhere near as high or bedraggled as on many other nights.

Jasminn grinned. "Tough night at the bars?"

The two women teased back and forth, until Kate said, "At least being out was more fun than sitting around dressed like that and drinking tea to keep yourself going. Big project for work?"

"Actually, it's something else. I'm trying to track down some guy, but I've got little to go on."

"What, you ditched Gabe and you're now desperate for a guy?"

"Ha ha, Kate. No, it's some guy related to the movement."

"What's he look like?"

"Just like you to ask that," Jasminn replied. "He's a bit shorter than Gabe, has dirty blonde hair and fair skin. I found a picture on my computer, but it's blurred and I can't be sure it's him."

Kate hurried into Jasminn's room. Jasminn followed and found Kate in her chair staring at the blurred image on the monitor.

"You like your men blurry?" Jasminn asked.

Now seeming more together, Kate held up a hand, silencing Jasminn, and continued staring at the picture. "I think I know this guy."

"You're kidding. How can you possibly tell from that blurry picture?" Jasminn asked.

Kate giggled. "Some nights everything's blurred—maybe I remember him blurred."

Jasminn's mouth turned down and she shook her head. "You are something Katie dear. I still don't see how you could tell."

Kate ignored her. "Is he a rich preppy sort of guy?"

"I know he's got money," Jasmin replied, "and yeah he seems kind'a preppy. He dressed that way."

"A while before you and I met, I think I hooked up with him."

"You think?"

"I don't keep a log, you know," Kate replied. "but I'm pretty sure. What's his name?"

"Alex."

Kate spun around twice in the chair in glee. "Yes, Alex! That's it! I told you."

Jasminn was amazed by this break. This could be a real shortcut—all due to Kate's wild night life. "What's his full name?" Jasminn asked. "Do you have his phone number?"

Kate shook her head. "It wasn't one of those things. We met at a party at some fancy place—I don't remember where. We talked for a bit, both got pretty drunk and went to a back room…you know. I never saw him afterwards, which is how it goes sometimes and was fine."

"Do you remember anything else about him?"

Kate thought for a second then giggled and said, "I think I remember his body. He had…"

Jasminn cut her off. "I'm definitely not interested in those details. Did he say anything that'd help me find him online?" Kate leered at her. "For my research," Jasminn clarified.

"I don't remember. It was a ways back, we were drinking and I'm sure most of it would have been the standard 'what do you do?' and other pick-up lines and small talk."

Jasminn shrugged, disappointed that her lucky break wasn't panning out.

Heading out of Jasminn's room, Kate stopped and said, "I can't be sure about this, but …"

"But what?" Jasminn urged her on.

"Assuming this is that guy, I think maybe early on he talked about politics—not my thing you know—and how involved he was on the right. Maybe trying to impress me. But maybe I'm mixing him up with someone else." She paused then confirmed, "No, I'm sure."

Kate went to her room to collapse while Jasminn stared after her. *Alex is a right winger, eh? It made no sense.* She'd wondered about this, but hadn't believed it. *Although it did fit some of what he'd said to her and the way he'd acted.* Forgetting her tea, Jasminn retook her position at her computers and commenced searching 'Alex' and 'Alexander,' she assumed that was his full first name, with right wing keywords and on right wing websites, and studying images as she searched.

Jasminn's high-level skills weren't of help in this search. Instead, this was, to her, a slow crawl through the muck of right-wing sites. After roughly two hours of grinding along, all of a sudden her face lit up and she yelled, "Yes! Got you motherfucker!" On her screen was a slightly out of focus pre-pandemic picture of a low profile alt-right group. A face wearing sunglasses looked directly at the photographer from the front row. Although the picture and the face weren't perfectly clear and the person wore sunglasses, Jasminn had no doubt that she was looking at a slightly younger version of Alex.

Jasminn felt a range of emotions and her mind leaped from one thought to another. *Victory! She'd found him—yet disappointment in him, and in herself and Gabe for being fooled. But could he have been part of the alt-right and had a change of thinking which swung him to the left? Doubtful, but how to be sure? Or maybe back then he'd been spying on the right? If he was really on the right, what was he up to? Spying on the left? And what was he doing with Peter?* So many questions. However, whatever the answers, she wanted to beat the crap out of him. She had to let Gabe know.

CHAPTER TWENTY-NINE

Dimitri's confession left Gabe lost as to why Peter had him attacked, but it did make it easy for him to decipher Jasminn's message about greasy hair. Nevertheless, he didn't know what prompted her to send it, and he was concerned about her. He'd replied "Understood. See you then."

Now, after two drinks with Matt, Gabe was home, but he couldn't sleep. He lay in bed looking at the lines in his cracked ceiling, visible in the city lights sneaking around the edges of his blinds. He reached a decision. He was through being told what to do and being beat up and used. He'd take the offensive. Pleased by this decision, although he had no idea how he'd pull it off, he finally drifted off to sleep.

The next morning Gabe was up early and got busy. He sent out email and text blasts saying he was taking several days' vacation from work and would be unreachable. He knew taking vacation days on such short notice and ghosting this way was against firm policy, but at this point he didn't care. After showering and dressing, he downed a protein shake, shoved his gym gear into his backpack, and was out the door well before his usual time. He trotted to the uptown subway and was waiting for Jasminn in front of her office building when she arrived.

"What're you doing here?" she asked, her expression shifting from an immediate smile to squinting to study his face closely.

"We texted that we'd meet today," he replied, adding "Is there somewhere in your office where we could talk privately?"

Jasminn brought him upstairs. Since she worked in a cubicle, to have privacy they squeezed between two servers in a cooled room barely larger than a closet. After Gabe hugged and kissed her, "Necessary in order to stay warm in this friggin' space," he said, Jasminn filled him in on her conversation with Justin.

She told him about Alex and how she found him online, then forwarded the picture of him with the right from a burner she'd taken for herself to one she had for Gabe. Gabe looked at her, his face drawn up, then his eyes wandered around the tiny space, bewildered. He wasn't wild about Alex but despite what Jasminn was telling him, Gabe hadn't expected this.

Eventually he shrugged. "I guess we'll have to thank Kate for how she spends her time."

"What do you think we should do about Alex, other than kneeing him in the balls?", she asked with a slight smile.

"Despite what you learned Jaz, as far as I know he's not after us. He's probably a lower priority." He told her about Peter hiring Dimitri to deliver his painful message, finishing by saying, "For now, unless things change, the DHS and Peter come before Alex." Even with what Justin had said about Peter, neither of them knew what Peter's reasons were.

Gabe added, "I've had enough. I'm going to fight back and end this."

She looked at him, baffled. "How?"

Gabe's hands fluttered apart. He wasn't sure.

"I know you don't want to run or hide, but I don't know how you can solve this," she said, stroking his cheek.

He took her hand and held it in both of his.

"I've got a few ideas. I don't know if they'll work, but I've got to try." He tried to sound confident. "I'm going now to work on my first one."

"Tell me," she said.

"I'm going to the library."

She gave him a look she'd given him many times over the years. Almost always she'd been joking, but this time she was serious. It was her "You're crazy look."

He answered her unspoken rebuke. "I'm not crazy. I need to research the Homeland Security department. I can't believe Smith's and Jones' actions are legal even with the national security claim, so maybe I can find some way to force the Department to leave us alone. I've nothing to lose. I had one other idea but hadn't put much faith in it. Now though, after Justin coming to see you, I'm definitely pursuing it."

"Whatever you intend, if it's tied to what I told you, please don't do it. I don't want to be responsible for you getting hurt." She said this in a caring tone which he was still adjusting to, but which he liked, a lot.

He put that aside. "As strange as this may sound, I think my best ally may be Justin, whether he wants the job or not."

"What do you want him to do?"

He shrugged and slid a hand under her shirt to rub her back, while saying. "I don't know, but at least he's not after me, he doesn't want anything from me now and he tried to help me by going to you. Plus, he's more knowledgeable about this than anyone else I can turn to."

"But he's under orders to keep away from you."

"He may be under orders, but I'm not. I'm going to do whatever I have to in order to get his help. What can he do, arrest me for harassing an FBI agent?"

She laughed and he was glad she did.

He took two of the burner phones from her, including the phone with Alex's picture, and they exchanged the burners' numbers to be able to be in touch, without it being a party line with Smith and Jones. After a few more hugs and kisses "to make sure she wasn't cold," they exited the server closet, receiving amused looks from people in the hall.

///

From Jasminn's office Gabe walked to a branch near Grand Central Station of one of his gym's many branches. He'd joined this gym when he'd first started at the firm. Most of his friends belonged to fancier clubs and more expensive gyms, but Gabe didn't see the point. Most clubs had basically similar equipment and, as Gabe pointed out to his colleagues, the weights weigh the same no matter the gym. The main reason he'd joined this gym was that it had branches, or clubs as they called them, located throughout the city, so he could carry around his gym clothes and squeeze in a workout if he wanted wherever he was.

He swiped his ID at the branch entrance and made his way to the locker room which was crowded with men dressing after their pre-work regimens. He locked his gym clothes and phone in a locker. If Smith and Jones really were keeping tabs on him through his phone, he could go off and do whatever, then pick it up later without them knowing where he'd been. If they challenged him, he'd say he'd had a long workout, or if he was gone too long, say he'd accidentally left his phone there. He accepted that they could hack the club's computer system to check on him, or maybe even review its security cameras' footage if they wanted to, but he'd just have to hope they didn't go that far. As a backup, he decided he could give his phone to Jasminn or Matt to carry around.

His next stop was a nearby branch of the city's public library. On his way in he glanced at Fortitude and Patience, the two large marble lions across the street in front of the library's main building. Looking at them he thought he'd need not just patience and fortitude but luck and ammunition.

The branch, like most of them, had free computers available for anyone with a library card. Gabe had never used them, but he needed to do so now to prevent Smith and Jones from tracking him. He knew that only 'safe searches' could be conducted on the library's computers. The computers couldn't access pornographic sites and whatever other sites whoever ran the system deemed unsafe. Gabe assumed this wouldn't include his target—Homeland Security's site.

All the computers were taken, so he printed his name on the wait list, then seated himself on a narrow wooden chair next to an elderly woman. Gabe looked sideways at her. Despite the warm weather she had on a long sleeved blouse and sweater and a floor length skirt with worn sneakers. She wore a hat that had clearly seen better days. He looked closer and saw that her clothes had stains and small rips. She clutched a large purse on her lap and several shopping bags stuffed to the top surrounded her.

Gabe looked away from her, but she shifted her body partway toward him and said, "You're new. I've never seen you here before."

"You're right." Without thinking, he added, "This is my first time using the computers."

She turned further to get a better look at him, giving him the opportunity to study her face. He had no idea how old she was, but her face was completely wrinkled. Not just normal wrinkled, but wrinkle after wrinkle and wrinkles folded atop other wrinkles. Her expression changed as she looked at him, and her wrinkles shifted as if they were a moving mosaic, but so many wrinkles made it impossible to read her expressions. When any part of her face moved, all her wrinkles moved.

"Excuse me," Gabe said. He'd been so taken by her wrinkles that he'd missed what she'd said.

"I asked, 'Do you know how to use the computers here?'"

Gabe smiled. "Yes, I know how to use a computer, thank you. Do you need help?"

Her face may have been indecipherable, but her tone of voice was not, and it made clear she thought he was a fool. "Young man, you don't understand. When you use these computers you're telling the government what you're looking at. That's fine if, say, you're ordering food, but dangerous if you're doing serious research."

Gabe didn't know what she was talking about, and unconsciously he slid to the far side of his chair away from her.

She asked, "You're not with the government, are you?" He shook his head, bemused. "Of course you're not. You don't look sharp enough." She studied him closely as she continued. "The government monitors these computers. You think they don't? Every site you go to, or try to go to, every keystroke you enter, they know. And if you're looking at things they don't approve of, or running searches they think are suspicious, they can come after you."

Gabe didn't know whether to be amused by or feel sorry for this obviously paranoid lady. "Isn't that's a little extreme?" he asked.

She snapped at him. "Hardly. Let's put it this way. If Karl Marx hadn't worked on the *Communist Manifesto* in the Reading Room of the British Public Library, but had worked on these computers, it never would have gotten written."

Gabe laughed, and quickly said, "I'm not laughing at you. I just think that's a great line."

She grunted and turned away, dismissing him as a naïve fool.

He tried making amends. "Why then do you use them?"

She turned back to him and with a faint gleam in her milky eyes and, amidst her wrinkles a sly grin, she whispered, "I know how to beat the system. They can cut me off, but they can't track me."

Fascinated and now enjoying himself, Gabe said, "As I told you, I'm new at this." He edged closer to her and whispered, "I'm doing secret research and want to make sure no one knows I'm doing it. Can you tell me how to get away with it?"

He thought he detected a smile through her wrinkles as she said, "You don't use your real library card." Although he couldn't read her face, she easily saw the confusion on his. "It's simple. You get library cards under phony names. It's not the staff's fault—they're nice and do a good job, but they can't catch these. I can't tell you how the cards are made because members of my secret society," she put a finger to her lips, "some produce them. But I do have a whole stack of them."

Gabe's mouth dropped open, taken by her and what she was telling him. Either he was in the presence of an excellent conspirator or a befuddled old woman, or both. He didn't know which.

She continued explaining to him how things work. "When I signed up a few minutes ago to use the computers I did so under one of my fake names. Look at this." She held up a library card for him to see, although she kept it out of his reach. The name on it was 'Bobby Brown.' She rushed on. "I know that's a man name, and of course I'm not that Bobby Brown. If anyone behind the desk ever challenged me, which no one ever has, it wouldn't be a problem. For this card I'd say my name is 'Bobbi' with an 'I,' and explain that the library erred when it issued the card." She paused for a second then ran on. "I've got lots of these and our society has fun coming up with names. Of course, we don't let that interfere with our mission."

Gabe didn't know what to say but finally replied, "That's really something Bobby."

"Bobby's not my real name." S shook her head at his lack of understanding.

Trying not to sound argumentative, he said, "I figured that."

She thought for a few moments before saying, "You said this is your first time using the library's computers. Looking at you, you're obviously not poor and probably have your own computer," she giggled slightly and continued, "so I'm guessing you want to do some online snooping you don't want tracked back to you. Am I right?"

Gabe gave her a slight nod.

She smiled broadly, her wrinkles moving all around. "In that case you shouldn't do it with your own card. Here, use mine and the computer they assign me. That way, the government can only see what Bobby Brown searched, but not what 'cute young man' researched."

She held out Bobby's card.

"Are you sure?" he asked. "What about your research?"

"Don't worry about me. I'm in no rush and I'm carrying several cards." She rummaged in her purse then looked at the cards she'd pulled out. "Maybe I'll be 'Hally Barry' or 'Kristie Stewart'." She smiled at him, clearly loving the game. "One more thing," she added. "Never tell anyone what you're researching. You don't know whom you can trust."

Before Gabe could say anything further, a man behind the desk announced, "Bobby Brown, computer number 7."

Gabe and the woman exchanged looks. He took the proffered card, thanked her, and then Bobby Brown spent several hours doing research online.

CHAPTER THIRTY

That morning Short Alex was working at the family store he managed. This combination hardware and army-navy store and the one his father managed were two of the largest of their kind in the New York City area. They couldn't match the chain stores' prices, but they were competitive enough. With that and their strong community ties and excellent customer service they maintained a loyal clientele.

By eleven he'd finished checking the outstanding purchase orders and vendor bills, and tested each security lock in the store's gun section. *Everything looks good,* he thought, *most importantly the special order.* Done, he made a quick circuit of the store, checking in with employees and making sure everything was running smoothly. Satisfied, he headed for the subway, knowing that as soon as he was out the door his assistant manager had changed the music broadcast over the store's sound system from Alex's blues to reggae.

It was a long but easy subway ride to Madison Square Park. By the fountain at the south end of the Park, Short Alex spotted his man. He was on a bench facing away from the sun and reading *The Times.* He wore a '60's era dark floppy felt hat and a light-weight gray poplin windbreaker. The hat's brim had been worked on, making it hang low in the front, and the windbreaker's collar was turned up. Together they obscured much of the man's face and cast shadows on the rest.

Alex sat next to him.

"How are you, Earl?"

"Doing fine. Lovely here, isn't it?"

Alex looked around at the park's well-tended green lawns and the trees with their broad green leaves. Water was popping up from the several jets in the nearby fountain's top tier then was gently trickling down the two lower tiers to the basin's calm water lit by the midday sun. He could hear little children in the park's playground, shouting as they played.

He nodded. "Want to stay here or go over to the café for a bite?"

"Stay put. Talking's easier when people aren't staring at me."

"What're you talking about?" Alex asked. "They'll be too busy looking at the really short guy with you."

They both laughed.

"We do make an interesting looking pair, don't we," Earl said.

Earl turned to business and asked about their special order.

"The shields should be here next week. They'll provide valuable protection."

"I don't want any details, but is the other stuff on its way?"

"On schedule."

Earl nodded and asked about Tall Alex.

"We watched him on and off for another day but saw nothing of interest so dropped it. We've also checked up on his and his family's backgrounds. His father's a successful hedge fund manager, and for school Alex went to one of the City's elite private schools then a Little Ivy. I'd say he's a well-to-do guy who's active on the left because he believes or because it's the in thing. Either way, I don't see any issue."

Earl then told Alex about his meeting with Gabe.

"Are you going to speak to others and maybe use him?"

"Most likely," Earl said. "You trust him?"

"I do, except I was taken aback that during that demonstration he was fighting up at the front that way, and that makes me wonder. We spent time together one night. I'd set it up to learn the story, but we ended up mainly talking the blues."

Earl shook his head. "You and your blues."

"Hey, he knew his stuff and he's a good guy. But I'm still going to find out the story."

They continued sitting, talking about the latest happenings on the left and the right. As they did almost every time they met, they both expressed their frustration with law enforcement for focusing so much more on the left although as far as they were concerned, the alt-right posed the far greater threat. While they talked, Earl occasionally looked around, peeking out from under his floppy brim.

"Don't look to your left," Earl said, "but there's a guy over there who's been watching us and now he's heading in this direction."

Alex didn't make the common mistake of turning in the direction Earl told him not to turn. Instead, he stood, stretched and did a slow three-sixty in the opposite direction. He completed his turn several seconds before the man reached them.

He was easily in his sixties, white, and wore jeans and a checked short sleeve button down shirt. He didn't appear hostile; instead, he seemed curious. He was looking at Earl, trying to get a good look under the floppy hat. "Excuse me, sir. You're Earl Reuben, aren't you?"

Cover blown, Earl pushed his hat back on his head, fully exposing his face, and looked up at the man.

"That's right. Can I help you?" Earl asked in a cool but not antagonistic tone.

For several moments, the three of them didn't move. The man wasn't large, but he was a lot bigger than Alex, and Earl wasn't much of a fighter. Regardless, Alex tensed, prepared to leap in if the man made the wrong move.

The man extended his hand and said, "Hello Mr. Reuben, my name's Professor Walter Kercheck. I thought that was you and wanted to come over and say hello."

Bemused but relieved, Earl rose, shook Walter's hand and introduced Alex.

"Is there anything I can do for you Professor Kercheck?" Earl asked, looking more closely at him. Earl's eyebrows raised and he asked, "Professor, do we know each other? You look familiar."

Walter's face broke into a smile. "You've got an excellent memory. Back when you were trying cases you defended a young woman in Chicago who was up for second degree murder arising from a march that got out of control."

Earl slapped one of his legs and he and Walter laughed while Alex looked at the two with puzzlement. "Now I've got it Professor, er, Walter. You came up from the jury pool. I'd used up all my peremptories and the judge wouldn't dismiss you for cause and as a result I was stuck with you on that jury."

Walter nodded and said, "NRA and all, and there I was." He added, "You were not happy," stressing the word 'not.' After a drawn-out moment, as if building the suspense, Walter looked at Alex and said with another grin, "We acquitted her unanimously."

Earl nodded, remembering it all, then said, "Walter we were about to go to the café there for some lunch. Would you be my guest and join us?" Walter accepted, and as they proceeded, Earl joshed, "They can't accuse me of jury tampering for buying you lunch ten years later."

They found a table and got their food. Walter told them he was now technically Professor Emeritus, having retired from his university as a sociology professor last year, and now wrote for a conservative website, but he said, not on the alt-right. Earl and Walter spent their meal, and then the desserts Alex got for everyone, debating politics. Alex listened, only chiming in occasionally. By the end of the meal and their talk, which was spirited but civil and respectful, neither of them had convinced the other to move any closer to the center. However, they agreed that the danger lay with both sides' militants, and it was up to people like them to deal with these groups.

After a time, Walter got up to leave. He and Earl shook hands and exchanged cards, promising to stay in touch. Walter gone, Earl said, "Nice fellow. I don't understand though how such an extremely bright man can have those right-wing views. Maybe more dialogue would help get people like him to rid us of some of those extremists on the right."

"Just on the right?" Alex asked.

"Of course just on the right," Earl replied. "We need the Antifa."

CHAPTER THIRTY-ONE

Gabe was sitting on the pavement, leaning back against the side of the Stuyvesant Town fountain near Justin's apartment building. It was about four in the afternoon. After his library research Gabe had picked up his phone, wandered around, then stopped at another branch of his gym and deposited his phone in a locker there. He'd been in Stuytown for a bit over two hours, waiting. He felt impatient but he'd wait as long as he had to. Every so often he'd get up, walk around and stretch, but he always stayed near the building entrance. He'd decided this was the best way to get to speak to Justin. *On top of that*, Gabe thought, *if Justin could corner Jasminn at her place, I can do the same to him.*

Another hour passed. Gabe grew more impatient and he was bored and thirsty. He also needed to relieve himself and the sound of the fountain made this worse. Eventually, he ran behind a building and did his business behind some bushes, deciding that if he ever went on another stakeout he'd bring a partner so they could spell each other.

People continuously passed by the fountain. Soon, glancing to his right, Gabe saw Justin. Gabe pretended to look in his backpack to hide his face. Then, keeping his face turned away from Justin, Gabe casually walked toward his building, beating Justin to its front doors. Finally seeing Gabe, Justin was stunned and stopped a few feet in front of him.

"What're you doing here, Gabe?" he asked.

"Obviously, I'm here to see you, Justin."

"Obviously. But out here call me Michael," Justin replied, scowling.

"OK, Michael. We need to talk. It's very important."

Justin shook his head and took a step toward the doors but Gabe blocked his path.

Louder, but still trying to be discrete, Justin said, "I'm not permitted to have contact with you. Please move."

"Was speaking to Jasminn permitted? Or what you told her? And are you permitted to use your FBI martial arts skills, or whatever they teach you, to make me move?"

Justin sighed, then scanned the surroundings. Taking a deep breath he said, "Follow me."

Justin led Gabe to the same boiler room where he'd taken Smith and Jones. Before Justin could say anything, Gabe rushed to tell him, "Justin, I mean Michael, I don't want trouble. You took a big risk speaking to Jaz and telling her what you did. Thank you for that."

"OK, you're welcome. Are we done?" he asked, gesturing toward the door.

"No. I need your help, Michael."

Justin didn't bother to explain that down there he could be called 'Justin.' "Gabe, it's not my job to help you. I take it you think you're in danger, and I wouldn't be surprised if you are. Go to the police or to Smith and Jones."

Gabe chuckled and shook his head. "Yeah, right, Smith and Jones. As if they're not the cause of all my problems."

Justin didn't respond, planning to wait Gabe out.

"You told Jasminn all about Peter and that you're watching him. Now, we both know that for some reason his agenda involves me. Rather than hiding from him, I want to tail him and find out what he's after and buy my freedom from Smith and Jones by serving him up to them."

Justin shook his head. "You're a very book smart guy and I'm told an excellent lawyer, but you lack street smarts. What makes you think you could 'serve him up' as you put it, or if you somehow managed to do so, that Homeland Security wouldn't want you that much more? You'd have proven your usefulness." He added with a note of anger, "You already impressed them when you helped blow my cover."

"At least for now Peter's my best shot, and if I don't have the necessary street smarts that's all the more reason why I need your help to find out what he's up to."

Justin slapped the top railing of the grate they stood on. "Damn it, no! I'm not doing anything for you. You should run away and hide somewhere."

"Yes, you are going to help me," Gabe yelled. "If not, since my career and life are being screwed up, I'll screw up yours."

Justin looked away, over to the boiler. After a bit, he turned back. "Alright, you win. One thing though. If we do find a basis to arrest Peter, I'm the one who brings him in so the Bureau and I get the credit. To help you with DHS, we'll tell them you played a major role. If nothing else, at least you'd be safe from Peter. Agreed?"

It wasn't all that Gabe wanted, but he thought it was the best he was going to get, and who knew how it might play out. "Agreed."

"I'll work out a plan for this. It may take a few days to get ready. Can I reach you without Smith and Jones knowing?"

Gabe smiled. "I'll give you my burner number."

///

The next morning Gabe called Uncle Steve. He asked one of Steve's two administrative assistants to set up a meeting for him right away. The assistant repeatedly said that Steve was extremely busy, but Gabe explained who he was and insisted the assistant tell Steve it was important. Within a few minutes, the assistant called back, and later that afternoon Gabe was at Steve's office. One of the assistants ushered Gabe into Steve's inner sanctum as Steve's manicurist finished buffing his nails.

Steve had his manicurist come twice a week. Gabe knew this was not merely vanity on Steve's part, but rather an intentional statement. As Steve had once put it, holding up his big beefy hands, "This is to put a shine on these meat hooks." They were workman's hands and could give bone crushing handshakes. They served as a reminder of his background, while the manicure was part of his statement about his current stature.

Standing by Steve's wall of windows, Gabe looked out over the Hudson and Jersey as the late afternoon sun shone on them. Both men were silent while the manicurist packed and left, and Gabe took a seat at Steve's over-sized glass-top desk. Only then did Steve ask, "What's the problem, Gabe?"

Gabe had decided he had to put a halt to Homeland Security manipulating him and eliminate any threat to Jasminn and Matt. He had a plan and Steve's aid was critical to its success. AS well, if he had to fall back on legal action, Steve would be a huge plus. Sitting across the desk from each other, Gabe told Steve almost everything, including the turn in his relationship with Jasminn. The only detail he omitted was his new arrangement with Justin. Steve took no notes and didn't interrupt, just listened closely, leaning back with his thick hands steepled on his chest. Sometimes he nodded and sometimes he got an angry expression and shook his head and sometimes he arched an eyebrow a tad. Uncharacteristically, and startling Gabe, at one point Steve launched forward and gave his desk's extra-reinforced glass top a vicious slap.

Done, Gabe sat back and waited.

Steve's initial response fooled Gabe. "I'm really glad about Jaz. I never understood what was holding you two back. Your aunt will be thrilled too."

Steve then focused on Homeland Security. "Of course, they've violated a multitude of laws, but if we play it that way they'll just play the national security card." As he spoke, he tilted his chair back so far Gabe was afraid that the chair would tip over. But, like so much in Steve's life, the chair was designed to serve him, and it held firm.

Gabe said, "I tried citing that and got nowhere and escalating it could be risky. I do have another idea though."

Steve flipped one hand slightly, signaling Gabe to proceed.

"I believe," Gabe began, "that the best way to handle this is through administrative channels. I researched DHS' senior personnel. I discovered that one of your college frat brothers, whom you also went to law school with, recently moved over there as its Deputy General Counsel."

Steve asked who, and in response to Gabe's answer, Steve rubbed an index finger against his cheek, remembering the fellow. "Ah yes,"

Steve said. "He didn't do too well in law school. I'm glad he's made something of himself."

Steve continued, his speech picking up speed as he worked out his strategy. "One of your firm's senior partners, Jill, was our year in law school, and while none of us were close, she and I both know the new Deputy. I think that I, assuming your permission, together with Jill, should meet with him. Depending upon everyone's schedule, in particular the Deputy's, it may take a few days, but we'll have the meeting as soon as possible. I'll make clear how outraged I am at what the Department is doing to my favorite nephew—I won't tell him you're my only nephew—and Jill undoubtedly will be furious about the Department's interference with her brightest young superstar. We'll add the standard threats about their illegal acts, our taking legal action and the unavoidable press leaks. I'm confident that the Deputy will want to cooperate fully, and they'll cease bothering you."

Gabe smiled and Steve said, "I gather that sort of approach is what you had in mind."

Gabe nodded. "Everything but the Jill part, but that's all the better assuming she'll go along."

"She will, and it will be fine."

If, instead of Gabe, the person on the other side of Steve's desk had been the CEO of one of Steve's multinational corporate clients, this was the point in the conversation when Steve would have made clear to the client how difficult the situation was, reminded the client of Steve's track record and acknowledged woefully that without Steve, and "Oh yes, his firm," the client would be in serious trouble, but now everything would go as well as it possibly could. Steve spared Gabe this speech.

Gabe had little doubt that Steve and Jill could handle the DHS at the senior level. "What about Smith and Jones? Will they just accept this?"

"If they don't want to be dismissed plus brought up on charges they will. Our new Deputy might even have the General Counsel's office punish them anyway to clearly establish his authority."

Gabe looked out the windows over Steve's shoulder. He placed one elbow onto his chair's padded arm, cupped his chin and asked, "What about the FBI?"

Steve disliked being questioned or challenged, even by his "favorite" nephew, and he held his head erect as he frowned. "It goes without saying that we'll have the DHS arrange for the Bureau to leave you alone too. In fact, I'll insist that they both mark this incident as "Classified" and attach an order restricting contact with you." Steve paused, took a deep breath, and smiled at Gabe.

Gabe nodded.

"So as my client," Steve continued, "do I have your permission to engage Jill as co-counsel and for the two of us to pay a visit to DC?"

Gabe nodded again.

"Good. We'll certainly talk before then, but I'll see you at our next Sunday dinner. And Jasminn better be with you. In the meantime, stay out of trouble."

Gabe thanked Steve and rose to leave. However, before he took a step, Steve said, "Ten Dollars."

"What?"

"Put ten dollars on the desk. That's the fee for Jill and my services. Expenses are *gratis.*"

Gabe smiled, plunked down a ten and as he was leaving thought, *the best ten bucks I've ever spent.*

CHAPTER THIRTY-TWO

It only took Justin a day to make the arrangements and get the equipment he wanted, so it was two mornings later when he and Gabe met. They rendezvoused at the staircase leading up to the Campbell Apartment bar at Grand Central. The night before, Justin had texted Gabe's burner, telling him what to wear and a list of clothes and assorted odds and ends to carry in his backpack.

As directed, Gabe showed up in a suit. Justin had said, "Often the best disguise is to look like what you are." That had made little sense to Gabe, but he didn't argue. Gabe had started the morning by storing his regular phone at the nearby gym branch so Smith and Jones couldn't use it to track him.

Justin walked Gabe through his game plan. As part of the Bureau's current observation routine for Peter, on those days the Bureau was tracking Peter, one agent would follow him from his home in Brighton Beach to Manhattan where he was handed off to Justin. From there, Justin was on his own. Over several calls Justin had managed to get this first watcher assigned for a week straight. He'd gone through the motions of asking for support in Manhattan but was turned down as he was sure he would be and, as he wanted due to Gabe's involvement.

"Here's your wireless," Justin said. "Put it in your pocket and wear the earplug. It works like a two-way radio but on a Bureau-dedicated frequency. I'll be the eyes on him and you'll keep back a block or so. I'll direct you where to go and will tell you if I need you to cover a spot."

Shortly afterwards, Justin picked up Peter and started tailing him, generally staying about a half a block behind.

Gabe spent that day and the next and several hours of the day after that as the caboose. He and Justin kept up more chatter than he expected and at first he'd thought people would think he was crazy, talking into the air. However, early on the first day he realized that with blue tooth and other wireless devices, lots of people did the same. Someone from the past would have thought they were all crazy, but now people walking down the street talking into the air and gesturing was nothing out of the ordinary. Several times when he wasn't connected to Justin, to break up the monotony, Gabe talked aloud, spouting gibberish, but nobody paid any attention. Gabe told Jasminn he found the situation surreal.

Everything changed on the third day. Gabe was stationed on the northwest corner of Fifth Avenue and Forty-Eighth Street when over their radio Justin said. "Peter just entered the Palace Hotel through the Fiftieth Street doors. Get to the northeast corner of Fiftieth and Fifth and keep an eye out in case he cuts back that way. I'll be at Fifty-First and Fifth, watching that side entrance and the front."

Gabe felt a thrill of excitement as he ran up the two blocks, He cut between people, jay walked and darted across Forty-Ninth against the red light, receiving middle fingers from the two cabbies he dashed in front of—just a typical New Yorker. At his designated spot he leaned against a lamppost and said, "I'm here. What now."

"Now we wait. And Gabe, don't breathe so hard into the mic. It's annoying."

A few minutes later Gabe asked, "How long do you think he'll be in there?"

Justin's reply made his exasperation clear. "How would I know? He could've ducked in to use their toilets, so not too long; or maybe he's meeting someone for lunch, in which case it'll be longer." Speaking as if he was talking to a little child, he added, "We'll just have to be patient."

However, their answer came right then as Peter exited back out onto Fiftieth Street. Standing there, he lit a cigarette.

Gabe said, "He came out over here. What do I do?"

"Stay calm. If he starts walking toward you, walk away. Don't let him see you. If he heads for Madison, follow him and I'll cut down on Fifty-First and try to retake the point."

Peter looked up toward Fifth, and Gabe thought Peter had spotted him or was about to head in his direction. Instead, Peter turned in the opposite direction, strolling toward Madison. Feeling a mix of relief and disappointment, Gabe told Justin which way Peter was headed, then began pursuit. At Madison, Peter turned right, heading south. Gabe continued following, trying to hide behind people without losing Peter. A half block later Peter entered a restaurant. Gabe knew the place; it was an expensive hamburger joint. Gabe stopped two storefronts short of the restaurant and informed Justin who'd caught up.

"What do we do now?" Gabe asked. One glance at Justin's face gave him his answer. "We wait."

Justin nodded. "He knows both of us. Neither of us is going to go in there and if he sees us say 'Oh, what a coincidence'."

"There's nothing else we can do?" Gabe had grown tired of the frequent waiting.

"There's one thing we can try. Do you have twenty dollars?"

Gabe looked sideways at Justin, but he pulled two tens and a twenty out of his pocket. He held up the bills for Justin to pick. Instead, Justin grabbed all them then studied the passerby's. Soon he saw a woman who fit his criteria. She looked to be in her late forties, wore a simple blue dress and carried a large shopping bag rather than a purse. Justin stepped in front of her and flashed his FBI badge. Gabe couldn't hear them, but saw the woman retreat a step and shake her head. Justin kept talking and held up the bills. She looked pensive as if deciding whether he was for real, then after more discussion, she nodded.

Justin handed her a ten and she traipsed into the restaurant. Justin moved to the front window and looked between the menus plastered on it. She stopped near the back and looked around for a few moments. A waitress approached her and said something. The woman shook her head and left, rushing to Justin who'd retreated from the window.

Gabe joined them just as the woman said, "I told the waitress I didn't see my lunch date, so I'd wait outside."

"Very slick," Justin said. "Did you see our guy?"

"Uh huh. He was sitting at a table with another man. It was sideways to me so I could see the other fellow too." She had a big grin.

Throughout this Gabe hadn't said anything, but then he asked what this other man looked like.

She smiled again and replied, "I work at an investment bank, and he looked like one of those fellows. He had on expensive gray slacks and an Italian-made cashmere jacket."

Gabe's face screwed up. "How could you tell all that?"

"I've worked there for over twenty years." She laughed." I know all the finest materials and manufacturers."

Justin interrupted. "Forget his clothes. What'd he look like?"

"Dirty blond hair, fair skin, kinda good looking. He was seated but maybe he's about this fellow's height," she said, pointing to Gabe.

Justin had his phone out, quickly slid his finger across the screen until he got to the picture he wanted and asked, "Is this him?"

The woman looked up at him, and her eyebrows raised. "I guess you FBI guys know what you're doing. Yeah, that's him. Now about...."

Looking over Justin's shoulder, Gabe stared at the picture while Justin smiled and said, "Yes of course." He reached into a pocket, pulled out the other Ten and the Twenty and handed them both to her.

Snatching the bills she asked, "Are they dangerous?"

"No," he replied. The woman's face fell slightly. "Just run of the mill white collar criminals. You've probably seen their type in your job."

"You know that I have," she said. She shoved the bills to the bottom of her shopping bag, then, as if this was an everyday occurrence, continued on her way.

"I thought you needed twenty," Gabe said.

"What can I say. She was a tough bargainer," Justin replied, the corners of his mouth turned up.

Gabe put aside the money issue. "Why'd you think to show her a picture of Tall Alex?".

"The description fit. Plus, Jasminn had told me that you two' d met with Peter and Tall Alex so I knew they had a connection."

"Oh right."

Gabe thought quickly. He'd forgotten that Jasminn had told him that she'd told Justin about meeting Peter and Tall Alex. He was sure though that she hadn't said anything to Justin about Alex being with the alt-right. Following Peter around wasn't getting anywhere, and if they found cause to arrest Peter, Justin was going to grab him for the Bureau. Gabe thought maybe he should change plans and focus on Alex and find a reason to deliver Alex to Smith and Jones. Not wanting to run the risk of losing Alex to the FBI, Gabe decided he wouldn't tell Justin about Alex being on the alt-right. He had one question though.

"Where'd you get a picture of Alex?"

"It's his booking picture from the night we were all arrested. I got it from the police."

Neither said anything more. They went and got their own lunches at a hot dog cart. Justin pulled out some money to pay for his. Gabe gave a fake cough and pointed with his chin at Justin's money.

"What?" Justin asked.

"It was my forty bucks you gave that woman. You can at least splurge and pay for my hot dog and soda."

Justin shook his head, but he paid.

Done eating, they waited, watching the restaurant.

"What do we do when they leave?" Gabe asked.

"If you were a real agent, I'd try to rush in a second team to follow Alex. Failing that, we'd split up and each take one."

Gabe said, "OK, let's do that."

Justin's lips tightened into a thin line. "You can't handle tailing someone on our own. Plus, you might get hurt."

"Damn it, Justin, let's get a few things straight. Yeah, you've got all this military and FBI training and experience. Maybe that makes you a combo hunting dog and killing machine, but I'm no slacker and can take care of myself. And you're not my boss. I'll do what I want. When they come out, if they split up, I'm following Alex."

Justin waved his hands in surrender. "Do what you want. But don't blame me."

After standing silently they walked to the end of the block to take up new positions.

Gabe asked, "Can we use these radio gizmos if they split up?"

"Unlikely. They're only for short distances. Unless those guys stay close to each other, you and I would get out of range. But we can still communicate via phone."

They split up and continued waiting. After what seemed a long time to Gabe, the two men left the restaurant. They tapped fists then Peter headed south while Alex took off going north.

Justin radioed, "Be careful Gabe, if he's working with Peter he could be more dangerous than he looks."

Gabe thought, *It may be worse than you know.*

CHAPTER THIRTY-THREE

Gabe took up the tail, keeping some distance behind Alex but trying not to lose him. Alex zig-zagged north on the avenues and east on the streets. Gabe wondered where he was headed. Justin had told him Alex lived on Park Avenue South and didn't work—one of the benefits of money—so Alex wasn't going to his home or an office. Soon Alex made his way up Third Avenue then turned right onto Fifty-Ninth Street.

Hustling to reach the corner and not lose him, it occurred to Gabe where Alex might be headed. *Shit. Is he headed to the tram to go to Roosevelt Island? What do I do then?* Gabe had no idea how often the tram ran but was afraid if they didn't take the same car Alex would be long gone by the time Gabe got across the river. He wasn't about to play comic book hero and hang on the car's bottom. If Alex did tram it, Gabe would just have to get on and make up a story.

Gabe closed the distance between them and by the time Alex reached Second Avenue, Gabe was not far behind. *And why shouldn't I take the same car? I just need a plausible reason why I'm going there.*

Alex was one of the first to board the tram. Gabe sped up and hopped in just before the tram's door slid closed. Gabe made his way through the other passengers toward Alex who was facing away, looking at Roosevelt Island.

"Alex, that you?"

Alex turned, saw Gabe and it was clear he was not pleased.

"Gabe."

"On the stairs I thought that was you. How you doing?"

Recovering, Alex replied, "All's good. And you?" Not waiting for an answer, he continued, "What're you doing on this thing?"

"Going to Roosevelt Island, of course," Gabe replied, grinning.

"I figured that. I meant why." Alex asked in a soft voice, "Does this have anything to do with Earl?"

"No. No heroics on the tram. Even if it did relate to Earl, you know he's got his top-secret mindset and I couldn't say anything."

Alex nodded, but the corners of his mouth turned down—if anything was happening with Earl, Alex wanted to know.

Ignoring this, Gabe went on, "My ride's work related. And you?"

"I've got a thing."

Not finding that particularly informative, Gabe followed up. "At the Tech Center? I hear that's where all the action is over there these days. Not that there'd been much action before."

They both chuckled since Roosevelt Island had been a dull, quiet family-centric place until the Tech Center changed that. The Cornell Tech Center had spurred technology development in the City by turning out entrepreneurial engineers and fostering start-up tech companies, so both of their excuses for going there sounded reasonable.

Alex's answer wasn't his usual smooth talk. "Yeah. At there. I'm seeing some people about a company they're launching. I'm also seeing some other people." He eyed Gabe closely. "And you?"

Gabe's work reference was a vague phony explanation, but he let it flow. "I'm playing tourist. Or to be precise, business tourist. I've done two deals involving companies generated by the Center and am starting another one. I've never been here, so figured I'd check it out."

They were both silent, taking in the three hundred-sixty degree panorama. The tram was moments from the station and Gabe was deciding how to play this. The prudent course would be to not say or do anything too aggressive, but he was frustrated by all that had gone on. He chose to push Alex and see if he learned anything.

As they stepped off at the Tramway Plaza, Gabe said, "You've got interesting friends. Makes me wonder."

Alex stumbled slightly; his face briefly went slack then he frowned. Composing himself, he said, "I don't know what you mean."

"Of course you don't."

They studied each other, Alex with a quizzical expression as he tried to figure what Gabe really meant, and Gabe with a firm stare. Without saying anything more, Alex walked away.

Gabe watched Alex rush off north while using his burner to message Justin, "On Roosevelt Island."

Gabe wasn't familiar with the island's layout, but he bought a map at the tram station and looked it over. The Tech Center was south of the tram, not north, so Alex wasn't headed there, at least not right away. It was clear that following someone there undetected would be difficult, even for a pro, much less for an amateur like Gabe whose subject knew he was there. The map showed only two main north-south roads. One was West Road, which went north along the island's west side. The other was Main Street which ran south on the east side and was where Alex had appeared to be headed. The two roads connected at several spots and there were a few smaller streets.

Gabe considered what to do. He was reluctant to follow behind Alex. He saw that a free Red Bus was waiting at the Plaza. From there the bus would go up West Road, then hook around and come back south on Main Street. Gabe hopped on the bus, hoping that along the way he'd spot Alex. It wasn't a great plan but was the best he had. The bus started off and Gabe sat back, keeping watch.

The bus had reached its route's northern end, looped around and was headed south. There was no sight of Alex. Gabe stayed on as the bus passed the Plaza and continued south under the Fifty-Ninth Street Bridge. Gabe planned on getting out at the Tech Center to look for Alex there. At that stop Gabe stepped off the bus, looked around and caught sight of Alex walking south along East Loop Road. The bus door had closed, but Gabe knocked, and the driver let him back on, giving him a puzzled look. Gabe pulled out his map to figure where Alex might be headed. Gabe decided to get off at the next stop for real, then wait to see if Alex went that far south. If Alex didn't show, Gabe would work his way back north. Reaching Southpoint Park, Gabe signaled to be let off.

"You sure this time?" the driver asked.

"I'm sure. Thanks for the ride."

Gabe took cover at a nearby building. He tried to estimate how long it would take Alex to get there. It was five minutes after Gabe's estimate, and Alex hadn't shown. Gabe was about to give up and head north when he spotted Alex heading further south.

The map showed that in that direction there was only the Smallpox Hospital, two small, unmarked buildings, and a park at the island's tip. Gabe knew the hospital was extremely old and had been a crumbled wreck for ages, though he'd heard some work had been done on it or was supposed to be done; he wasn't sure which.

Alex kept walking and Gabe followed, moving faster to shorten the distance between them. Alex reached one unmarked building. Gabe wondered if he'd go in, a mysterious building potentially being a good destination for a mysterious trek. Alex walked past it, not giving it a glance. *That leaves the hospital or the park,* Gabe thought.

Gabe jumped as his burner rang. "Yeah," he answered, assuming it was Justin.

"That's a nice way to answer your phone." It was Jasminn.

"Sorry, Jaz. I assumed it was Justin."

"Where are you?"

"Roosevelt Island."

"What're you doing there?"

He replied, "I'm tailing Tall Alex."

She was silent. After a long pause Gabe said, "Jaz? Jaz, you there?"

"I'm here. Why're you following Alex? I thought you and Justin were watching Peter."

"Peter and Alex met. When they split up Justin stayed with Peter and I took Alex."

"And now you're there on your own watching Alex, who we're guessing is extreme right wing and could be dangerous? Gabe, drop this and get out of there. I'm scared you could get hurt."

"Don't be scared. He doesn't know I'm following him, and if he did and started something I can deal with him. Hey, I can't stay on the phone, but I'll meet you and Matt at my apartment tonight as planned. If you beat me there, use your key."

Gabe disconnected before Jasminn could argue further and he silenced the ringer. Several other people were walking in Alex's direction and Gabe mixed in with them, giving him some cover. A metal fence surrounded the hospital's remains and, still a bit behind, Gabe could see Alex remove his cashmere jacket and carry it as he squeezed through an opening in the fence, then vanished among the ruins.

Gabe didn't want to rush in on Alex's heels. Instead, he lingered along the side of a small building near the hospital. He took off his suit jacket, stuffed it in his backpack and hid that behind the building. After waiting a few minutes, he worked his way through the same gap in the fence. Once through he moved cautiously. He didn't want Alex to spot him, but if Alex did, Gabe would say he'd come to check out the hospital ruins—the same reason he'd say he assumed Alex was there.

He went inside the hospital through a collapsed section of the exterior wall. *Inside,* an interesting term he thought, *since the hospital's ceilings and roof had collapsed, and the ground was open to the sky.* He didn't know which way to go, so randomly walked down what he figured was once a hallway running along the outer walls. Large sections of the top of the hallway's inner wall had toppled. However, from about Gabe's height down much of it still stood, although it had numerous cracks and holes. The surface beneath Gabe's feet was partly dirt and weeds, but mainly it was fragments of crumbled bricks and pieces of the wooden ceiling and slate roof. Thin trees and wiry bushes were situated about, having taken root over the years. Gabe watched each step, walking slowly and gingerly, taking care not to shift the debris and make noise.

He reached a doorway to an open space, perhaps once the building's main reception area. First peering in and seeing that Alex wasn't there, he stepped in and looked around. The condition here was little different than in the hallway, except the ground had fewer brick pieces and more remnants of the ceilings and roof. The trees and scrub were larger, benefiting from the sunlight the open area provided.

Gabe backed out and continued down the hall, coming to a cross hall heading deeper into the hospital. He took this hall and soon reached another intersection which he figured was close to the hospital's rear. Suddenly he heard faint voices coming from the far end of the new hall. Staying close to one wall and treading even more carefully, Gabe made his way toward the voices. At the end of the hall were the remains of a doorway. The voices were coming from inside.

Gabe edged close to that opening. Seeing a small hole near the bottom of the wall, he crouched down. Through it Gabe could only see the ground and the bottom of a wall across another open space. At first no one was in sight, and he couldn't tell from the voices how many people there were. Then several pairs of legs moved into his peephole's view, and across the room Gabe could see four pairs of pants up to about the knees—three pairs of camouflage pants and Alex's gray slacks. They were talking quietly and with a strong breeze that had picked up, Gabe could only make out fragments of what they were saying.

One voice said, "I still say we're damn lucky to have gotten away with leaving the cases here…" Gabe missed a few words. "…would have…disaster if … found."

Gabe recognized Alex's voice but could only catch bits. "I wasn't…. The place is closed…and with its shitty condition, tours aren't…. Plus there's the fence and not…come here."

The first voice replied, "Yeah, but…."

Alex said, "Did you want to…and play guard? If the FBI…you'd…in jail. Not only…they learned who you are…endangers the …. This way…worst…large setback,…lost, but they couldn't tie it to us."

Another voice: "Maybe…but.. would have felt better…a storage facility."

A third unknown voice said, "Risks there too. Those places…cameras and…of documentation. Afterwards…places' security…and the FBI pored over and as careful as we…lead."

"Look," Alex said, "It's done. We did… this way … and now…. almost ready to use them…. No point…now."

Alex's gray slacks headed toward Gabe, Alex kicking debris as he went. Gabe pulled back and looked around but had nowhere to hide. When Alex stepped through the doorway, Gabe would be discovered.

One man spoke loudly enough so Gabe could hear him. "Alex, you going back the way you came?" The rustling ceased. "Once we get the cases loaded do you want to come with us in the boat? We could drop you. Say at the Thirty-Fourth Street docks?"

"Maybe, let's see," Alex yelled, "Let's do this."

Gabe heard the rustling of Alex's steps moving away from him, then heard the men sliding on the remnants and booting pieces of bricks as they left, leaving a trail of voices and scattered debris. The sounds faded, but Gabe stayed put. He was wet with sweat, his thighs ached from crouching even for that short a time—nerves he guessed--and his mouth was bone dry. He slumped to the ground amidst the bricks.

Gabe looked through the hole—no pants in sight. Taking a deep breath, he slowly edged around the remnants of the doorframe and saw only empty space. Determined to push on, he headed to the doorway where, from the kicked rubble, he could tell the men must have gone. He moved quickly but quietly, following them down a hall. Gabe judged that he was nearing the hospital's southwest corner. He reached another broken doorway and stepped out to look.

Quickly, he ducked back, inwardly cursing himself for being a fool, and hoping he hadn't been spotted. Not hearing anyone heading his way, he poked his head out. The men weren't looking in his direction and mustn't have seen him. Through the rubble, they were rolling a handcart with a tarp covering a large load. Grunting, they shoved the cart over a door sill onto a gravelly area, then into a field of high grass. Gabe followed, tiptoeing past a second handcart with another tarp-covered pile. He looked out. It had rained during the night, making the men struggle to push the cart in the mud. Their attention focused on their work, Gabe slipped out and hid behind a tree near the edge of the grass.

The men and their cart were heading to the East River. Gabe could make out at the shore a boat's weather-protector top bobbing on the river. It was clear they were going to load their cargo—cases, one of them had said—onto the boat. The men were deep in the high grass, and it would take them several minutes to reach the boat and transfer their load. Gabe figured he'd have some time and ran back to inspect the second cart's contents. The tarp was lashed tight and at first Gabe couldn't get under it. Circling the cart, he spotted a dull metal gleam and saw that in one corner the tarp was not fully drawn. Straining, he managed to inch up the tarp, sliding it enough to uncover part of a dark green metal case.

He stopped, listening for the men, but heard nothing so continued tugging. The tarp caught briefly then snapped free and slid up further, exposing a large padlock. Gabe picked up a brick to smash the lock but stopped mid-swing. He doubted he'd break the lock, but he'd certainly leave marks, alerting Alex and the others. Plus, the case's far end was still under the tarp, so he couldn't open it even if he got past the lock. Abandoning the idea of a break-in, Gabe pulled the tarp back down.

He was breathing hard from the tension and his struggle with the tarp when he heard the men returning. He ran out and fled the ruins. Back outside the fence, Gabe ducked behind the building he'd used earlier. He grabbed his backpack and ran north, not stopping at any bus stop, instead continuing all the way to the Tram Plaza.

Soon he stood hanging onto a metal post in a rising tram car, still breathing hard while looking back at the shrinking Smallpox Hospital, wondering what Alex was planning and what he should do. His initial thought was they were dealing drugs, although nothing evidenced that. He realized what the cases reminded him of and recalled Alex saying something about being 'ready to use', and another man saying 'afterwards' and talking about the FBI. Gabe thought that the crates probably held guns and they must be planning an armed attack. But an attack by the Antifa or the alt-right and an attack on who or what? At first Gabe wasn't sure, but as he thought about it he became certain it was the alt-right—there was that old picture of Alex and what he'd supposedly said to Kate and Jasminn's reaction to what he'd said to her. *And.* he thought, *those guys with Alex seemed a lot more alt-right, not extreme left.* Gabe didn't believe the left would launch any armed attack but decided it didn't matter what side they were. Either way, the danger was real.

He called Justin, insisting he'd discovered a crisis and demanding that Justin meet him. He gave Justin the gym's address, twice refused to say anything more, and ended the call. Gabe continued staring back at Roosevelt Island, too busy thinking to pay attention to the view.

CHAPTER THIRTY-FOUR

Gabe exited the gym after retrieving his phone. Once out the door someone grabbed his arm and pulled him hard, dragging him into a neighboring doorway. It was Jones. Gabe tried to tug free but couldn't break the agent's grip.

"Cute trick, Kid. Where've ya been?" Jones demanded.

Gabe was rattled but stuck to his story.

"Here. Working out. Let go, Jones, damn it," he cried. He tried to break free, but Jones' grip was too strong.

"We know your phone was here, but you weren't. Clever, but we don't like games. Now, one last chance." Jones yanked Gabe's arm for emphasis, "Where were you and what were you doing?"

Gabe didn't answer. He stopped struggling, breathing hard but glaring at Jones. A sudden pain in his lip and the inside of his mouth stunned Gabe. He hadn't seen Jones' blow coming but felt the pain and the blood seeping from his split lower lip.

"Let him go, Jones."

Jones looked up and saw Justin standing there. Jones' face broke into a grin. He said, "Look who it is. You're not allowed near the Kid, Mr. FBI Man. Get lost." Jones taunted, "You could be reported."

Justin pointed at Gabe. "When I write you up for hitting him?"

Jones was focusing on Justin and Gabe used this to surprise Jones and yank free. Gabe backed away from Jones, spitting blood and wiping blood from his lip with his shirt.

"Jones, cool down before I wipe that smirk off your weasel face."

Jones laughed and the corners of his mouth lifted in a smirk. He and Justin moved into fighting stances, both ignoring Gabe.

Gabe looked at them and cried, "Are you two crazy? You can't fight now." He looked at Justin. "What I have to tell you's more important than you and Jones settling who's tougher."

Without shifting his eyes from Justin, Jones asked, "What's important? And what're you doing with this guy?"

Gabe continued pressing his shirt to his lip. With a partly muffled voice, he said, "Both of you back off and I'll tell you."

After hesitating, both men stepped back and relaxed their stances.

Jones said, "A parking garage's a few doors down. Let's talk there."

Jones led the way. He and Justin kept watching each other and Gabe followed, still holding his shirt to his lip. Jones stopped halfway down the garage's ramp, out of sight from above and below. Under a flickering light he looked from one to the other.

"So?"

"I'll explain," Gabe said, spitting out more blood and giving Jones an angry look. "I tailed Tall Alex this afternoon."

"Why?"

"Because I don't trust him." Jones rolled his eyes, but didn't interrupt. "I followed him to Roosevelt Island. There he joined three men. They were loading onto a boat cases they'd been hiding at the old Smallpox Hospital. I couldn't see the other men's faces or hear everything, but I heard some. They were talking about the cases. I'm almost certain they contain guns, although no one said that exactly."

Justin and Jones exchanged concerned looks.

Gabe continued. "My first thought was drugs, but then they said other things like being 'ready to use them' and the FBI investigating 'afterwards'. The worst is that I saw part of what I think is a weapons case."

Jones and Justin looked at each other again. In the garage's fluorescent light the dislike which had clouded their faces had given way to concern, and their game faces snapped into place.

"You definitely didn't see what's in these cases?" Jones asked.

"All I saw was part of the outside of one, nothing else."

Between spitting blood and wiping his lip, Gabe told them everything, including what he heard the men say, watching them cart a load to a boat; and partially uncovering the one case, which he described.

When Gabe finished, Justin said to Jones, "I assume you know about the missing WMDs."

"Yeah, and that sounds like those could be their cases."

Confused, Gabe asked, "What are WMPs?"

"It's 'WMDs'," Justin said. "Weapons of Mass Destruction. These are military weapons which by law civilians generally can't have. They include certain automatic machine guns, but also arms like rocket launchers and SAMs. This isn't public, but some have disappeared from military bases recently. Luckily, we're only talking hardware. No bio or chemical agents are missing, but still, this is serious."

"And you think these are those WMDs?" Gabe asked, looking from one to the other.

"We've no way to know, but it could be, and since it sounds like Alex is preparing to use whatever they've got, we can't take a chance," Justin replied.

Jones added, "We'd go after them even if they just illegally possessed regular arms, but WMDs drastically ramp up the stakes."

"They didn't say where they were taking the cases?"

"No." Gabe thought both agents appeared controlled but and excited. Jones was bouncing ever so slightly on the balls of his feet.

"Alex has to be put under twenty-four hour watch. You can get a team on that, can't you?" Jones asked Justin.

"I'm sure I can under the circumstances."

Gabe almost asked Justin about Peter, but since Justin hadn't mentioned him, Gabe kept quiet.

Justin said to Jones, "Antifas being armed like this is serious. We've got a lot to do. There's a hotel a block up. Let's set up there."

Gabe said, "Wait a second. You're assuming they're Antifa. I think Alex's fooled everyone, and he's actually with the alt-right."

Both agents looked at him in surprise.

"He's Antifa, Kid," Jones said.

"No, we think he's undercover for the right," Gabe replied.

"We?" Justin asked.

Gabe realized his mistake, but it was too late. "Jasminn and me."

Justin sighed, unhappy that she was this involved.

"How'd you two come up with that?" Jones demanded, not concerned about Jasminn, shifting his feet, and anxious to get moving.

Gabe showed them the picture on his phone of Alex with the alt-right group.

"This is an alt-right group as you can see from the insignias and stuff. See that guy there?" Gabe asked, pointing, "That's Alex."

They examined the picture.

"The blurry faced guy wearing sunglasses?" Jones asked.

"It may not be crystal clear, but it's not blurry. That's him. It proves what I'm saying."

"Hardly. That could be lots of people," Jones said.

Gabe was starting to panic. "I know you want it to be the left so you can claim they're the big menace, but it's the right behind this. This picture proves it plus I saw them and heard them. I'm telling you. You're wrong."

Justin tried to calm Gabe down. "Gabe, you say that's Alex. We can't be sure, but send me the picture and I'll forward it to the right people at the Bureau. Maybe they can determine that one way or another. We can't decide what side these men are on based on your impression. Either way though, right now our focus must be on finding and recovering those WMDs, whoever's got them."

Gabe couldn't disagree.

Justin continued, "Gabe, you go home and stay there. Since Alex saw you on the tram he might be suspicious and come after you to see if you know anything."

The three of them walked up to the street, Jones and Justin flanking Gabe until they'd put him in a cab and sent him home.

CHAPTER THIRTY-FIVE

Gabe's lip and the inside of his mouth were still bleeding when he got home and he thought *That goddamn Jones has one hell of a punch.* Jasminn and Matt were waiting for him there. When Gabe came in, Matt saw the blood, grimaced and turned away. After a stunned look, Jasminn grabbed ice cubes and paper towels, lay Gabe on the couch and started ministering to him. Matt avoided the others' eyes, went to a window and unmoving, stared out over the rooftops.

"Gabe," Jasminn asked, "Who did this to you?"

He muttered, "Homeland Security. Again."

Matt slowly turned to face them.

"This time only Jones had the pleasure. I guess Smith was busy."

Matt bent over part way, brought one hand to his mouth and bit its knuckles, then covered his face with both hands. Gabe and Jasminn stared. They'd never seen him like this.

"What's wrong big guy?" she asked.

He didn't answer. His shoulders heaved and he began crying.

Jasminn rushed over and reached up, placing a hand on his shoulder. "What is it?"

Matt sobbed for several minutes before she got him calmed him. He wiped his nose on one of his shirt sleeves then on a paper towel Jasminn shoved in his hand. His head remained lowered and his shoulders hunched. Barely loudly enough for them to hear, he said, "I'm sorry, Gabe. This's all my fault."

Confused, Gabe asked through his paper towels pressed against his mouth, "What's your fault?"

"Smith and Jones."

Gabe dropped the paper towels and bolted upright. "What're you talking about? How do you know them?"

"It's my fault you're in this situation. I'm sorry Gabe, I never thought anything like…."

Matt collapsed onto a kitchen stool, laying his crossed arms on the countertop and burying his face.

Gabe was on his feet, his mouth hanging open. Standing over Matt, he demanded, "What'd you do?"

It took some time before Matt was calm enough to explain. As he finally started, he avoided looking at them and skipped over a lot of details. Partway into it, Gabe took a seat at the counter opposite Matt, his eyes fixed on his old friend. He felt betrayed. While Matt spoke, Jasminn stomped around, punching the furniture. At one point Gabe had to restrain her from hitting Matt. At last she eased up and Matt could speak calmly, and he finished. Gabe was in shock but, despite being the victim, he gave no sign. He was also mad at himself for never questioning how Smith and Jones knew he was at the demonstration that night.

Matt finally looked up and made eye contact with Gabe. "Gabe, I knew this wasn't right, but I really believed it'd just be a little thing—and afterwards that'd be the end of it and we'd be rid of them. They warned me not to tell you. I'm such a fool."

"No, you're more than a fool. You're a big fucking dumbass and a coward," Jasminn yelled, spit flying from her mouth. Gabe had to hold her back again. "How could you do this to your closest friend?" Her face twisted in disgust. "Big Matt is really big chicken shit spineless Matt."

"I fucked up," he replied, braving only a quick look at her. Looking at Gabe he pleaded, "But I'll fix things. I'll go to the police and tell them everything."

Gabe had stayed quiet, but now he said, "We've got to think about this. I'm working on getting Smith and Jones off Jasminn and me, but now we have to protect you too."

"I can't believe you said that," Jasminn yelled at him, "You should kill this motherfucker. Your friend stabs you in the back to save his own ass and you're talking about protecting him?"

"I'm sure he didn't intend it that way." Turning to Matt he said, "You did screw up big time though."

To Jasminn, Gabe said, "There are several parts to this. I absolutely want them off our backs, and off them permanently, and yes I'm pissed as hell at Matt, but I don't want him going to jail."

"Right this minute, his staying out of jail is not high on my list of priorities." She was furious and wasn't getting past her anger.

"Understood. I'm not feeling too good about him right now myself, but still... "

"You're talking about me as if I'm not here," Matt said, almost whimpering.

"To me you're invisible and might as well not be here," she shot back.

Gabe broke it up.

"Matt, I want to record your story. I want you to go through it again in detail. Start at the beginning. Explain how they tricked you, then forced you into this. That means you have to say on the video what you did. Understand? Even though you say it wasn't your fault, it's an admission and in the wrong hands could be used against you."

"I understand. If I'd stood up in the first place this wouldn't have happened. "He looked from one to the other. "I'll do whatever you say Gabe. Whatever happens to me doesn't matter."

Gabe said he hoped it wouldn't come to that, while Jasminn said, "Thumbscrews and the rack. For starters."

Seeking to ease the tension and Jasminn's anger, Gabe quipped, "At least she didn't suggest the Iron Maiden."

Gabe took his and Jasminn's burners and set them up facing Matt to record audio and video. He played safe and plugged the phones in so they wouldn't run out of power during the taping.

Matt said he was ready. At first he spoke slowly, stammered and paused and didn't look directly into the phones, but he calmed down and improved as he went along. He started by stating his name and the name of the medium-sized but well known firm he worked for. He explained he traded options on futures on a blockchain algorithm similar to cryptocurrency and included a few other details, although few outside his field would understand any of this. He added that the quants and the computers hadn't yet taken over this space as it was too small for them.

He paused to look at Gabe and Jasminn. Off camera Gabe nodded and Jasminn motioned for him to continue, holding back from giving Matt the finger. Matt went on, saying how, as part of his normal trading, over a two-week period he'd downloaded onto his office computer several data nuggets, explaining this was standard for this type of trading. He explained that if a nugget had any bug or other malware, his company's computer system was supposed to block it. It turned out that the data nuggets' creators were better than his company's security experts, and when he downloaded the fifth nugget this triggered all the nuggets, and they began functioning together.

His voice got softer, so they waved for him to speak up.

"Right after I downloaded the fifth one, a message appeared on my screen. It wasn't an email or a message from another comm app. It was more like wallpaper. I was too stunned to take a screen shot, but I remember it. 'Thanks for your help Matt. We can now seize control of the company's systems whenever we want. We've deposited your first $20K. Write down this bank name, location and account number. You know our agreed password.' I was shocked but wrote them down. It ended, 'Much more money to come. Don't worry, security can't see this.' The message stayed up less than two minutes before vanishing. To put it mildly, I was freaked. I searched my computer for the message or anything else suspicious in order to delete it but found nothing.

"For the next few days I waited for my world to cave in—for tech people and security guards or the FBI to swarm in and haul me off. But nothing happened. I thought about contacting the bank named in the message, but didn't, figuring I shouldn't create a record of any communications. Anyway, I'd no idea what this password was, so couldn't have checked if money had been deposited. I didn't know what to do or even whether this was real or a really sick practical joke.

"That Saturday, to distract myself, I went to ball at an uptown court. I show up and people start yelling 'White Rocket'."

Jasminn and Gabe looked at him, confused. They'd never heard this nickname, but they kept quiet and Matt kept talking for the video.

Matt noted their surprise so explained. "I got that name because of my hops, but I keep it local. It's only for those courts. Anyway, I'm a star there so am picked right away. Amazingly, I'm playing great, really aggressively, I guess taking out my frustration on the other teams. We win five straight, take a break, and I get another 'White Rocket' chant.

"I'd noticed two guys watching through the fence. They clearly didn't belong. Scouts and agents sometimes show up looking for prospects, but these guys didn't look like either. During that break they sent a kid over saying they wanted to talk to me. Normally I'd wave them off, but the next game got held up because two players on the other team were fighting each other, so I went over.

"Before I get to say I'm not interested in whatever they're offering, one of them said something to the effect of 'We're not here for your ball playing. We're here about the message. The one that popped up on your computer.' He went on. 'Let's talk about whether you go to jail for taking twenty thousand dollars for helping us hack your company's computers.' I was stunned and denied doing anything. They kept saying that's not how the company's computer guys or the FBI would see it. We went back and forth. I skipped the next game, pissing off my team.

"They identified themselves as Smith and Jones and showed me Homeland Security IDs, shocking me that the government could be behind this. Smith did most of the talking, although Jones did most of the threatening. They admitted they'd framed me. They promised if I went along everything would vanish and I'd never hear from them again. I couldn't believe this was real and had a hard time not hitting them.

"Smith told me what they wanted. He claimed they were investigating extreme left-wing groups and they'd sent in their own undercover people but gotten nowhere. I asked what this had to do with me. They said I'd been ID'ed at some protests--as if it's hard to pick out a six-eight guy with blonde hair. Smith said, though, that they'd decided they couldn't use me as their spy.

"Jones said that they set me up because they wanted to enlist Gabriel Bentley but were sure he wouldn't cooperate if they simply asked him. They said they needed to force him. I said I wouldn't do anything against Gabe, and asked why Gabe, anyhow. Smith said he fit their criteria—smart and involved with some protests so he wasn't a stranger to people on the left. They said they'd seen that he had important ties, although I didn't know what they were talking about."

Gabe assumed they were referring to his actions at the demonstration at Gracie Mansion.

"I still said 'No', but in addition to threatening me with my supposed role in their hijacking the company's computers—and that was when they told me about the whole data nugget set-up—they then threatened to physically harm Jasminn Cummings. They swore that if I went along they wouldn't hurt Jasminn or Gabe. I didn't trust them, but I had no choice and agreed to do the one thing they asked. This was to message Gabe to come to a protest when they told me to. I felt like shit but didn't see any other option. Then, several days later, when they instructed me to do that and told me what to text, I did it."

Matt stopped, and they stopped the recording.

Jasminn walked around to Matt and hugged him from behind. "Sorry Matt, I didn't know."

Gabe held up one of the phones, saying, "I know what to do with this."

A little later a courier picked up the phone and delivered it to Uncle Steve along with a short note from Gabe.

Despite Gabe's efforts to make Matt feel better, Matt soon went off with his tail between his legs, as Jasminn put it.

Gabe and Jasminn spent a long time talking about Matt, then he told her about Tall Alex and what had taken place with Justin and Jones and the WMDs. They spent the rest of the night trying to put aside Smith and Jones and everything that'd happened, but they couldn't and ended up in Gabe's bed taking turns hugging each other.

CHAPTER THIRTY-SIX

Earlier, after putting Gabe into a cab, Justin and Jones went to the hotel Justin had mentioned. He and Jones flashed their badges and asked for the manager. Within a few minutes they were set up in a far corner of the lobby restaurant which the manager reopened for them. From there they hit their phones and coffee and sandwiches soon appeared.

Justin's alert about 'WMDs' set off alarms at the Bureau. In most circumstances, Justin's limited information wouldn't have been enough to trigger an instant and powerful response, but the letters 'WMD' were magic, black magic. They immediately got him twenty-four hour surveillance on Alex. A Bureau division began monitoring for any use by Alex of his ATM or credit cards. The NSA was brought in and tasked to track his phone. The Bureau's New York office was put in charge of the on-the-ground work. In preparation for the moment of reckoning, an FBI SWAT team was called to assemble at a staging facility. This team was to remain at the ready until the WMDs were found and recovery was authorized. While this went on, other Bureau and Justice Department personnel handled the legal necessities and bureaucratic niceties. They contacted the Mayor's office and the New York City Police and began coordinating activities, including having the NYPD send a SWAT team to join the FBI's team. The situation was added to the President's intelligence briefing for the next morning.

The Bureau still believed Alex was Antifa, so in addition to recovering Alex's presumed WMDs, the agencies planned for the possibility that Alex's group didn't have all the missing WMDs, but that other Antifa groups were also planning attacks using them. Who these other Antifa groups might be was highly uncertain. In response though, the FBI and Homeland Security went on high alert throughout the country and obtained warrants for raids on suspected Antifa members.

Jones' task was simpler. From the moment he and Justin concluded that an imminent WMD attack was possible, preventing it and recovering the WMDs became the FBI's responsibility and, to the extent the Bureau chose to involve them, the local police. Homeland Security had little role unless brought in by the Bureau. Justin surprised Jones by offering to let him and Smith take part in what lay ahead.

///

Jones' first call had been to Smith. When the call came, Smith had been at his Weehawken apartment, slouched on one end of his couch while a rom-com played quietly on the television and his current lady friend slept on the couch with her head on his lap.

Jones' call shook Smith and he'd sat upright, trying not to wake the woman and lightly stroking her hair while he mulled things over. *This was bad…in many ways.* He thought, *One positive aspect was that the Bureau was blaming the Antifa. The other plus was Justin including them.* Smith intended to use that to clean up some problems. Gently, he'd slid his lady's head off his lap and rested it on a pillow. He went out to the patio, thinking about Gabe and Tall Alex. Jones hadn't explained how they'd become intertwined, but their connection required special consideration. Jones also hadn't said whether the FBI was protecting Gabe, but that was their decision, and if they erred and didn't, it would be the Bureau's responsibility.

He texted Jones to get them DHS SWAT gear and a car. Both agents had standard issue handguns, but Smith decided to take his personal long barrel Magnum Research Desert Eagle in addition. If he needed to use a gun, he wanted one with maximum stopping power—certainty of results being the goal.

Smith decided that there was no point in his crossing the river until they had Alex in their sights. He hoped that wouldn't be until after he got to spend a little more time with his lady friend—after all, one never knew how things would play out.

Before returning inside, Smith made one call: "It's me. Some issues have arisen. I'll take care of them and fill you in afterwards."

///

Gabe sensed movement. He and Jasminn were in his bed and she was asleep. He lay still, thinking whether he had anything to use as a weapon, but nothing was close. Sounds were coming closer, then he heard whispering—there was more than one person. Gabe was scared.

He wouldn't wait for the unknown people to reach them. He jumped up, screamed and leaped at them. He thought he was engulfed by Peter, Tall Alex and Short Alex, then a light went on.

A voice cried, "Gabe."

It was Jasminn. He was sprawled across the bed, drenched in sweat, and her arms were wrapped around him, softly crooning over and over, "It's OK, Gabe. Everything's OK."

He clung to her, confused.

"You must've had a nightmare."

She kept soothing him until he calmed down and he described the dream. They agreed it didn't take Freud to figure out why Peter and Tall Alex were in Gabe's nightmare, but they couldn't figure out why Short Alex was with them. Gabe showered, and for the rest of the night they lay there holding each other until finally falling asleep.

///

Saturday morning was beautiful. The sky was a bright blue, not a cloud in sight, the sunlight had a golden tint and the temperature was pleasant. Gabe and Jasminn slept late, and when they awoke all thoughts of Gabe's nightmare were gone. However, as they dressed and ate they couldn't get over what had happened yesterday—Gabe tracking Alex and finding the WMDs and Matt's confession.

"What do we do about Alex? There must be something. We can't do nothing," Jasminn said.

"Like what?"

"I don't know. You've got Alex's number. We could call him."

"And say what? 'Hi, let's get together if you're not too busy with your WMDs.'?"

She gave him a dirty look. "Hey, I'm trying to help."

"I know you are," he said, putting his arm around her, "and I love how brave and determined you are, but I don't see what we can do. The FBI and Homeland Security must be all over this; watching Alex, if they haven't already arrested him or brought him in for questioning."

"How about you call Justin and see if we can learn anything?"

Gabe tried, but Justin didn't answer so Gabe left a message.

"We're supposed to meet Matt to practice for that tournament," he reminded her.

"Do you really feel like playing, and wouldn't it strike you as ridiculous for us to go play basketball or think about the tournament when we know all of this is going on?"

"Yes, it does, and if there was anything we could do to help, we should be doing that instead, but I can't think of anything. In fact, it's clear that Justin and Jones want us to stay away. Also, there's Matt. If we don't show he'll be convinced it's because of what he did and he'll be that much more broken up."

They went back and forth but finally decided they should go as originally planned although neither really wanted to. Having decided, they headed uptown for Jasminn's basketball gear. Gabe wore his and carried a change of clothes in his backpack.

The court where they were to meet Matt was near Jasminn's apartment. She and Gabe beat Matt there. They hadn't been practicing and Gabe still wasn't one hundred percent physically, so unless the White Rocket blasted off they'd gone from front runners to long shots.

Matt was late, so Gabe texted him. While waiting they half-heartedly played two-on-two against two high school seniors they knew from the court. Both teens were headed to mid-level Tier II schools on basketball scholarships, and while Jasminn played well despite her mood, Gabe didn't and they lost every game.

By their third loss, Matt still hadn't shown or texted back so Gabe called him.

Matt's phone rang several times before he answered it, "Hey."

"Why aren't you here?"

"Gabe, I can't play with you guys." Matt's sadness came through the phone. "There's no way after what's happened. You can't want me."

Gabe spent several minutes unsuccessfully trying to convince Matt that they still wanted him, "After all," he said, "who wouldn't want the White Rocket?"

Jasminn had followed Gabe's side of the call. After he disconnected, she said, "You're much more forgiving than I am."

Without Matt they called it a day. The teens took a break and they left together. Parting, one said, "Sorry about Matt not playing. With him you guys were the odds-on favorites. Maybe next year."

Gabe and Jasminn went into the building, its reinforced front door locking securely behind them.

None of them noticed the two men lurking behind a nearby parked truck.

CHAPTER THIRTY-SEVEN

Tall Alex wasn't superstitious, but the gorgeous morning struck him as a good omen. Today they would strike a powerful blow, with more to come. He had only one concern, but was confident his new ally would handle it. Alex had plenty of time, and he didn't rush. He went to a café where he enjoyed brunch and a bloody mary—he figured why not. Done, he left a generous tip then started strolling west and south. He took his time, enjoying the weather.

Unknown to Alex, the Bureau surveillance team had staked out his building and started following him as soon as he left it that morning. Their hope was that he'd lead them to the WMDs, rather than them having to take him in and sweating him for their location. Alex and his secret entourage continued along until he received a text from Peter: "Spotted. Waiting for opening." The NSA captured a copy of it and forwarded it to the FBI, but neither agency knew what it meant.

Smiling, Alex hailed a cab, directing the driver, who was a member of the surveillance unit, to take him to the Spring Street Salt Shed—the surveillance team picking up Alex's destination through the cab's mics. The Salt Shed is one of the many structures in which the City's Sanitation Department stores the salt it uses to combat snow and ice on its streets. The Salt Shed is unique though—rather than being a typical-shaped building, it more resembles a salt molecule. It has a steep sloping roof reaching seventy feet at its peak and is connected to a repair shop operated by the department to service its vehicles.

"You an architect going to check out the Salt Shed?" the driver asked, hoping to get Alex talking.

"No. Just meeting somebody by there."

The driver tried once more to prompt Alex to talk, but he got nowhere so gave up, not wanting to make Alex suspicious.

Now knowing where Alex was headed, an FBI van took off, using its siren to cut through traffic. It let out agents near the Salt Shed and was parked a few blocks away before the intentionally slow-moving cab got there. Soon additional agents arrived, and they dispersed, taking up positions across the highway in Hudson River Greenway. Other agents set up on side streets, surrounding the Salt Shed, but staying hidden.

"Pull over here," Alex said, directing the driver to drop him in front of a metal gate. The gate was crisscrossed by thick metal beams and blocked the Shed's Canal Street entrance. Using a call box next to the gate, he was buzzed into the wide courtyard designed to handle salt trucks, then made his way into the Shed. An agent across the street broadcast "Subject," as Alex was now called, "has entered the Shed."

Within minutes, an FBI Mobile Command Center, disguised as a double-length cable news truck, parked two blocks below the Salt Shed. Special Agent in Charge Tina Perez of the FBI's New York headquarters had command of the operation. She was set up in the Command Center with her team of Special Agents and technical personnel. With them were liaisons from the Mayor's office and the Police Department. As the agent on the case, Michael Yang—as the Bureau knew Justin—was there.

The consensus in the Command Center was that whatever Alex had removed from the hospital yesterday, presumably missing WMDs, was now in the Shed. *Why else would Alex go there?* The SWAT team leaders urged an immediate offensive. Due to political concerns, the Mayor's representative opposed any action absent proof the WMDs were there. Perez was determined not to let any WMDs slip through her fingers, but she didn't want a large-scale urban SWAT action on her record unless essential so vetoed an immediate offensive. Instead, she ordered the surveillance group and the SWAT teams to conduct a full reconnaissance and develop an assault plan for her consideration in case an assault became necessary.

The Bureau and other agencies took additional steps. They set up a hidden camera to monitor the main entrance, and one on the second floor of the adjoining repair shop, and At Perez's request, the Mayor's Office had the Buildings Department provide blueprints of the Shed.

Justin let Jones know what was happening, and soon Jones and Smith joined him at the Command Center. Perez permitted them to sit in, although she made it clear they had no authority.

Every so often men would appear at the Shed's gate, buzz and be let in. The FBI assumed that a force was assembling in the Salt Shed. SWAT pushed for immediate action. Perez held off, but as more men arrived, she began to waver. Her decision might have been different if she'd known that men were already there before the Bureau had arrived.

In the early afternoon the two SWAT team leaders briefed Perez. Bradford Rosen was the FBI Special Agent in Charge of the Bureau's team, and Captain Pulaski headed the city's force.

As everyone crowded around in the Command Center, Rosen reported on the key factors for an assault. "We've gone over the Shed's blueprints. The Shed is stronger than any structure we've assaulted going back as far as I know of. I'll tell you up front, storming this building creates a significant risk of casualties on our side, especially if a well-armed trained force is in there and prepared. The walls are six feet thick concrete with an interior metal lining." The assembled group exchanged looks.

"The place has no windows. Its main entrance is through the courtyard truck entrance which is over twenty feet wide so is an exposed field of fire. It has a roll-down metal door, basically a giant garage door. We think blasting that door is our best way in. Despite its size, the Shed has only two regular doors, one leading in from the courtyard and the other from the repair shop. Except for those doorways, and blasting the roll-down, it'd be like attacking a fortress."

Rosen's audience muttered among themselves.

"What about the two doors?" Perez asked.

Rosen nodded to Pulaski who stood and answered her. "Entering through regular doors is the norm, but slows force insertion, making our people more vulnerable as they enter and slowing our buildup. We generally counter this with gas, flash/bangs and other deterrents. Smoke helps. However, this interior is so large that all these would only be effective on anyone near a door when we triggered them—those deeper inside wouldn't be affected and potentially could fire immediately."

Someone asked, "From in there can they see out?"

Rosen replied, "Not from the repair shop, but 'yes' from inside the Shed. There're cameras on either side of the truck door covering the courtyard. Assuming someone's watching their monitors, they'd spot us at the gate. A ground assault from there would not have the element of surprise."

For the first time since he and Jones had arrived, Smith spoke up. "What about visual access to the inside?"

Rosen shook his head. "It's no good. We can access the opening to the main vent from the repair shop, but the vent's too steep for our robot."

Perez huddled with her closest assistants then ordered the SWAT teams to remain ready if needed. They continued waiting.

CHAPTER THIRTY-EIGHT

Back from the court, Gabe and Jasminn showered at her place, then left to go eat. They got only a few steps when Gabe's nightmare was realized. Peter stepped out from behind a parked van and stood several feet in front of them. Jasminn instinctively looked behind them. Dimitri was standing there, blocking the sidewalk. Jasminn's eyes widened— Dimitri had a sweatshirt slung over his right arm but sticking out from underneath it a gun barrel pointed at them.

"Gabe," she gasped.

Gabe looked back quickly and saw the gun. He snapped his head back to Peter and saw a gun poking out of Peter's windbreaker.

Gabe started to say something, but Peter commanded, "Quiet. Not a word."

An old station wagon pulled up. Peter led them over, pointed to its large cargo section and ordered, "Get in." He made them lie on the section's bed while he sat up front and, having learned from Jasminn, he took their phones, removed their sim cards and batteries and tossed these out the window. Dimitri sat next to them, his gun in hand.

"What the fuck you doing, Peter?" Gabe demanded.

"Shut up," Peter growled.

Dimitri rapped Gabe on the shoulder with his gun, reinforcing the message, then threw a blanket over them, concealing them from any prying eyes. The blanket was thin and it let light in, allowing each of them to make out the shock and fear on the other's face. Jasminn grabbed his hand.

///

Just minutes after Gabe and Jasminn were grabbed, in D.C. Uncle Steve and Jill finished meeting with Homeland Security's Deputy General Counsel. The Deputy hadn't wanted to give up his Saturday, but Steve had insisted. On the street outside the Department's offices, Steve hit Gabe's name on his phone's contact list. Instead of Gabe answering, the call went directly to voice mail: "Gabe, Jill and I took care of everything. Orders will be issued and despite the usual bureaucratic b.s., both agencies will be off you within twelve to twenty-four hours. Just stay out of trouble in the meantime. Tell Matt that the Department will handle his firm, so he'll be fine too. In addition, you'll be assigned protection until this is cleaned up. All's well."

///

In the FBI's Command Center, after a long wait and lots of grumbling, everyone got excited when, for the first time since the vigil started, a car pulled up to the gate. It might mean nothing, but at least it was activity. A man exited the car and used the call box. Through the camera they'd set up in the repair shop, the people in the Command Center could see his face.

Simultaneously, Jones and Justin cried out, "That's Pietrov."

Justin continued, explaining, "He's a foreign agent. We thought he might be working with Alex. This proves it."

The gate slowly rolled back, letting the car into the courtyard. As it did, Jones startled everyone by shouting, "The Kid's in there."

The door to the truck entrance rose enough for the car to drive underneath, then it immediately rolled down. Smith told the others who "the Kid" was, and the camera's recording was backed up, replayed slowly and zoomed in on the car's cargo section. To Justin and the Homeland Security agents there was no doubt that the face peeping up from the back was Gabe's.

The Mayor's representative asked, "Any chance this guy works with the Subject and for some reason they're sneaking him in?"

Smith shook his head. "Not a chance. Gabriel's not Antifa. He's the one who tracked the subject to the WMDs and alerted the Bureau." Smith eyed Justin. "Alex must be on to him and had Pietrov snatch him. That wouldn't have happened if the Bureau'd protected him."

Nobody argued.

Perez said, "If you're right, then on top of the WMD situation we have a kidnapping and hostage situation."

Afraid of the possible political repercussions of an armed assault, the Mayor's representative urged, "We should still wait. There's no reason to assume anything will happen to him."

The Bureau personnel gave the speaker looks ranging from disbelief to disgust.

Perez said to him, "That's not how we operate." She announced, "but we've got to find out what's going on in there."

Rosen said, "The robot's no good, but one of my men could go in through a vent. He could carry a wireless camera and look through the vent's grillwork." He thought for a second then continued. "Whoever goes in, he'd have to strip off his body armor and everything else that could make noise. If they heard him they'll shoot and he'd be defenseless. Maybe as bad, it'd tip them to our presence."

At this point Perez was more concerned about knowing the situation inside the Shed than she was about these risks. "Do it," she ordered, "and prepare for an assault. We should be ready to launch it immediately, depending upon what we see."

Rosen left the Command Center followed by Justin.

"Tough assignment, Rosen."

"Yeah, Yang," Rosen replied, turning toward him and pulling a pack of cigarettes from one of the many pockets in his fatigues. He took one and held out the pack to Justin.

Justin shook his head. "Hey, Rosen. Tell me. Have you been paying close attention to the Shed's walk-ins?"

"Of course." Rosen paused for a moment. "Actually, I'm somewhat surprised by them. They're almost all big tough looking guys and there haven't been any women."

"And many look like ex-military," Justin said.

"I saw that. Not my sense of the typical Antifa," Rosen said, edging off as he was anxious to get to his men.

"Maybe because they're not Antifa."

Rosen stopped, faced Justin and studied him closely, shielding his eyes from the sun. "What're you suggesting?"

"They could be alt-right."

Rosen's brow furrowed and he raised his voice. "Yang, this is an action authorized against an armed Antifa group."

Justin held up both hands, signaling for Rosen to stay calm. "I know. Look, the focus is the WMDs, but I have evidence suggesting that the Subject may be alt-right. I didn't put much credence in it before, but seeing those guys who've been showing up and Pietrov having Gabe makes me think…."

"You've brought this to Perez's attention?" Rosen asked.

"I just tried to, but she's focused on the WMDs, and she's right. I'm telling you because when your guys go in, they shouldn't assume they're dealing with an untrained disorganized group. They should know they may be taking on hardened soldiers."

"Thanks, Yang. That matters. We'll be prepared."

Rosen started walking away.

Justin called out after him, "One other thing."

Rosen looked back partway.

"When you go in, I want to be with you. I've been involved with this from the start and have to see it through."

Rosen respected Justin for this. "Fine with me, but Perez has to approve it."

"I'll bet the Homeland Security guys will want in."

Rosen sighed, not wanting them. "Again, it's Perez's call, but I'm going to object. If they are included, they'll definitely be last in. I'm not risking them getting in the way of my men.

///

Covered by two guards carrying machine pistols and stiff from being crammed in the car's rear, Jasminn and Gabe stretched their muscles and looked around. They saw mountains and smaller piles of dirty, brownish-colored salt. They were mystified as they had no idea what the piles were for or where they were. They could see the activity going on—mainly men wearing black bloc or in the process of donning i and loading rifles and machine guns.

Gabe quietly said to Jasminn, "Looks like a heavily armed extreme leftist group. I assume those are some of the WMDs Jones and Justin were worked up about, but this makes no sense to me."

She said, "This must be Alex's operation, but what's Peter doing with him?" She thought. "Maybe Alex doesn't know Peter's a foreign agent and thinks he's on Alex's side, whichever side that really is."

"I don't know, and I don't get why they brought us here."

He could see Jasminn hugging herself, the pronounced wrinkles in her brow and the tremble in her lips. She was scared, and although he wasn't showing it, Gabe was just as scared. He put an arm around her to comfort them both.

"We'll be OK," he said, not convincing either of them.

Meanwhile, other than their guards, no one paid them any attention and they continued to look around unmolested.

CHAPTER THRITY-NINE

In the repair shop, Rosen's men took command of the vent's access area. Rosen knew the best man for the assignment was Agent Barnes, and Barnes volunteered as soon as Rosen told his team what was needed. Barnes was thin but wiry-strong and was an experienced free climber.

Barnes stripped down to his underwear. His boots would make noise against the metal vent and socks would be too slippery, so he'd go barefoot. He put on a wireless headset, they strapped a wireless video camera to him, and then hoisted him up into the vent's opening.

Barnes told Rosen, "Don't worry, sir. This is no big deal compared to rock faces I've climbed," then he set off. Barnes didn't point out that normally he wore special shoes and other gear and didn't climb in just his skivvies, as another agent had put it. In turn, while Rosen thought the climb was doable normally, he was sure Barnes had never climbed while risking being shot at, but he said nothing.

The inside of the vent was slick and there was nothing Barnes could use for leverage. The vent started out rising sharply, almost a sixty-degree incline according to the building plans, ran horizontally for a short distance then angled up again until it ran flat. Barnes ascended the first upward slope by wedging his hands, elbows, knees and feet against the sides, and used them as leverage to climb and stop himself from slipping back. At the top of this rise he boosted himself onto the first flat stretch. Barnes rested briefly then scuttled across this section to the first grillwork which was at its far end. He looked through the grill but saw nothing other than a large mound of salt. He could hear voices but couldn't make out what was being said. He shrugged, whispered a report back to Rosen, and began the next climb. This one wasn't as steep, only forty degrees, but halfway up a screw gashed his left foot and big toe. He lost his hold and slid a body length before managing to brace himself. He held his position, not moving, in case the people inside had heard him and were searching for the noise's source. Despite the muscle pain from straining to hold his position, he silently counted slowly to sixty. Not having been fired upon, he started working his way up again. This time he felt for sharp objects before resting his weight anywhere. His foot bled steadily, but by keeping his weight to its outside it didn't hamper him much.

Barnes reached the top of the second rise. Without resting he crawled along the second horizontal stretch until he reached the next grill. He carefully peeked through it, pulled his head back and whispered into his mic, "Jackpot."

Barnes' camera's lens was attached to the head of a cable, like an eraser on a flexible pencil. Barnes worked the cable so its head barely poked through an opening in the grill. With that, a technician in the Command Center could rotate and angle the lens, adjusting the camera's view. As a result, they could now see much of the Shed's interior. Salt mountains and some smaller mounds were piled against most walls, sloping inward down to the cement floor. Some of the piles had open spaces between them—looking down on them, one member of Perez's staff commented that they resembled cement fjords. Perez gave the woman a harsh look; topography lessons not being what she wanted.

The center area was intended for unloading and loading salt, but no salt trucks were there. However, the building was far from empty. The people in the Command Center could see three vans off to one side and roughly forty men within view. Most wore black bloc, although without face coverings. Some were in the process of putting on black bloc over their own clothes and more outfits lay piled on the floor as if awaiting more men. Two crumpled tarps were visible lying next to two barren handcarts and metal cases spread out. A myriad of weapons lay next to the cases and most men held weapons—for the benefit of the non-Bureau viewers Perez identified these as fully automatic machine guns. FBI observers picked out two rocket launchers and a SAM, open cases with grenades and more automatic machine guns.

The sight of the WMDs and men wearing black bloc incited a wave of excitement in the Command Center and a flurry of action, including calls to officials in Washington and a heated debate about whether to strike. They now knew that at least some of the missing WMDs were in the Shed and they presumed that the men in black bloc confirmed that this was an Antifa operation. Nevertheless, Perez decided to hold off a little longer, hoping something would improve the situation.

After the center section of the Shed with the WMDs had been carefully studied, Perez ordered the technician operating the lens to rotate the camera. She found Gabe and, to their surprise Jasminn, off to one side under guard. Seeing her, Justin bent his head and shook it, mad that she'd gotten in so deep that she'd ended up in there.

CHAPTER FORTY

While Barnes was in the vent, the SWAT teams and the police were busy. Previously, to avoid alerting anyone, none of the nearby streets had been blocked off. In preparation for an assault, hoping no one would alert the Shed's occupants, the police closed off the surrounding streets. Loaded dump trucks were parked nearby, waiting for an order to block the Shed's gate.

Earlier, SWAT personnel had carefully tried to open the door from the shop into the Shed but had discovered it was bolted on the inside. They'd laid an explosive strip around the door's edges and upon command SWAT would blow the door. Pulaski took half the city's SWAT team and stationed them with him at this door. Perez had given Smith and Jones permission to be part of this assault. Dressed in DHS SWAT outfits, they waited there. Like the other men, Smith had a grim determined look while Jones grinned, looking forward to what lay ahead.

At the same time, the remainder of the city's SWAT team, the FBI's team and Justin ascended to the Shed's roof from the rear, out of sight of the Shed's occupants.

Rosen, two explosives experts and two others walked to the edge, seventy feet above the courtyard. The edge extended out above the courtyard, past the Shed's entrance. This put the double-wide metal door behind the edge, preventing them from dropping straight down. The explosives men strapped on harnesses with ropes attached while others attached hydraulic braces to the roof.

Ready, the explosives men stepped far back from the edge, ran and leaped out over the front edge as far as they could. Their jumps drove them outward and gravity did its job and dropped them. The harnesses absorbed most of the long drop's impact and then the ropes swung them back toward the Shed, sailing underneath the roof's edge and toward the large metal door. Approaching the door the men used rods with hooks to snag the metal lip along the sides of the entranceway, working the hooks in tight. They slowly pulled themselves hand over hand along the rods until they each reached a side of the door, about halfway down.

They proceeded to work their way up the sides of the entrance, drilling holes into the cement, driving in pitons to aid their ascent. Knowing the cement's thickness, the men weren't worried about being heard from the inside. As they were making their way to the top of the door and then across it to the middle, they wedged plastic explosives into the tight space between the door and the cement blocks. Done, the men on the rooftop hoisted them up. As they ascended one of them thought, *That'll have to be one hell of a door for this not to knock it off its ass.*

///

Gabe and Jasminn had been moved to one side between two high mounds of salt. Tired of standing, they sat on the cement floor, leaning back against one of the salt piles. Their guards were apparently not very concerned about them as one walked away and the other paid them little attention; mainly scrolling on his phone with one hand while holding his machine pistol with the other.

"Somehow we've got to contact the outside," Gabe said. "The FBI needs to know that these weapons are here and that these guys are preparing to use them."

"How do we do that without our phones?" Jasminn asked. "You got a glimpse out. Any idea where we are?"

"It was only a quick look since Dimitri shoved my head back down," he said. "From the glimpse I got it's an odd-looking building. I didn't know what it was but looking at all these piles I think this might be what they call the Salt Shed which is downtown somewhere."

He shifted on the cement floor, trying to get comfortable.

"Your butt sore?" she asked.

He couldn't help himself. "Yes. Some of us don't have as much padding there as others."

She punched him in the shoulder, drawing an uninterested glance from the guard. Angling her head in the guard's direction, she asked Gabe, "Do you think we could somehow get his phone?"

Gabe chuckled. "Sure, just go over and ask to borrow it."

"We've got to do something," she insisted.

"Like what? I could take him if he wasn't armed, but he is. Or do you think he'd fall for the old bathroom trick?"

She replied, "Oh, damn. You shouldn't have said that. Now I've got to go."

He glanced at her and shrugged.

"Hey," she said. Louder, she cried, "Hey, Mr. Guard!"

He looked at them.

Her face was scrunched up. "I need a bathroom." she said, in obvious discomfort. "I've really got to go bad."

The guard replied, "Hold it in."

"I've been doing that. I can't anymore. What do you want me to do? Go right here?"

He studied her suspiciously, not about to be tricked, but she was grimacing and stood up partway, crossing her legs. Even though he would use his pistol on her if need be, not letting her use a bathroom violated an unspoken code of conduct.

He pocketed his phone and said, "Move slowly and I'll take you there. But don't try anything or I will shoot you."

Gabe rose too, and with the guard close behind they went where he directed, going around a pile of salt. Reaching the pile's far side they weren't visible to the rest of the Shed and for a moment Gabe was out of the guard's sight. Gabe grabbed a handful of salt and, as the guard came around the pile Gabe stepped to his right, whirled and threw the salt at the guard's face. Some went in the man's eyes and reflexively he reached for them, dropping the pistol. Following the motion of his throwing arm, Gabe spun the rest of the way toward the guard and leaped on him. The two of them went down, Gabe on top, overwhelming him. Gabe reached for the dropped pistol, when he was struck high on the back between his shoulder blades.

The blow knocked Gabe off the guard and he collapsed on his stomach. He lay there in agony for several minutes with his eyes closed and oblivious to what went on around him. With Jasminn's help he finally sat up. Facing him, but at a safe distance was the other guard who held his machine pistol pointed directly at Gabe's chest.

"If I wasn't under orders, I'd have shot you," he said.

Gabe looked around, getting his bearings.

"Are you OK?" Jasminn asked.

"I think so. What happened?"

She pointed to the guard. "He clobbered you with his gun butt."

The guard said, "Correction. I tapped him lightly. If I'd really hit him hard, he wouldn't be moving at all. What I said: orders."

"What about you?" Gabe asked her.

"I'm alright. Amazingly, while you lay there, they let me use the bathroom."

"I'm so glad," he muttered and rested against her.

CHAPTER FORTY-ONE

Gabe was still groggy but with Jasminn's help he'd made it to his feet when a man in full black bloc, wearing a mask and carrying a pistol hanging loosely by his side appeared around the salt pile. The masked gunman said something to the guard, who then left, leaving Jasminn and Gabe alone with this new figure. His pistol was pointed at them and with his free hand he tugged off his mask.

Gabe exclaimed, "Alex?" while Jasminn's eyes were focused on the gun.

"Come on Gabe, do you really expect me to believe you're surprised? Somehow you figured it out," Alex said. Gesturing with the pistol, he ordered, "Sit."

They seated themselves on the floor, Gabe grunting as he did so.

Alex looked from one to the other, but no one said anything.

"Tell me how you found out that I'm with the alt-right. Was it on Roosevelt Island or did you already know and that's why you followed me there?" He rushed on, "Who've you told?"

Gabe ignored Alex's questions. Instead, he asked, "What're you planning with those WMDs? That's a lot of firepower."

"I'm surprised you know what they are, and it is indeed a great deal of firepower. But answer my questions," Alex demanded, his lips drawing tight.

Jasminn surprised both men. "I'll tell you, you dumb shit."

Alex's eyebrows arched and he flashed a small smile.

"You're like lots of guys. You think too much with your dick. Some time ago, to impress some woman so you could screw her, you told her you were a big *macher* on the right. She remembered, and so we knew where to hunt you. I'd say you're a *putz*, not a *macher*."

She paused, expecting Alex to react. When he didn't, she added, "You've also been made a fool of by your good buddy Peter."

Alex's forehead wrinkled giving him a puzzled look.

"I'll bet he convinced you he's part of the alt-right and that he infiltrated the left to help the right just like you. Well, it turns out he's a foreign agent. The FBI knows all about him. It seems he's helping to further pit the left versus the right and help divide the country. All this time, despite all you alt-righters' "America First" talk, you've been played by a foreign agent." She shook her head. "What a fool."

Alex stood frozen for a few moments, then he relaxed, shrugged, and said, "I'll deal with that, but he's been useful. Hey, he brought you two here like I asked."

Gabe waved his arm toward the rest of the Shed and asked, "What's your plan with all this?"

Alex was silent. *Should he tell them?* He thought *Telling them would be like in some Bond movie*, but decided, *Why not?* "Chelsea Piers is two miles straight up the highway. Tonight, at a banquet hall there, some of the Conservative Party's major figures and donors are having a 'Keeping America the Greatest' dinner there—black tie. They've got several big name rock and country music stars performing. They're sold out. It's going to be quite the *soiree*."

Gabe's jaw dropped as he realized what Alex intended.

Alex read his face. "That's right, me and my black bloc team here will be making a surprise appearance. And after we're done, America will rise in revolt against the Antifa and the entire left."

Gabe said, "That's why the black bloc. This is an alt-right false flag operation."

Alex smiled and said, "Everyone will be opposed to the left and more people will join the right. The leftist movement will be shattered and its leaders who we've been hunting will be irrelevant—they'll either end up in jail or on the run and powerless."

"You'll be killing your own people," Gabe said.

"A regrettable but necessary sacrifice. I think of them as heroes for the cause."

Jasminn's hands were curled into fists and through clenched teeth she barely managed to get out, "You bastard. And how many people will you kill?"

"I expect maybe a hundred, or two at the most."

"Asshole," Gabe cried and started to his feet.

"Uh uh," Alex warned, pointing his pistol at Gabe. He continued, "Now Gabe, tell me who you've told about me or I'll have to shoot the delectable Jasminn."

Gabe continued to rise, but a slight wave of Alex's gun stopped him.

///

From the time Barnes poked his lens through the vent's grill, the Command Center's personnel had been monitoring the activity in the Shed. The rotating lens gave them a three hundred-sixty degree panorama. On each rotation, they'd seen Gabe and Jasminn under guard. When the lens came around on one rotation, they were starting to walk with the armed guard behind them. The woman operating the lens kept it on them, wondering where they were going. Some of the Center's crew were watching when Gabe attacked the one guard before being hit by the other.

The operator shook her head, thinking *the guys got balls.*

The lens resumed its rotation, sweeping over the vans again. The woman immediately halted it and called out, "Special Agent Perez! You need to see this!"

Everyone looked at the monitors. The men were starting to load WMDs into the vans.

One of Perez's lieutenants said, "They must be getting ready to move out."

A police liaison said, "If they try, we'll stop them on the street."

"No! No! We can't have warfare in the streets. You have to stop them before they leave the Shed," the Mayor's representative cried.

"It'd be easier to stop them once they exit the fortress," another aide advised Perez.

Perez joined the argument. "What if they fire their rocket launchers and hurl grenades outside? We've blocked off the area and the police have it surrounded, but civilians could still be injured or killed and there'd be a massive amount of property damage. Much worse than if we stop them inside. Plus, there's always the risk, no matter how small you may think it is, that a van gets through our blockade."

Perez made her decision and opened her mic to reach Rosen and Pulaski. "This is Special Agent in Charge Perez. You are ordered to commence assault immediately. WMDs are being loaded into the vans. Destruction or capture of the WMDs and the vans is the highest priority. Enemy combatants are heavily armed. You are authorized to use all necessary force. The two captives are being held in the northwest corner. Rescue them, if possible, but do not endanger the mission. Proceed immediately."

CHAPTER FORTY-TWO

Standing atop the Shed's roof, Rosen received Perez's order through his headset. He looked over his men. They were all heavily armed and had at the ready a band of either flash/bang, smoke or gas grenades and several had shields slung over their backs. They'd checked each other's gear twice and were all calm and ready to go—no one needed to be pulled from the ranks.

Rosen ordered the men in the first wave to take their positions. Six men clamped onto each of the ropes, one rope above each edge of the truck door and one in the middle. The lead men carried one-man battering rams.

After one last look at his men, Rosen nodded. to an explosives man, who uncapped the his detonator's switch and pressed it, setting off the explosives along the truck door. With a tremendous roar most of the door's upper part was instantly gone, disintegrated by the blast, and its few remaining pieces hung limply. The door's bottom section, ten feet roughly, hadn't vanished in the blast, but the force had separated much of the bottom's sides from the Shed's walls and crumpled parts of its top, curling them down. The impact destroyed many of the paving stones in the courtyard and despite the thick cement the men on the roof felt the vibration from the explosion. The sound was audible for over a mile and glass within a hundred yards shattered.

The lead men nodded to each other, and started toward the edge, picking up speed as they went. The others on the ropes joined the sprint as the rope tightened in front of them. As they leaped out, their momentum swung the ropes away from the Shed then back past vertical and into the smoke enshrouding the entrance. Almost simultaneously, the leads struck the bottom section of the door with their battering rams, their momentum adding force. The blows separated the door further from the sides. Momentum swung the men back away from the door. The first men dropped the battering rams and slid down to the courtyard. The other men on the ropes followed them. Once the first group hit the ground, the second wave and then a third wave followed.

The blast openings along the sides and the crumpled top served as the insertion points. The SWAT team immediately pushed their way through them, some clambering over the top. As each man went in he pulled the cord on his grenade band and hurled it, sending flash/bangs, gas and smoke grenades flying into the Shed. Once inside, most of the attackers rushed to spread out and tried to spot the Shed's occupants through the smoke, while others ran and took up prone positions on salt mounds or the cement floor then laid down suppressing fire.

As soon as the main explosion sounded, Pulaski's men triggered a second detonator setting off the explosives packed along the door leading into the Shed from the repairs area. The door blew apart and the bolt formerly keeping it shut was gone. The SWAT force swarmed in through the cleared doorway and followed the same tactics as the first group. Per Pulaski's order, Smith and Jones were the last into the Shed.

The strategy was initially successful—the men inside the Shed were taken unawares. The explosions had echoed throughout the Shed, momentarily deafening the men inside. They were shocked and confused, not knowing what to do at first. The few within direct range of either blast were flung to the ground, stunned and several wounded or killed.

The smoke from the explosions blowing into the Shed and the smoke grenades made it difficult to see and heightened the confusion. The SWAT teams' other grenades and shots added to the defenders' disarray. As feared, most of the men inside the Shed had been far enough away from the doors and spread out enough over the Shed's large interior that the initial assaults didn't quash all resistance.

Some of the men under attack started returning fire and within moments all the uninjured were doing so. At first they fired blindly into the smoke. As the smoke thinned, both sides began to be able to make out their enemy and the shooting became more focused. The defenders' guns were automatics, and some of them held down the triggers, spewing bullets nonstop until their cartridges were exhausted, then reloading from their plentiful supply.

Those defenders with military training mostly fired in short bursts, focusing on targets rather than shooting wildly. Dimitri was one of these, and he hit two agents. The SWAT team recognized the greater danger from these experienced fighters. They became the main targets. A bullet from Pulaski's rifle caught Dimitri in the neck, killing him.

Rosen spotted a rocket launcher and ordered his troops to destroy it. Several unleashed a hailstorm of bullets, reducing the launcher to expensive pieces of useless junk.

A member of the city's unit spotted a figure in black bloc lying underneath a van and aiming another rocket launcher at a group of the SWAT team. Right as the man fired the launcher, the city's sniper put a bullet through his forehead, killing him and causing the launcher to jerk. The rocket missed its target and instead exploded in a salt mountain towering next to the group. The explosion didn't injure them, but it buried them under an avalanche of salt, taking them out of the fight until they dug their way out. The SWAT units weren't carrying any weapon powerful enough to destroy the vans with one shot, but Rosen directed concentrated fire at their front hoods, soon destroying their engines.

The only shelter was the salt piles, the vans and the car used in kidnapping Gabe and Jasminn. A few members of the attacking SWAT forces were injured, but to that point they'd suffered no fatalities. The same wasn't true of their opposition as several were killed.

Blasts went off to Rosen's right. There, several SWAT members were down, one not moving and some others who'd obviously been hit. The injured scrambled back for better cover, dragging their unmoving comrade. Rosen alerted his forces, "They're using grenades!" The attacked became the attackers, throwing grenades at the SWAT teams and forcing them further back behind the salt mountains.

The SWAT teams didn't carry explosive hand grenades or any other weapons of comparable firepower. Facing stronger weaponry, Rosen was weighing their options when, without orders, several agents dashed out from behind a salt mountain, using their shields to provide cover. They reached WMD cases in the Shed's exposed center, grabbed several and started dragging them back. The gunfire from both sides increased and grenades landed near the men. Justin was one of the injured and he pulled a crate with his right arm while his left arm hung at his side. The group's rear man's left foot dangled from his leg at a grotesque angle. After what seemed like forever to Rosen, the men made it to shelter.

One of these men radioed Rosen. "We got boxes of grenades and one armed single-use AT-4."

Rosen thought, *Holy shit! We've got an anti-tank weapon!* He planned how to proceed then issued his orders. As the men in black continued their grenade assault and bullets flew both ways, a barrage of grenades began flying out of the fjord where Rosen's men with their stolen crates were sheltered. The grenade counterattack forced the Shed's defenders back. One of Rosen's men stepped into the open and fired the AT-4. Per Rosen's orders he aimed at the floor in front of the enemy's position. The sound was amplified by the Shed's cement walls and was ear-splitting. The effect was devastating. Shards of the cement floor flew out in an expanding arc in the direction of the Shed's defenders, hitting many. Several were injured and a few were killed. Eventually, the gunfire and grenade attacks ceased and there was a long silence punctured only by the cries of the wounded.

Rosen's communications gear could function as a megaphone, and he broadcast a demand through the silence: "Surrender now or we will fire more shells. Throw out your weapons, then step out with your hands up, and get down on the ground."

Rosen was betting that their foes didn't know what weapon had been used against them, and specifically that it was a single shot launcher, and was their only one. Nothing happened at first and Rosen was afraid they'd called his bluff, then slowly men began to step out from behind salt piles with their arms raised. One was an uninjured Peter who throughout the fighting had hidden behind a salt mound in the rear since he had no intention of dying for this mission.

///

From the battle's beginning, Smith had avoided the action. He'd stayed out of sight while working his way along the Shed's walls and the sides of the salt piles toward the northwest corner where Gabe and Jasminn had last been seen.

///

When the first explosions went off, Alex had motioned for Gabe and Jasminn to retreat deeper between the salt mounds and remain on the floor. He followed them partway back, further into the gap, maintaining a salt mound between them and the fighting. The gunfire echoed off the walls in a loud steady stream blocking out other sounds. Alex faced the tip of the mound, where anyone would come from, and alternated pointing his pistol in that direction and behind him at his captives. Suddenly, a figure clad in SWAT gear charged around the mound into sight. Before Alex could react, the racing figure fired two shots at him, one striking him in the chest and the other in the abdomen. The force flung Alex into the air and back. He hit the floor and skidded toward Gabe and Jasminn, coming to a rest a few feet in front of them. They stared down at him and gasped, their eyes wide, thankful for being saved but shocked.

Alex lay still, his eyes shut. Blood flowed from his chest onto the floor and more blood puddled from the gut shot. Sweating, Gabe crawled on shaking arms to him, leaned over and put his ear to Alex's mouth.

Gabe could only hear faint breaths and quiet moaning. He sat up, lifted Alex's head and rested it on his crossed legs.

Keeping his pistol pointed at Alex, the shooter yanked off his helmet.

Gabe gasped. "Smith!"

Jasminn's head swiveled from Gabe to Smith.

"Is he dead?" Smith called, gesturing with his pistol toward Alex.

"No, but he will be unless he gets help. Call for aide," Gabe yelled back, his voice shaky and hard to hear over the shooting.

Smith ignored Gabe's cry and maintained his position; staying back from them, several feet off from the salt mound's tip.

"Come on Smith, call for help."

Alex groaned and mouthed something. It was barely audible, and Gabe hunched over trying to hear him. Alex's eyes opened part way. He was facing toward Smith and peered, struggling to make out the figure through blurred vision. He groaned again, then whispered so softly Gabe barely made out what he said, "Smith…with us…. helped…."

The sound of Smith's Desert Eagle drowned out the rest as two more bullets ripped into Alex's torso. Gabe heard the bullets' path near him and felt their impact through Alex's body. He screamed and jerked away, letting Alex's head hit the floor where it collapsed sideways; his empty eyes facing the salt mound.

Gabe and Jasminn stared at Alex for several seconds, then their faces rose in tandem and they eyed Smith.

Smith lowered his pistol and shouted, "I had to. He was reaching for his gun. You two would be dead."

Jasminn's lips tightened and Gabe's chest rose and fell rapidly. They stared at Smith, knowing he was lying.

"Gabriel, what'd he say to you?"

Gabe shook his head and looked away. "Nothing."

"Gabriel!"

Silently Gabe turned to look at Smith, and Smith read the answer on Gabe's face.

Smith gave a deep sigh. "Sorry it has to be this way, Gabriel," he said loudly, bending his knees slightly for balance, raising his Desert Eagle and pointing it at Gabe. Gabe couldn't move, hypnotized by the pistol, thinking, *I can't believe it's ending like this. Not after Jaz and I have finally found each other.* Jasminn lunged toward him, trying to shield him but he pushed her back into the salt mound.

A voice yelled, "Smith! Don't do it!"

A figure in SWAT gear dove into sight from behind the salt mound. Faster than Gabe could follow, Smith spun his gun toward the figure, rose slightly and twisted in that direction. Two shots were fired. One was the loud blast of Smith's Desert Eagle, the other from the SWAT pistol.

The man in the SWAT gear crashed to the ground and lay there. Gabe saw blood spurting from below his helmet. Smith knew where to shoot to avoid his target's armor, and his shot had struck in the narrow opening between the top of the man's vest and the bottom of his helmet. It was a superb shot, but Smith's bullet had just missed the man's neck and struck his right clavicle, shattering it. The Desert Eagle's power had driven the bullet through the scapula, shattering that as well, finally exiting the man's back and embedding itself in the rear of his vest. The man lay unmoving and silent.

The SWAT man's shot had been thrown off by Smith's rotation. He'd targeted Smith's right ear for an in-and-out shot, but his shot was low, separating Smith's facial artery, breaking the right side of his jawbone and coming out through his left cheek.

Smith glanced at the body of his attacker then focused back on Gabe and Jasminn.

They could see the grimace on Smith's face and the blood on both sides, but he was still standing. He switched the Desert Eagle from his right hand to his left and clutched the right side of his face with the now free hand. His face's right side was drooping, and he was trying to hold it up as blood flowed from it. Smith stepped toward them, moving slowly as pain shot through his face. As he got closer, he slowed to a shuffle and his body wavered, but the Desert Eagle remained firmly pointed at Gabe.

Jasminn was still huddled against the salt mound. In one motion she scooped up a clump of salt and flung it underhanded at Smith. In pain and staggering, Smith had been focusing on Gabe and the salt caught him by surprise. He grunted. Some of the salt hit his face, burning the open wounds and hurting his eyes, but it didn't blind him. He swung his gun toward Jasminn. Gabe dove to his right, grabbed Alex's gun, swiveled toward Smith and fired. Gabe's first shot hit Smith just below his right eye, freezing him. Gabe's next two shots were wild and missed, but the first one was enough. Smith dropped to his knees, and the Desert

Eagle fell from his hand, clattering on the floor. Then Smith fell over on his side.

For a moment Gabe stared at the gun then he let it slip from his hand. He and Jasminn rushed together and grabbed each other tight.

After a long moment she said, "We have to check them." She picked up Alex's gun and carefully approached Smith while Gabe circled around Smith's body and went to the other downed figure.

Jasminn kicked the Desert Eagle away from Smith then nudged his body with her foot. Smith didn't move, Cautiously, and with the gun pointed at Smith, she bent down and with her free hand, while grimacing, put her fingers on the side of his neck.

"He's dead," she yelled, her arm shaking.

Gabe stood above the other body. The man was alive; groaning slightly and his hand was gripping his right shoulder. Gabe knelt and carefully removed the man's helmet, trying not to move him. As the helmet came off Gabe gasped then cried out, "Jones!"

Jones stared up at him, grimacing in pain but his eyes were alert and he looked into Gabe's face. "Is Smith dead?" he asked, his voice little more than a whisper.

"Yeah, he's dead." Gabe paused for several seconds. "Thanks for saving us, Jones."

In a faint voice, but with a hint of a smile Jones said, "That's the job. But I still don't like you Kid."

CHAPTER FORTY-THREE

The aftermath of the battle in the Shed was its own operation—no shooting or hurling of grenades, but critical nonetheless.

About twenty defenders of the Shed had surrendered. SWAT forces and police reinforcements had herded them into a far corner where they were searched for weapons and put in restraints. Once at the city jails, the booking process revealed that most were known members of alt-right groups. Subsequently most were transferred to federal detention centers to await trial. Peter was among those arrested, but the Bureau spirited him off separately.

Gabe and Jasminn were both shaken, and even though Gabe had one new bruise on his back neither needed medical care. Perez's people wanted to hold them for questioning, but they argued to be allowed to leave. The argument was resolved when four Homeland Security agents appeared carrying documents showing they'd been appointed as a security detail for Gabe and Jasminn—Uncle Steve had arranged to include her in the protective order—and the detail had authorization to take them.

Several vans with Homeland Security agents and separate ones with FBI teams arrived. Within hours, the WMDs, including the remnants of the blasted rocket launcher, had been collected, inventoried and removed under heavy guard. In addition, the Bureau's initial layout of the 'crime scene' was well underway. Only then were the coroners allowed to remove the dead—twelve Shed defenders, including Alex, and four from the SWAT forces, including Smith.

Well into the evening, Perez and Rosen watched the goings-on in the Shed under bright police lights. She'd congratulated him several times for a job well done.

"You know," she said, "this isn't the last battle over the Shed."

Tired, emotionally drained, and experiencing a post-combat low, Rosen wasn't thinking on all cylinders. He looked at her for an explanation. For the first time that day she smiled, then said, "Oh, there are several battles to come. The first is over publicity and credit. So far, there've been only vague media reports of a massive gun battle and camera crews have exterior shots. However, no official statement yet about what happened, who was responsible, and most importantly, who gets the credit. The word 'joint' in 'joint task force' will be tossed around a lot, but at the end of the day, some agency will emerge with the lion's share. She smiled again. "There'll even be a fight over the costs of repairing the Shed, including the doors you guys blew." Her smile broadened. "I hope there's room in your budget."

///

Two days later Gabe and Jasminn went to Gabe's favorite local coffee house. He was bummed to find some guy in his favorite wingback chair. As Jasminn and he seated themselves on a small sofa, he thought that he'd mostly be sitting there with Jasminn going forward, not by himself in "his" chair, and he was fine with that. His favorite waitress came over, smiling at him. She and Jasminn looked at each other and Gabe felt an immediate charge in the air. Jasminn drew a little closer to him and the waitress's smile slipped for a moment. Gabe introduced them, and the women quickly discovered they had some common interests beyond Gabe. He thought *I've lost my wingback and now I've been demoted to number two.* But it was alright.

After Jasminn's new friend delivered their lattes and biscottis, Justin arrived. He had a different look--wearing slacks and a button-down shirt. His hair was shorter, he had a close shave and his bearing seemed military.

"How's it feeling?" Gabe asked, pointing to Justin's left arm which was in a sling.

"It would violate FBI protocol to complain but," he said, "it hurts like a son of a bitch."

They all laughed.

Jasminn said, "We heard you were incredibly brave, getting those cases."

"I was just part of a team, doing my duty," he replied modestly, and meaning it. "I heard that you two are quite the heroes—distracting Smith and then shooting him."

"Mine was pure luck," Gabe said, "I'd never even held a gun before."

Justin shook his head. "I know that's what you said in your official statement, but it wasn't luck Gabe. It was clutch. You rose to the occasion and did what had to be done. I think that's the sort of person you are." He looked at Jasminn. "I think that's the sort of people you both are."

Jasminn and Gabe looked at each other, slightly embarrassed but flattered.

Justin continued, "How're you two doing?"

"Great," Gabe said, "glad that it's over. Except for them, that is."

He pointed across the room where two members of their security detail sat drinking American coffee and looking out of place.

Justin smiled. "That'll just be for a little while. I'm sure the powers that be want to be sure things've fully cooled down and that no one on the right's after you, or hopefully even knows you were involved."

"What about the WMDs? You recover them all?" Jasminn asked.

Justin answered quietly, forcing the other two to strain to hear him. "We don't know. People are going through stockpiles, but it'll take time. One thing we've discovered from serial numbers is they had stuff we didn't know was missing."

Jasminn asked, "What's that mean?"

"It confirms there are more stolen WMDs than we knew. There's a lot more checking to be done."

Gabe let out a loud whistle causing people to glance over at him.

After a moment he said, "Okay, tell us. What'd you want to speak to us about?"

Justin face became flushed. Jasminn thought he was embarrassed.

"Well," he said quietly, "both as part of protecting you, and frankly trying to keep secret what Homeland Security did to Gabe and Matt, no one wants any of you three mentioned publicly in connection with this. But, we do need a credible story about finding the WMDs and unearthing Alex's true role. Obviously, that's thanks to you two, but since you're not to be mentioned, the higher-ups have decided that publicly I'm going to receive the credit."

He looked down.

"Stealing our thunder?" Jasminn asked, trying to sound angry despite a grin spreading across her face.

Lowering his voice like Justin had, Gabe asked, "What about Smith and Jones?"

"You'll hate this, but Smith will be treated like the SWAT guys who died—protecting our country. He'll receive a posthumous medal and be buried with honors."

"That sucks," Gabe cried, sitting back hard against the sofa, sending pain through his still sore back and causing him to yelp.

"Yeah, it does, but it's been decided that that's how it has to be. There's so much outcry against the right right now that the last thing the government wants is for people to learn that a government agent was involved with the alt-right. Imagine if it got out that he'd played a role in their planned terrorist attack."

Gabe said, "I get it, but that still sucks. He deserves to be branded a traitor, not treated as a hero. Think what he did to help Alex." After a brief pause he asked, "Precisely what did he do?"

Justin shook his head. "Can't tell you. Anyway, we're only starting to work through the details, but let's just say the WMDs didn't walk out or get to Alex on their own."

The waitress checked up on them and Jasminn used that break to change the topic. "So what happens to you now, Michael?"

He smiled at being called by his real name. "You're right. My cover's blown. 'Justin' will cease to exist and I'll go back to being Michael. I'll be reassigned to another job within the Bureau at another location. We'll be leaving New York. I feel bad mainly because my daughter will have to leave her friends. Unfortunately, that's part of this life."

"And Jones?" she asked.

Justin sat back. Pain shot through his injured shoulder and arm, but he gave no sign other than the slightest tightening of his lips. "That's a tough one. He's lucky to be alive and I'm told he's expected to make a good recovery. I don't know what'll happen to him though. On the one hand, he committed numerous crimes against you and a defense of national security probably isn't going to fly for what he's done. On the other hand, he risked his life to save your lives and shot his own partner in the line of duty." He paused, then added, "I really don't know."

Justin thanked them again for everything they'd done and their bravery and service to their country, then said he had to report to FBI headquarters for further debriefing. The three of them rose. Jasminn and he gave each other half smiles and hugged briefly, Jasminn making an honest effort not to hurt his arm. Justin and Gabe shook hands and Justin gave him a light pat on the back.

///

That evening Gabe and Jasminn were at Gabe's apartment. He was packing for their mini-vacation. In the morning they'd be heading to the Hamptons to stay at Uncle Steve's beach house for a few days. Knowing what they'd been through, Steve urged them to get away and use the house. Jill had squared Gabe's prior absence with his firm and arranged it so he could take a few more days, and Jasminn was using some of her many vacation days—as she always said about working for a not-for-profit, "the pay sucks, but the bennies are great."

Gabe was hunting for his bathing suit when he said, "I should get word to Earl that I'm out. I don't have his contact info though."

She said, "Tell Short Alex."

He looked at her.

"I mean tell Alex. He can tell Earl."

"How do you know he knows Earl?"

"He told me. Alex is a lot more involved than he lets on. Of all of you they locked up that night looking for important players on the left he was the one."

"How do you know?"

"I was going to tell you. He called me earlier today and we spoke some," she said, "and we'll talk more after the Hamptons. He asked if I wanted to get more deeply involved. Don't worry, he wasn't talking about anything extreme."

Gabe was surprised but before he could follow up, Matt showed up.

"To be continued, Jaz," he said as he buzzed Matt in.

After Matt joined them and they'd hugged, they sat around and Gabe asked, "Why'd you tell me earlier you were positive we were caught up in the Salt Shed shootout?" He added with a smile, "We're not involved with every major violent incident in New York."

Matt shrugged and looked embarrassed. "I had a feeling. What actually happened after you left the court that morning?"

Jasminn proceeded to tell him, although toward the end she said they'd beaten the high school players and he rolled his eyes in response. When she told him about Peter and Dimitri, he burst in.

"Shit. So if I hadn't been an asshole and had showed up for practice, I would've been there and you wouldn't have been grabbed." He kicked a kitchen stool in frustration, splintering one of its legs.

"Come on Matt," she said, "you couldn't have done anything. It was two guys with guns."

Matt shook his head. "Doesn't matter. Nothing'll happen to you guys when I'm around." As he said this Matt kicked out again and took off another leg of the stool. This time the stool went down.

Gabe laughed. "What, you think you're that huge ex-military guy from those books?"

"Or that ex-ballplayer p.i. from those other books?" Jasminn asked.

Matt didn't say anything, he just grabbed the two of them for a big three-way hug.

Eventually the story was fully told and emotions calmed down, then Matt said. "Knowing you'll be together makes it easier to tell you my news."

Homeland Security had cleared matters with Matt's employer, so he wasn't in trouble and still had his job. As a result, neither Jasminn nor Gabe had any idea where this was headed but they were concerned— why was Matt still so upset?

"What's happened made me do a lot of thinking," Matt said. "I've thought about my attitude and how I've conducted my life."

They both looked closely at him, introspection never having been Matt's thing.

"I resigned today."

"Why?" Gabe asked, perplexed. "You're in the clear."

"Look, I know what you guys and lots of others always thought about my work ethic when it came to b-ball. Maybe I didn't care enough or maybe I was afraid to go all out in case it didn't work. Whatever, I let down a lot of people, especially you two. I'm gonna go to a sports training facility. I'll spend several months working harder on my conditioning and my game than I ever have. Then I'll go overseas, probably Europe, and hook up with a pro team there—even at our age they still reach out to me occasionally. I'll show everyone what the White Rocket can really do. I don't have that many good playing years left, but I've got enough, and I promise you I'll be on an NBA roster soon. And Jasminn, when I do, I'll wear your college number."

The other two were speechless. Introspection. Commitment. This was a new Matt, and they were thrilled for him, ending up in another three-way hug.

///

The Hamptons trip worked out as Jasminn and Gabe had hoped. Beforehand, neither had any doubts about their feelings, and their time together proved them right. They laughed, they loved, they had sex until Gabe had to beg for time outs, and they were together. Even their security detail didn't ruin their joy. Early on they agreed that back in the city Jasminn would move in with him.

On their last day in the Hamptons, over a rosé while sitting on the deck and watching the sunset, Gabe said, "After all these years together, waiting's stupid. We should get married right away."

"Damn right," she replied.

///

Back in the city, Gabe was preparing for his return to the office. Showered and shaved, he once again donned his custom-made white shirt, his fine black suit with its pinpoint white stripes, then a pair of designer socks. He followed that with his cordovan boots, a leather belt and finally a French silk patterned tie. Looking in the mirror he realized that this was what he'd worn a little over a month ago for his first post-pandemic face-to-face negotiation. He laughed, remembering that he'd thought of himself as dressing for battle.

Still gazing in the mirror, he mused about what had happened since then—not the beatings and subterfuges nor Smith and Jones, but the most important things: *His finally admitting to himself his feelings about Jasminn, telling her about them and her saying she felt the same for him. They're no longer being just teammates and friends but being a deeper team. Each prepared to do whatever it took to help and care for the other.*

It felt good. It just felt so so good.

///

Harry Einner of the DHS did not feel good about his upcoming meeting. In his mind it wasn't his fault, though they'd been his operations.

He was picked up at 8:30 pm sharp in a plain black sedan and driven to an area just outside D.C. The car pulled up in front of a townhouse. It had an awning with low hanging sides running from the front door to the curb, and when Harry stepped out of the car he saw that the awning hid him from any onlookers.

Before he could knock on the front door, a tuxedoed man opened it. The man obviously knew who Harry was and whom he was there to see since, without a word, he led Harry to a room in the rear. Harry entered, the door closed behind him and the Senator was instantly by his side, shaking his hand and putting an arm around his shoulder, clutching him tightly.

"We're all disappointed, Harry, but don't worry, everyone knows it wasn't your fault," the Senator said.

Harry gave an ever so quiet sigh of relief, although a part of him didn't fully believe the Senator. The Senator guided Harry with an arm around his shoulder and seated him in a fine leather club chair. As a further reversal of their customary roles, the Senator had Harry's preferred drink at hand.

The Senator sat in a chair angled toward Harry. Still working to relax Harry, he asked, "Have you ever been here?"

Harry tried his drink and, in his nervousness, swallowed too much. He fought back a cough. "No. I don't even know what this place is."

The Senator chuckled. "We're in a bordello. The finest one within at least fifty miles of Dupont Circle."

Harry stared in surprise. He started to take more of his drink then stopped himself, knowing he needed his wits. "I didn't know they still existed."

"This one does, and I guarantee you it's the finest. When I first arrived in Washington this was one of the very first places one of our fellow travelers took me. Believe me, it surprised me too."

Harry glanced around the room, noting the expensive furniture, thick fabric wallpaper and the deep blue velvet curtains covering the windows.

The Senator saw Harry was impressed and he said, "It's also extremely expensive, but it's my good fortune that such does not pose a problem for me. However, perhaps the best thing about it, even more than the ladies, is that due to its clientele it's perhaps the most private place in all of Washington."

Harry nodded, still surprised by the setting and concerned about their meeting.

"Now Harry, about what happened in New York, I know what the media's said, and I attended a briefing by one of your superiors. I'm sure the media knows little, and I don't believe your superior shared the unvarnished truth with us mere Senators." He smiled. "Accordingly, please take me through the highlights."

The Senator sat back, lit a cigar and waited for Harry to begin. The telling took a while, but Harry told him; the one operation to root out left wing leaders, explaining Smith and Jones' operation and how they used Matt and then Gabe; the false flag terrorist attack operation;

and how everything failed. He concluded by telling the Senator about Smith killing Alex and then Jones and Gabe killing Smith.

When Harry was done, the Senator sat quietly, occasionally sipping his rye and mulling things over. Finally, he spoke. "If I may summarize: we've lost some of the WMDs, the false flag operation failed and the left-wing leader operation failed. Oh yes, and we lost Smith and that Alex fellow. None of which, of course, is the worst of it."

Harry was puzzled by that last statement but said nothing. He knew if the Senator wanted his thoughts, he'd ask for them.

"The worst part is that, at least for a good while the extreme right wing, and the conservative movement as a whole, will be in disfavor. They'll, we'll, be the subject of intense public pressure and demands will be made to crack down; the middle of the road electorate will shift somewhat to the left and there'll be new government task forces, government investigations and arrests."

The Senator took another sip before continuing. "Now, we and our fellow believers will fight back, primarily on the media front. We'll have to deal with the congressional hearings which will undoubtedly take place. It will take time, but we'll handle this, and eventually for much of the electorate this will become as insignificant or as false as the fabled events of January sixth."

The Senator looked at Harry who recognized that his concurrence was being called for and he gave it.

"For the immediate future," the Senator said, "no actions should take place. We must let things cool down. In the meantime, we should plan for when the time is right again. Let the others know."

Harry nodded, acknowledging his instructions. Assuming he was dismissed, he stood.

"Wait," the Senator said.

Harry dropped back into his seat.

"I know we've got plenty of loyal men and women in your department, but you thought highly of Smith. Do you have any one in mind to replace him?"

"Not yet, but several people might fit the bill. I've got to dig deeper into them and give it more thought."

The Senator nodded then pressed a buzzer by his chair. Instantly the door opened and the tuxedoed man was standing there.

"The gentleman is done. Please show him out. And let Madam know I'll visit with the ladies for a while."

THE END

Printed in the USA
CPSIA information can be obtained
at www.ICGtesting.com
LVHW020526111023
760703LV00009B/314